THANE

AARON RANDOLPH

** * **

This novel is entirely a work of fiction. The names, characters and incidents portrayed in it are the work of the author's imagination. Any resemblance to actual persons, living or dead, events or localities is entirely coincidental.

Second edition

Cover art by Mat Van Rhoon
Editing by Felicity Anderson

ISBN: 979-8-9889423-3-7
ISBN-13: 979-8-9889423-3-7

This book is dedicated to Tatum, closest to a daughter I ever had,
and to Hor-Hay, the best friend anyone ever had

Acknowledgement

This book and I owe a lot to a lot of people, such as Mat Van Rhoon, the legend who gave me such incredible feedback and was also inspired to create the brilliant cover art completely unprompted. Meryn Holtslander helped me with some medical questions and served as obvious inspiration for one of the character's names. My other beta readers Erin Scabareti, Madi Sarlo, Todd Fuller, and Aaron Connors all provided invaluable contributions. The Ultra Hope Girls Discord server and my BFYTW podcast brothers Stevie and Augie were constantly cheering me on while I wrote it. And of course, my parents Linda and Charley for always supporting whatever insane thing I decided to do this time.

But I insist this book would not exist at all without Caroline Orejuela. When I was absolutely lost, she took time out of her incredibly busy voice acting work to read my first eight chapters, and she gave me exactly the encouragement and inspiration I needed to finish the book. Her insights since have raised this story to another level, and I am profoundly grateful. Everyone should be so lucky to have a friend like Caroline.

Prologue

Samantha stared up into the night sky as she'd done so often in her youth. It wasn't every night you could see every individual star so clearly.

Of course, the morbid side of me wonders just which of those bright lights will kill us.

Samantha shook her head and glanced instead at her phone. Her phone used to be her mortal enemy, an endless annoyance as department heads e-mailed constant reports, budgetary requests, scheduled meetings, all just part of the job - but now she'd give almost anything for such blessed mundanity. Instead, she now clung to her phone, reacting to every vibration instantly in search of hope, feeding off it like an infant at a mother's breast.

Reluctantly, Samantha opened her e-mails, and her thumb hovered over the latest arrival. It was grayed out, but as of the last 24 hours, she found herself re-reading everything she received at least three or four times.

Almost against her will, Samantha's thumb pressed against the screen.

National Aeronautics and Space Administration
Office of the Administrator
NASA Headquarters
300 E Street S.W.
Washington, DC

Deputy Administrator Samantha Mulroney:

With Japan, we now have confirmation from three independent sources with more on the way. It's not a fluke, or a glitch. I've got everyone from Kennedy to White Sands asking for orders and all I can think to tell them is to keep gathering information for now.

* * *

Has the President been briefed? Did Jim get anything from the pols?

Dr. Jennifer Shepard
jshepard@nasa.gov
Chief of Staff
NASA Headquarters

Samantha angrily dashed a tear from her eye. She'd sent back a terse "you'll know when I know", mostly because she didn't know how else to respond. Independent confirmation from that many sources was not a good sign. Still, Jenn had deserved better, and Samantha resolved to check in with her later and apologize.

As if it matters. As if anything does.

Samantha's thoughts turned to Jim. James Arnold was the Administrator at NASA, having been selected by the current president to serve and confirmed by the Senate. He'd hand-picked her to be his Deputy, even though she thought she wasn't the most qualified choice. Jim's belief in her had been unwavering, and they were sworn in on the same day.

Those feelings were returned and then some. Samantha had been on his staff since James was a state senator for New York, to the point where she ran his last U.S. Senate campaign. Samantha smiled in spite of herself.

As if her memories had summoned him, her phone began to play Alice in Chains' "Man in the Box", and Samantha instantly pulled up the text message that had just arrived.

> Just got out of meeting with President. Didn't go well. Surprise, surprise, there are those who think it's some kind of hoax, but nobody important is taking them seriously, and any second now, Bob's going to have every world leader there is ringing his phone off the hook.

Samantha started to type a reply, but then "Man in the Box" played again.

> Bob gave the go-ahead
> on Project Thane.

Samantha froze for a second, then typed as fast as her fingers would let her.

> are you sure?

> Positive. Thane is a go.

> jim, thane has been
> around since the sixties
> and it wasn't a great idea
> then

> If you've got another
> idea, I'm all ears.

Samantha sat back down hard, completely unaware she'd begun to stand up during the exchange. Thane was an anachronism, a joke that had been floating around NASA longer than Samantha had been alive. Layne Staley sang again.

> Sam. I've always needed
> your guidance, but I can
> safely say I've never
> needed it more than now.
> How do you think we
> should proceed?

She stared at her phone, unable to piece even two words together in her mind. After a moment that felt like an eternity, she instead turned away from the phone and looked up. Samantha stared up into the night sky as she'd done so often in her youth, but this time she let the tears flow freely.

It wasn't every night you had to decide the fate of humanity.

Chapter 1

Cris was awakened by the vague sensation of pain. He'd narrowed it down to his right leg and was starting to open his eyes when he was struck with a massive charley horse in his calf. Cris let out a little yelp and immediately started clutching his leg. Over the next few seconds, he just breathed heavily and endured the pain until he remembered to flex his foot, pulling his toes towards his body for some relief until the pain subsided, and he could start massaging his calf muscle.

Why does this keep happening to me? Is it me, or maybe my bed?

It was about then that he realized he wasn't *in* his bed. It was a reasonably comfortable bed, a bit smaller than he was used to, and a bit Spartan. As he looked around, he realized the entire room fell into that description. Blank white walls with no windows, a simple white table and chair made out of ceramic, and a long mirror were the only appliances.

Cris muttered, "What the hell...?"

He threw back the white cover and sheets, and found he was still in the clothes he remembered wearing last night – a simple black T-shirt with a blue short-sleeve shirt unbuttoned over it, jeans, and his favorite comfy shoes. He checked his pockets, but found them empty. No phone, wallet, keys, or change. Everything had been taken from him.

Okay, now I'm getting a little worried. Did somebody kidnap me and lock me in here?

Cris' thoughts flew back to last night.

I finished typing up a story last night. It was a big one, too. Contractors for the Hewley building did substandard work with non-union scabs and marked it all up to spec. Not only could it bring down the contracting company, but the Hewley building will have several new building code violations to deal with, and that could make me an enemy of the richest man in Arlington. But could even he have arranged this?

There were two doors, a small one by the mirror, and a large door with no doorknob at the head of the bed, and both doors seemed to be made out of the same ceramic material as the furniture. He tried the small door first and found a small bathroom with a sink, toilet, and tiny shower stall.

That answers that question, at least.

Cris closed the door and was going to check the other one when the mirror caught his attention. He stopped to take a closer look and realized there was some kind of smooth collar made of that same ceramic around his neck. It didn't appear to have any openings or buttons he could discern, and it was too small to get his head through. He tugged at it for a bit but quickly realized it was pointless.

He dug his thumb under the edge of the collar to try to feel the inside, but the lights in the room turned red, and a deep klaxon blared at him from seemingly out of nowhere. As Cris whirled around in panic, the lights reverted to white, leaving red words on the wall.

DO NOT TAMPER WITH THE COLLAR
OR YOU WILL BE PUNISHED

Cris let his hand fall from the collar as the words vanished and the wall became pure featureless white again.

What the hell kind of nightmare have I gotten into?

He went to the other door, but it was completely smooth, and appeared to be made out of similar material as the rest of the furniture. He tried to open it, but he didn't have much luck without anything to grab onto. He balled up his fists and banged on it.

"HEEYYY!! LET ME OUT OF HERE!"

It felt simultaneously cathartic and futile. *If they could kidnap me in the middle of the night without me even noticing...what else are they capable of?*

Cris walked slowly back to the bed and sat down heavily. His eyes wandered back over the featureless room. Feeling the injustice of it all, he thought a little snark for his oppressors was appropriate. "You couldn't be bothered to give me a magazine or something?"

Without warning, words again appeared on the wall opposite, this time colored blue.

PLEASE BE PATIENT
YOU WILL BE RELEASED SHORTLY

Oddly polite for kidnappers, Cris thought, as the words faded away. He checked the wall behind him, looking for a projector of some sort, but the wall was just as blank and empty as the one the words had appeared on. *Maybe it's not a wall, but one big computer screen?*

Cris decided investigation was the right tactic in a situation like this and proceeded to pore over the room. The walls were smooth to the touch. The room was pristine, no dust or dirt that he could detect, like the room had been carved into existence the moment he had been brought to it.

It was puzzling. The imprisonment, collar, and threat of punishment indicated malevolence - the polite message that he'd be released soon indicated the opposite. *Unless it's a monkey's paw kind of thing...I get released, but there's just a pack of hungry tigers outside that door.*

At that exact moment, the door slid sideways into the wall with an audible hiss.

Cris was tempted to bolt for the doorway, but given his last thought, he warily stood up and walked towards it instead. What he saw stopped him just short of crossing the door's threshold.

Outside his door appeared to be a hallway, and directly opposite his door was another open doorway. Just beyond, a visibly frightened girl his own age stared wide-eyed back at him.

Chapter 2

She had long red hair pulled back into a ponytail, a small pointed nose, and her eyes were two different colors. Her right eye was a warm green, but her left was icy blue. Her eyes locked with Cris' as they exchanged a look of fear and uncertainty.

Cris had never been in this situation before, so the best he could manage was, "Hi."

The girl did not respond.

"And just who the hell are you?"

Now their eyes shared surprise. Almost as one, Cris and the girl leaned out of their rooms and looked toward his left.

Five other people of various ages and physical attributes stood in the hallway. Cris noted that all of them had collars like his. The first to pipe up was an older gentleman wearing glasses, an off-white shirt and matching pants, and a decidedly non-matching pair of rainbow-colored suspenders. "There's no need to be rude."

A tall, physically imposing young woman with long brown hair wearing blue medical scrubs stepped up to the man. "I have been kidnapped, there's EVERY need to be rude." It was the same voice as before.

A shorter young woman in a yellow sundress with short, spiky brown hair and black leather wristbands on her crossed arms pointed out the obvious in a slick Southern drawl. "From the look of things, I'd say all seven of us have been kidnapped, y'all."

Scrubs, more curious than aggressive, turned to face Wristbands, "What makes you say that?"

"We all came out of identical rooms and have these stupid collars on."

Cris looked at the room behind the girl opposite him – Wristbands was right. It was completely identical to his room.

Wristbands fiddled with her collar. "They could've at least made mine black. Or pink."

A short, bald young man in camouflage pants and a tan t-shirt spoke up, "Yo, that'd be badass. Can I get mine in digital camo?" Behind him stood an unassuming young woman with shoulder-length brown hair, big brown doe eyes, glasses, a tie-dye t-shirt and jean overalls, which made her look younger than Cris guessed she was.

He looked back at the girl opposite him in her pretty orange-with-tiny-purple-flowers blouse and jeans. He couldn't shake the feeling that she was familiar somehow. *But I'd definitely remember a girl with mismatched eyes.*

Dismissing the thought, Cris looked to his right to see another door. This one was larger than the door he came through, but it had no knob or other method of opening that he could detect. Just in case, he tried pushing on it, and when that didn't work, he tried to lift it, but there wasn't enough space to get his fingers under the door.

Scrubs shouted, "I wouldn't bother, buddy. From the look of you, I'm a lot stronger than you, and I couldn't get my door open."

Suspenders clapped back, "That is not evidence that he will fail. Just evidence that you failed."

Scrubs laughed, "Oh, what are you, the pinnacle of success? How much luck did you have with your door?"

Suspenders did not waver. "I've gotten through it, haven't I?"

"Because the kidnappers let all of us out."

"That is not proven either."

"Just stop!" That voice had come from the girl in the overalls. "This arguing is pointless and it's getting us nowhere. We're all in the same boat, so we should work together instead of sniping at each other." Cris noted she had a rich, full voice and momentarily wondered if she, too, was a singer.

The girl with the multi-colored eyes finally spoke in hushed, uncertain tones. "Should...should we introduce ourselves?"

Scrubs shook her head. "No. If the kidnappers are listening in, or worse, if one of us is the kidnapper or an agent for them, we might be revealing info they could use against us."

Camo Pants raised his hand. "I don't know about you guys, but they took me from my bed in the middle of the night – from a military base — and neither I nor anybody else even noticed. If the kidnappers don't already know my name, I'm pretty sure they could easily find out, yo."

That's a chilling thought. Kidnapping a soldier from a military base requires a lot of money, incredible audacity, insane luck, or a combination of all three.

Suspenders nodded. "The young man is correct. While revealing more damaging information would be unwise, it is most likely safe to share our names and other general details."

There was a moment of uncomfortable silence.

Cris decided to break the ice. "I guess I'll go first, I don't have anything to hide. My name is Cris Thorpe, I'm a reporter from Arlington, Virginia, and the last thing I remember is going to sleep in my own bed."

Suspenders raised a hand as Cris finished speaking. "Before we go too much further, was everyone else taken while sleeping in their own bed? And was everyone sleeping alone?"

Everyone else nodded their heads.

"Myself as well. Anything else you'd care to add, Mr. Thorpe? Any idea why you're here?"

Cris shook his head. "I mean, I literally just submitted the biggest story of my career so far, and it would've angered one of the richest men in Arlington, but to do all this? It would cost and risk more than any damage my story would do. It doesn't make any sense."

Scrubs snorted. "Tell me about it. I'm Meryn, and if my scrubs didn't give it away, I'm a registered nurse. And I'm from Buffalo, New York. I have no enemies. I'm involved in nothing bigger than keeping my fur babies fed and happy."

Cris couldn't help but ask, "Cats or dogs?"

Meryn smiled for the first time. "Both."

Camo Pants wore a similar grin. "Aww."

"Ahem." Suspenders appeared to be nonplussed. "I'm Ethan Winters, I'm a Professor of Applied Mathematics at the University of Cambridge in Massachusetts. And suppose you wanted to design a better flying vehicle or program the next generation of artificial intelligence. In that case, you might want to kidnap me, but giving me a grant would be far less expensive."

"What up, yo!" The small and wiry Camo Pants guy certainly didn't lack for energy. "I'm Jamie, Jamie Gamble. I'm a pilot in the United States Air Force. I'm not comfortable saying the exact location, but I am stationed in the northeastern US. Oh, and I don't know why I'm here. I mean, I'm a good pilot, but I'm still in training."

Overalls cleared her throat. "My name is Victoria. I'm a librarian and an actress from Carlsbad, California. I'm not sure why I'm here."

Ethan jumped in, "Not sure, or you don't know?"

Victoria's expression soured. "I'm still reeling from a nasty breakup, okay? But she doesn't have the resources to do something like this, and also, why on Earth would she kidnap all of you?"

Wristbands shrugged her shoulders. "Hey, y'all, I'm Mai. I'm a mechanic from Jonesborough, Tennessee. No idea, never hurt nobody."

All eyes turned to the girl next to Cris, who still seemed unsure, but after a moment, "Hi, yes, I'm— my name is Alera. But you can call me Al."

Everybody waited expectantly, but nothing followed. Alera looked around nervously.

Cris tried to help. "Hi, Al. What do you do, and where are you from?"

Alera nodded gratefully. "Oh! Yes! I'm a student. At Castleton State College." A moment passed. "In Vermont."

"What do you study there?"

"Oh. I'm still undecided. But I'm leaning towards astronomy or programming."

Cris smiled. "I took programming classes when I was a kid, I loved it, but I didn't have the discipline. Can you think of any reason anybody'd want to kidnap you? You're not, like, a software company heiress or something, right?"

Alera surprised Cris with a laugh. "Oh, God, no. My mom's a single mother. She works as a waitress and housekeeper."

Ethan summed up, "Everyone is from the USA, but not everyone is from the same region. Five of us are highly skilled, but two are not."

Victoria glared at him. "Which two exactly?"

Cris picked up the thread, "Can anyone else think of anything we all have in common? Anything significant? Wait, we were all sleeping alone? Is everybody here single?"

Everyone nodded except for Victoria. "I mean, I am now..."

Cris mouthed "Sorry," to which she appeared to mouth, "It's okay."

Meryn snapped her fingers. "Oh, hell. I have no family, very few friends. Maybe they picked us because no one would miss us?"

Cris shook his head, but Jamie spoke up before he could, "Naw, good idea, but my parents and sister would miss me quite a bit. Besides, I bet your friends would miss you quite a lot, and your fur babies DEFINITELY would."

Meryn flashed another smile. "Aww. Thanks, Jamie."

Ethan was turning pink. "Sentimentality does not help us. If we truly are strangers with nothing in common, then why were we brought here against our will?"

Cris was looking at Alera when he spotted something out of the corner of his eye, and he spun to his right. Three words had appeared on the door as if in answer to Ethan's question.

PREPARATIONS ARE COMPLETE

Chapter 3

Cris waited. What for, he wasn't sure. An explanation? An attack? But there was no further addendum to the announcement on the door. *Compared to the last message I saw, this one feels sinister.*

Mai fiddled with her hands. "What preparations? Preparations for what?"

The words faded from the door's surface, and the door slid open with a hiss. Beyond was a large room with a table and chairs and what appeared to be a bunch of armchairs in a circle. Cris cautiously approached the opening but stopped when he heard Victoria's voice.

"I don't think we should be so quick to do whatever the kidnappers want."

Ethan frowned. "Right now, our primary goal should be to gather as much information as possible. And we've exhausted about all we'll get from this hallway."

Jamie raised a finger. "Also, I dunno about everybody else, but I got a warning when I tried to take my collar off, something about punishment. I don't know what they mean, but it doesn't sound fun."

Meryn added, "Can confirm. Not fun."

Alera gasped. "You were punished?"

Meryn nodded. "I kept trying to take this stupid collar off because I thought the warning might be a bluff. And out of nowhere, I felt like my entire body was on fire. It must've lasted only a few seconds, but it felt like an eternity. Then it stopped, and the wall told me I had one strike."

Everyone was silent as they digested this new information. Cris looked at Meryn's face and saw the raw anger in her eyes. *I was foolish for thinking of our kidnappers as "polite". Anyone who would do that to another human being is clearly a sadist.*

The group slowly filed into the new room. Cris noticed it was just as pristine as his cell. There was a large round table with seven chairs in one half of the room, and the other half contained seven comfortable armchairs in a circle. More interesting were the doors. Like the previous hallway, there were seven doors, three along each side, and the largest door was at the head of the room. The doors were all different colors, red, blue, yellow, green, orange, pink, and – the largest – white.

Jamie was the first to speak. "Trippy. What's this, like kindergarten or some shit? We here to learn colors?"

Cris laughed. "You, uh, you don't talk like many soldiers I've ever met."

Jamie grinned. "That's right, yo. There's only one Jamie!"

At that moment, the klaxon blared once, and words appeared in blue along the wall.

MAKE YOURSELVES COMFORTABLE

Meryn snorted. "How kind of our torturers."

Ethan walked over to the armchairs. "Suit yourself. But the smartest move here is to do as they say, otherwise we risk further punishment." Ethan sat down stiffly in the nearest armchair.

The others followed, Alera and Mai sitting first opposite Ethan. Cris and Jamie were next, and sat together between the girls and Ethan. Meryn, seeing one of the only two seats left on the other side of Ethan, made a beeline for the other seat. Victoria let her pass and calmly sat between them, though Cris thought she looked mildly displeased at the arrangement.

Jamie commented first as he reclined, "Well, they're comfy, at least."

Victoria leaned forward. "Al, I just noticed – your eyes are so pretty."

Alera blushed and looked down at her legs. "Oh! Thank you."

Meryn joined in. "She's not wrong, Al. Heterochromia's pretty rare."

Jamie scratched his bald head. "Hetero what now?"

"Heterochromia. It's when a human or animal's eyes have multiple colors. Al here has complete heterochromia, meaning each eye is a separate and distinct color."

"Is...is it like a disease?"

Cris interrupted, "No, it's not a disease, it's just a genetic feature, like being tall, brown-haired, or bald at a young age."

Jamie laughed and rubbed his smooth head. "Added sexiness then, I get it."

Everyone laughed except Ethan.

"Hello!"

Cris jumped out of his seat as the voice of what sounded like a teenage girl came from directly behind him. But when he turned to look, he saw nothing that wasn't there before. "What the...?"

The voice carried on with a cheerful lilt. "Forgive me if I startled you. No,

I'm not actually here. I'm a virtual instructor, or V.I. for short, but please, feel free to call me Vi."

Cris walked around the room. *It's like the voice is following me...as if it's just coming from the empty air in the middle of the room.*

Mai stood up, fists balled, looking up at the ceiling. "Why have you kidnapped us?"

Vi merrily answered, "You are here to perform a series of tasks. I apologize for any inconvenience."

"It's a bit more than an inconvenience!"

Cris, still looking for a speaker in the ceiling or floor, asked, "What do these tasks involve?"

Vi appeared to be endlessly jovial. "You will learn more about the tasks when it's time to do them."

Ethan cleared his throat. "What purpose do these tasks serve?"

Vi chirped, "Successful completion of tasks will result in rewards."

"What kind of rewards?"

"Food, drink, and/or entertainment."

"But we're not allowed to leave?"

"If you successfully complete the final task, you may exit through the white door."

I knew it! Cris looked again at the white door. It looked heavier and sturdier than any other door in the hallway or the large room.

Ethan leaned forward. "And if we fail?"

Vi answered, "Failure to complete a task or attempting to tamper with your collars will result in a strike."

Everybody froze.

Victoria asked, "What do the strikes mean?"

"Strikes are a measure of disobedience and/or failure. The number of strikes a person has is indicated on the back of their collar."

All eyes turned to Meryn as she immediately tried rotating her collar, but nothing ever appeared.

Cris walked around behind Meryn. Sure enough, a large red X was on the back of her collar. "I'm guessing it stays on the back no matter how much you try to turn it?"

Vi affirmed, "That is correct."

Meryn asked, "You see it?"

Cris nodded, "Yeah. It's a red X."

Ethan leaned back. "And there's an accompanying punishment for strikes, yes?"

Vi merrily pronounced, "Your first strike will result in the collar sending an impulse to the brain's pain center, activating it while simultaneously sending an impulse to the neurons in your central amygdala to silence them. The resulting pain will be extreme and all-encompassing. The impulse will last for one second."

Meryn stood up. "Bullshit! That felt like at least ten seconds, wasn't it?"

Vi corrected, "Regardless of how it felt, Meryn, your punishment only lasted for one second."

Cris turned to the empty air in the center of the room. "You know all our names?"

Vi answered, "Yes, Cris, that is correct."

"Are you an artificial intelligence?"

"I am a virtual instructor."

Cris stared. *What kind of a non-answer is that?*

Ethan shook his head. "We're getting off-topic. What happens when you get a second strike?"

Vi continued to deliver grim portents in the same tone of voice as an overly peppy store cashier. "Your second strike will result in the collar sending another pair of impulses to the pain center and amygdala, resulting in extreme pain, but this time the impulse will last until you fall unconscious."

Meryn's jaw dropped, and Alera covered her open mouth with one hand.

Cris asked, "How long will that take?"

Vi cheerily answered, "The time needed varies, depending on the individual's constitution, but roughly forty-five seconds to a minute should suffice."

The looks of horror and shock on everyone's face accompanied Meryn's shout, "OH MY GOD!"

Ethan appeared the least perturbed, but his voice wavered a bit as he asked, "And the third strike?"

Vi brightly responded, "The collar will send a targeted electric shock to the nerve fibers inside the brain stem."

Meryn gasped.

Vi continued, "This results in a painless and instantaneous death."

Chapter 4

The room erupted with noise. Meryn, Mai, Jamie, and Victoria were all on their feet and shouting simultaneously while Alera sobbed. Ethan didn't make a sound as he stared off into the distance, and Cris could only manage a light gurgle as a wave of nausea rolled over him. *This is absolutely insane – if they're willing to straight up murder us without a second thought, then what horrific things are the tasks going to make us do?*

Mai had tears in her eyes. "JUST LET US GO!"

Meryn had hate in her eyes. "SHOW YOUR FACES, YOU FUCKING COWARDS!"

Jamie was also raging, "THIS IS FUCKING FUCKED UP, YO!"

Victoria cried, "PLEASE! I DON'T BELONG HERE! I'VE DONE NOTHING WRONG!"

Cris stumbled away from the cacophony and knelt behind Alera's chair. Al was still weeping. The sudden urge to comfort her struck him, but he was keenly aware of the fact that they barely knew each other.

"Hey, Al." The words were out of his mouth before he knew what he was going to say.

Alera didn't look back, but she raised her head.

It felt trite and empty, but he had nothing else. "We're going to be okay."

Alera remained silent. To cover the awkwardness, Cris stood up and sat beside her.

"There's a....an orphanage. In Falls Church, just outside of Arlington. My sister runs it, and I help out when I can."

Alera had stopped crying, at least.

Cris looked in her eyes and said, ultra-seriously, "So we have to be okay. Otherwise, some orphans will cry."

Alera gave a half-smile and finally spoke. "Is that true?"

Cris looked away. "No. All of them will cry. We barely feed them."

Alera's green and blue eyes widened for a fraction of a second before she burst out laughing, and Cris joined in.

Cris through laughter said, "I'm sorry, that joke is SOOO dark!"

Alera wiped her eyes. "It was good, though."

Cris wanted to tell her they'd be okay again, but instead, he just locked eyes with her and nodded.

The shouting had calmed to loud voices. Meryn still demanded, "Tell us what the hell is going on! Answer me, Vi! VI!"

Ethan raised his voice for the first time. "Have you considered asking her a question?"

Everyone quieted.

Ethan's volume returned to its usual level. "She doesn't respond to commands or statements, do you, Vi?"

Vi returned, "That is correct. I have been programmed to answer questions and give the subjects their instructions."

Cris glanced at Ethan. *He doesn't miss much. He's not terribly gifted socially, but he is sharp.*

Meryn asked, "Why did you call us subjects just now?"

Vi answered, "Because that is how you are labeled."

Victoria questioned, "Is this all some kind of experiment?"

Vi chirped, "I do not have that information."

Jamie shouted, "So, who the hell locked us in here?"

Cris could hear Vi smiling. "The main computer controls the locks."

"That's not what I asked."

Ethan decided to take over. "Vi, who programmed the main computer?"

Vi merrily responded, "I do not have that information."

"Vi, what information do you have that we don't already know?"

"I have information on the planned structure of each day, information on the dormitory, information on the two types of tasks the subjects will be facing, and information on the subjects themselves."

"Let's take those in order, shall we? What's the planned structure of each day?"

"Each day begins with breakfast at seven A.M. here in the common room. Subjects will have access to standard breakfast fare including several cereal selections and juice. Subjects have free time until noon, at which point they'll be required to perform the first task of the day."

A stray thought broke Cris' focus. *This sounds weirdly like school.*

Vi continued, "After the first task, dinner will be available, and subjects will have free time until seven P.M., at which point they'll be required to perform the second task of the day. After the second task, the subjects will have free time until eleven P.M., at which point the common room will be locked until breakfast starts the following day."

Jamie snorted. "Probably so we don't beat their asses while they're bringing out our food."

Ethan ignored him. "Vi, what information on the dormitory can you give us?"

Brightly, Vi advised, "You may now use the dormitory as you see fit. The rooms you woke up in belong to you, and the doors to each room will now respond to the presence of their owner and no one else. There are no rules about staying in your own room, but if multiple people share a room, you do so at your own risk."

Meryn took over the interrogation. "What are the two types of tasks we'll be facing?"

"Your first task of the day is a practical task. These tasks require skill, knowledge, and teamwork to succeed."

Mai interrupted, "Do you have an example of a practical task?"

"I do not have that information."

Meryn resumed, "And the second type of task?"

"The evening tasks are social tasks. These will require courage, judgment, and interpersonal skills to succeed."

Alera wryly remarked, "Sounds delightful." Cris looked at her and lightly snorted.

Ethan stood up from his seat. "And while I admit to some trepidation, perhaps we should ask Vi for information about ourselves."

Meryn crossed to him and shot back, "No! We already agreed not to divulge too much about ourselves."

Ethan retorted, "This is information our kidnappers already have. Not only can it not do us additional harm, but it would be wise to find out what they know."

Meryn regarded him with lifeless eyes. "I think I genuinely hate it when you're right."

Ethan's face remained unmoved as she walked away. "You're not the first. Nor will you be the last. Vi, what information do you have regarding the subjects?"

"Jamie Gamble. Twenty-three years old. Air Force Pilot stationed at Wellens Air Force Base in Wayland, Massachusetts. Flight and Aeronautics expert."

Jamie straightened and saluted the room and then grinned lopsidedly. When Cris looked back at Alera, her hands had clasped the armrests, and she had become tense.

"Victoria Latimer. Twenty-four years old. Librarian. Carlsbad, California.

Culture expert."

Victoria was looking up. "I mean, yeah, I guess I sort of am. I know a lot about movies, plays, books, TV shows, video games, comic books, you name it."

Vi carried on. "Meryn Sarovitch. Thirty-four years old. Nurse. Buffalo, New York. Medical expert."

Meryn nodded. "I am working on my doctorate."

"Mai Shibata. Twenty-two years old. Mechanic. Jonesborough, Tennessee. Science and Technology expert."

Mai said nothing, just clasped her hands and shifted a little.

"Cris Thorpe. Twenty-five years old. Journalist. Arlington, Virginia. History expert."

Cris was a little puzzled. "I guess that's true. I've just always been able to remember names, places, and dates."

Vi continued. "Ethan Winters. Fifty-seven years old. Professor of Applied Mathematics. Cambridge, Massachusetts. Logic expert."

Ethan adjusted his suspenders but said nothing. Out of the corner of his eye, Cris noticed Alera shaking.

"Alera Zeller. Twenty-one years old. College student. Castleton, Vermont."

Alera stood up.

"Murder expert."

Chapter 5

All eyes were on Alera for several heartbeats.

She stammered, "M-, may I explain with a bit of a cliché'?"

Meryn still stared wide-eyed at her. "Okay. Shoot."

"It's not what you think."

"You know what my next question's gonna be, right?"

Alera took a deep breath and looked Meryn right in the eyes.

"I like murder."

Meryn stepped back. "That does not help."

Alera scoffed, "I mean, I like reading about it, hearing about it – not performing it."

Everyone continued to stare suspiciously at her.

"L-Look, it started when I was a teenager, and I started reading young adult novels about teenagers getting killed by serial killers, but before long, I started researching actual, real-life murders, and I'm still fascinated to this day. I listen to, like, eight or nine different true crime podcasts, and I have one of my own."

Mai visibly relaxed. "Really? What's it called?"

Alera was the most excited Cris had ever seen her. "It's called 'Don't Walk Alone'."

Mai shook her head. "Ooh, never heard of it, but I love that name. I listen to 'Midtown Murders' myself."

"Me, too! Alan and Sarah are amazing!"

Meryn still looked at them both with some doubt. "Mai, you can, uh, vouch for this?"

Mai nodded, "Yeah, doll face, it's real. True crime podcasts are huge. I may not be as big a fan as Al is, though."

Alera had talked more in the past minute than she had in the last hour, but she was not out of steam yet. "Look, I know it's unhealthy – my mom and everybody I know have said so – but I can't help it. I just really like dark stuff."

She looked over at Cris. "I even like dark jokes. But I've never hurt anyone, and I have nothing to do with any of this."

Ethan crossed his arms. "Well, labeling you a 'murder expert' has certainly focused our suspicions on you, which makes me wonder what our kidnappers are trying to deflect suspicion from."

Jamie looked confused. "Well, who else is suspicious?"

Ethan turned. "You tell me, Miss Shibata."

Mai spun to face him. "Huh?"

Ethan slowly stalked towards Mai at the end of the room. "We're trapped in a building of some sort with technologies that none of us have seen before, like voices emanating from nowhere. I haven't seen anything resembling a speaker anywhere in here, have any of you?"

Midst a chorus of head shakes, Jamie added, "And the words that just appear on the wall without a projector!"

Mai made a noise of disgust. "So? These are technologies that exist. How does that make me suspicious?"

Jamie had joined Ethan in staring down Mai. "You're the science and technology expert – you could have set this whole thing up!"

Victoria put herself right in Jamie's face. "Hey! There's no proof that she did!"

Cris interposed himself between Mai and Ethan. "The bad guys could have easily labeled her that way to make us suspicious of her, just like Alera. I'm surprised that didn't occur to such a logic expert."

If Ethan was offended, he didn't show it. "I discounted it when she verified she knew that the technology existed. While it doesn't prove her guilt, it does make her the most suspicious of us."

"I think it's more likely that none of us are involved. What would be the point of planting an agent among us when it's pretty clear our captors can already see and hear what we're doing?"

Ethan looked Cris dead in the eye. "Control."

Cris raised his voice. "What, they can't control us enough with strikes, pain, and death?!"

"EVERYBODY STOP!!" Meryn's scream echoed from the other side of the room. Her eyes blazed as they all turned to face her. "Listen to yourselves. We're doing exactly what they probably want. Tearing ourselves apart with doubt and mistrust weakens us and strengthens their hold over us."

Ethan's voice never wavered. "And what makes you believe that's what our captors are after?"

Meryn didn't take her eyes off Ethan's face. "Vi, are we being recorded?"

Vi, as cheery as ever, informed, "Video and audio of each room are recorded and saved on the main computer."

There was a second while the others digested that.

Ethan asked, "Vi, why wasn't this divulged when we asked you what information we did not have?"

Vi responded, "That information could only be given when directly asked about."

Meryn resumed, "Now do you get it? They could've blocked that information from us, but they didn't. I have to assume that means they eventually expected us to find out. Which means they want us to be paranoid. And these psychopaths are at least telling us that they're willing to kill us, and I know from experience that they're willing to hurt us. So I don't want them to get what they want."

Cris nodded in agreement.

Meryn continued, "If they want us to be paranoid, then I want to trust you." She looked at Ethan in particular. "I want to trust ALL of you."

Ethan looked away, lost in thought.

Meryn concluded, "I think we need to band together. Because if we don't, we could all die."

Tempers subsided quickly, and everyone split off. Cris had sat in an armchair until Ethan realized there was likely more information Vi was holding back until asked about. The interrogation and the constant repetition of "I do not have that information" drove Cris from the room.

He headed for the room he'd woken up in, and sure enough, the door slid open at his approach. Cris walked in and sat down hard on the edge of the bed, letting out a long sigh. *Alone at last. Unless...?*

Cris asked, "Vi, are you here, too?"

Immediately, a perky and familiar voice assaulted his ears. "Yes, Cris. I am available in every room of the complex."

"Great. Can't ever be rid of you. Perfect."

Wait. Does that mean-

"Vi, is this room soundproof?"

"All dorm rooms have soundproof walls, though sound can escape through the door."

"Does that mean anybody can ask you a question, and the rest of us won't know?"

"Unless someone listens at the door, that is correct."

Ethan could have had a hand in programming this AI. But so could Mai. Maybe this is literally only for one or two of us, and the rest are all in on it. Cris sighed to himself. *By the time I figure any of this out, I'll probably be dead.*

There was a knock on the door.

"Come in."

Nothing happened.

Oh. Right.

Cris walked up to the door, and it slid open, revealing Jamie. "Yo! What up?"

"Uh, nothing. Just kinda thinking, I guess."

"Cool. You mind if I think with you?" Jamie smiled up at Cris.

Cris couldn't help but laugh at his earnest face. "Why not? Come on in."

Jamie walked past Cris into the room, looked around, and sat in the lone chair, legs splayed out. "Yo, I like what you haven't done with the place." He giggled at his own joke, and Cris couldn't help but laugh.

"Yeah, my decorators are busy keeping us trapped here and dancing to their tune."

Jamie's smile faded. "Yeah, well, we're gonna fuckin' change the music."

"I sure hope so. Why are you here?"

"Dude, if I knew, I'd say so."

"No, I mean, here, in my room."

Jamie laughed. "Sorry. I don't know, man. I don't know anybody, and you seem pretty chill."

Cris leaned against the wall and crossed his arms. "Thanks. So what's your deal?"

Jamie leaned forward. "I don't really have a deal, man. I'm a traveler of the green, son. You?"

Cris shrugged. "I'd partake a time or two in college, but weed was never really my thing. No offense."

"None taken, brother. Weed isn't for everybody. Sure would like some now to settle my nerves, though."

"I hear you. I know your base is in Massachusetts. Where're you from originally?"

A wide grin appeared on Jamie's face. "Niagara Falls, baby!"

His enthusiasm is super infectious – but considering how quickly he jumped to accuse Mai, I'd say that passion's got two sides to it.

Cris raised an eyebrow. "That's not far from where Meryn's from."

"Yeah, I know. Not sure what it could mean, though, not everybody's from the northeast, but maybe something happened around there that still links everyone somehow? I don't know, man, it just hurts my brain." Jamie massaged his bald head.

Cris was looking right at Jamie when he felt a wave of tiredness ripple through him, and his eyelids suddenly got heavy.

Jamie looked up bleary-eyed. "What? I'm not gonna sleep..."

Jamie slumped in his chair as Cris's legs gave out, and he collapsed.

What is happening—

Then everything went black.

Chapter 6

When he came to, Cris was still on the floor. He looked up to see Jamie still in the chair, stirring. He groaned aloud as he pushed himself up to a sitting position.

Jamie was wiping his eyes. "What the fuck was that? Nap time?"

"I don't know. We should check on the others."

"Agreed."

Jamie followed as Cris stood up and activated his door. As they emerged into the hallway, Mai and Victoria exited their rooms, yawning.

Victoria asked, "Did everybody else just fall asleep out of nowhere?"

As if in answer, from the large room, Meryn yelled, "Uh, guys? Dinner's ready!"

Everyone filed into the large room to see Meryn, Ethan, and Alera standing next to the round table, upon which now sat three pitchers of what appeared to be ice water, a small stack of plastic cups, and a platter piled high with hot dogs in buns.

Alera pointed out, "I guess this is why they knocked us out? So they could bring the food in?"

Jamie seemed dismayed. "Just hot dogs and water?"

Mai laughed. "I'd've figured you'd be used to rations."

Jamie scratched his head. "I mean, MRE's are amazing, but I'm used to having some food options on base."

Victoria added, "Well, technically hot dogs are keto friendly as long as you skip the bun."

Mai shook her head. "Whatever, doll face. I'm starving."

Ethan held out a hand. "Wait. It's entirely possible that they drugged the food."

Mai grabbed a hot dog. "Well, here's hoping they used some good drugs." She took a big bite, chewed, and swallowed while everyone watched. Mai shrugged and added, "Tastes like perfectly normal hot dog to me."

Ethan said nothing but did not take his eyes off Mai.

"What?"

"Remember that lack of proof is not proof of lack." With that, Ethan walked away from the table.

"Weird-ass old man..." Mai muttered under her breath.

Well, if she can be brave, so can I. Cris poured some ice water into a glass and drank. "Nothing weird that I can detect."

Meryn shrugged. "Dig in, I guess?" She grabbed a hot dog for herself and grabbed a plastic cup while Alera dutifully poured her and the others a drink from the pitcher nearest her. Cris grabbed a hot dog and pulled out a seat at the table. The others eventually followed suit as everybody except Ethan ate their fill. Before long, the feast turned into a conversation.

"I mean, I guess I've always wanted to be a reporter, ever since I was a kid." Cris drank the last dregs of water from his cup. "Couldn't really tell you why."

Meryn nodded. "I hear you. I just sort of fell into nursing. I didn't really know what I wanted to do, even in college, but I've just always liked taking care of people. What about you, Victoria?"

Victoria's face lit up. "Oh, I'm a HUGE nerd!" She laughed, and the others followed suit. "I've been a big reader forever, and I got into acting and singing in high school. But I enjoy all sorts of things. I play video games, I read comic books, and when there was an ad for a job at my local library, I just jumped on it."

Mai smiled. "I guess that's sort of true for me, too. I've loved cars since I was a kid, and I got into computers around the same time I started working on cars. I've built a bunch of computers. Haven't built a car from scratch yet, but that's on my list. What about you, Jamie?"

Jamie leaned back in his chair, nearly falling over, but caught himself. "Whoa. I'm from a military family, but we're probably more chill than most. My folks are retired and traveling constantly, and I guess I just always wanna go fast. Mama says I was constantly running everywhere, and I drive like an absolute lunatic. Wasn't much of a jump to flying jets."

Meryn asked, "What's that like?"

"I guess I'd describe it as sheer joy and euphoria, with occasional moments of pure pants-shitting terror." He laughed.

Alera piped up. "I'm still sorta undecided about what I'm gonna major in."

Victoria asked, "But didn't the voice say you're twenty-one?"

"I started college later, when I was twenty. If I were gonna lean one way or another, it'd be programming. I really enjoy seeing something I've programmed come to life, even if it's something as silly as a button lighting up."

Cris leaned over the table. "Does that mean there might be a murder mystery game in your future?"

Alera's smile threatened to split her face. "I've been thinking about that for ages! I just don't know how it would play – I think I could totally make a bad-ass murder mystery game!"

Meryn pushed her chair out from the table and stood up. "And what about our enigmatic math professor?"

Ethan chuckled dryly. "What do you think? I went to gifted math classes my whole life and was usually the best in those as well. Attended college classes at fourteen and won a full ride at sixteen. Spent some time in the private sector but returned to teaching in my mid-forties."

"Why'd you leave the private sector?" Cris asked.

"I'm only willing to share publicly available information at this time, Mr. Reporter."

Cris laughed. "I'm not asking for a story, just curious."

"Well, not only is it private, but it's also irrelevant."

Meryn leaned back in her chair to look at Ethan. "It's been about a half an hour, by the way. If Mai had been drugged or poisoned by her hot dog, odds are she would've presented symptoms by now."

"Are those odds one-hundred percent?"

"More like ninety to ninety-five percent."

Ethan crossed his arms. "I'll hold off, thanks."

Meryn leaned forward again. "Okay. Enjoy your cold hot dog."

The others continued to talk for some time until everyone decided to sit in the more comfortable armchairs. Ethan took the opportunity to finally eat, and the evening passed somewhat pleasantly with no more conflicts or major revelations. However, it was fairly obvious to Cris that everyone was anxious and worried about what tomorrow would bring.

Eventually, Vi spoke up. "Attention. It is now eleven P.M. In five minutes the door to the common room will lock. Please proceed to your dormitories. I would advise being in bed by midnight as that's when your collar will signal your brain to produce the neurotransmitters that will induce sleep."

Victoria's eyes widened. "That's convenient. I usually have difficulty getting to sleep without my air conditioner."

Vi did not react. "A similar signal will be sent at seven A.M. to induce wakefulness, though you may awake before then."

Jamie turned to face everybody. "Welp, I'm gonna call it a night. See you tomorrow when we're going to crush these tasks, yo."

Cris nodded, "Yeah, we are. Good night everybody."

Everyone headed off toward the dorms, except for Ethan.

Alera turned back and asked, "Uh, Ethan, this door's gonna lock you in in a few minutes."

Ethan half turned his head. "I think I might sleep in the common room tonight."

Alera shrugged and rejoined the others.

Cris opened his door and looked back as Alera opened hers. He just smiled and nodded. She returned the smile, and they both went into their rooms.

As the door slid shut, Cris took off his clothes and hung them over the back of the chair. He sat on the edge of his bed. *I don't know what Ethan's up to. Maybe he's trying to test the collar's ability to send the sleep signal if he's not in his dorm. Or he could be setting some kind of trap.*

Cris lay down, pulling the covers over himself. He mused about this for some time before sleep overtook him.

Cris awoke with a start. He was momentarily concerned that he was not in his own bed until the previous day's events came back to him. *Oh. Right.*

Cris pulled out the covers and swung himself up into a sitting position. "Good morning, Vi. What time is it?"

Vi chirped, "It is 7:01 A.M. Breakfast is available in the common room."

Cris stood up and saw his clothes folded neatly on the seat of the chair. *Someone came in my room while I slept!*

"Vi, what happened to my clothes?"

"Your clothes were washed and dried last night."

I mean, I guess that's better than being forced to wear the same stinky outfit for however long...

Cris dressed and walked into the hallway. Almost immediately, Alera opened her door.

She said, "Oh! Good morning!"

Cris replied, "I was going to scope out breakfast, care to join me?"

"I, uh, I guess that depends."

"Okay. On anything in particular, or...?"

Cris heard a slight commotion, and then Victoria emerged from Alera's room and stood beside her in the doorway.

"She might be referring to me."

Whoa.

Chapter 7

Cris' mind whirled. "Uh. Oh! Uh, well, I didn't know, and I can, um—"

Victoria held up a hand. "Easy, it's all good, nothing happened. I just didn't want to be alone, and Alera was kind enough to let me stay with her."

Cris held up his hands, mirroring Victoria. "It's none of my business at all. I just thought—hey, you know what? What say we all just grab breakfast together?"

Victoria smiled at him. "Heck yeah!"

She then grabbed Alera and Cris' hands. Before he could even register surprise, Victoria walked them into the common room. The three of them joined Ethan and Meryn inspecting the dining table, though Victoria did not let go of Cris' hand.

The breakfast choices were a little less sparse than dinner the night before. There were five different kinds of cereal, two boxes each, some sugar in a little white porcelain container, three half-gallons of milk, whole, two percent, and almond, paper bowls and plastic spoons.

Meryn was quick to gripe. "No coffee?"

Vi chirped, "You may request coffee for future meals if you succeed at your tasks."

"How do you expect me to succeed at anything without coffee?"

Vi answered, "I have no expectations of success or failure."

Meryn sighed. "Yep, that's what a day without coffee does to you."

Ethan did not wait this time, he grabbed a bowl and filled it with a marshmallow-laden cereal, and reached for the 2% milk when Cris asked, "No hesitation this time, Ethan?"

Ethan continued pouring the milk into the bowl as he said, "The food was not drugged last night as far as we could detect. It seems statistically unlikely they would drug us on the second meal and not the first." He pulled up a chair and sat down, tilting his head to one side and rubbing his neck. "I should also add that I attempted to find a seam in the walls or floor last night, and Vi informed me that attempting to tamper with the walls, floor, or ceiling would result in a strike."

Mai raised an eyebrow. "Why'd ya sleep in the common room?"

Ethan ceased massaging himself. "Doing what our captors don't expect might lead to them slipping up, but in this case, it just led to a stiff neck. I'll be sleeping in my dormitory from here on."

"So ya CAN admit when yer wrong!" Mai's face reflected excessive amazement.

Cris poured some crispy rice cereal and added milk and half a spoonful of sugar, but before he could pull a chair out, Victoria nudged him with her elbow and said quietly, "Let's go sit in the armchairs."

Cris could hardly disagree with that, so he sat down in an armchair. Victoria quickly joined him, and Alera sat on her other side. Cris decided to break the ice. "So, Victoria, I actually guessed you were a singer before you told us yesterday."

Her eyes widened. "Really? How?"

He shrugged. "You just have a really rich voice. I figured either you were a singer or a professional speaker or something."

Victoria laughed. "Well, thank you, kind sir. Do you sing yourself?"

"Only occasionally, for fun. Karaoke, for example."

"What do you like to sing?"

"I do, like, three songs." Cris laughed. "Paranoid Android by Radiohead is my anthem. But I've been known to do a pretty mean Interstate Love Song by Stone Temple Pilots and an eerily excellent Jack Black impression in Tribute by Tenacious D."

Victoria and Alera both laughed. Victoria followed with, "Oh, my God! I forgot about that song! It's so much fun!"

Alera added, "Victoria sang for me last night. Her voice is AMAZING."

Victoria looked simultaneously flustered and pleased. "Oh, stop."

Cris swallowed his cereal. "What do you like to sing, Victoria?"

Victoria answered, "Oh, you know, I like my musical theatre!" She sang the last two words.

Cris' eyes widened. *If just two words sound that good...*

Meryn was seating herself opposite the trio. "Ooh, is Victoria gonna sing?"

Victoria sighed, but Cris noticed a half-smile as well.

She sang "I love your funny face, your sunny, funny face, for you're a cutie with more than beauty. You've got a lot of personality N.T., a thousand laughs I've found in having you around, though you're no Gloria Swanson, for worlds I'd not replace your sunny, funny face..."

Everyone in the room applauded. *That was AMAZING. Even Ethan was impressed. She has such incredible control over her voice.*

Cris just said, "Outstanding."

Victoria nodded and flashed him a smile, "Thank you."

Ethan shouted from the table, "That is a tremendous gift you have, young lady."

Victoria tipped a hat she wasn't wearing. "Thank you, kind sir."

The compliments kept flowing, and while Victoria's grin stayed wide, she did not seem embarrassed in the slightest. *She genuinely loves singing for people. I can't match her skill, but I totally understand why she does it.*

The conversation turned to Victoria's training and favorite musicals from there, and Cris noticed Alera was paying rapt attention. *Apparently, nothing happened, but I guess that doesn't mean nothing will.* Alera then caught Cris looking at her, and she smiled at him briefly before turning back to Victoria.

"What about you?" Victoria asked Cris. "Have you had any training at all?"

"No, I'm more of a car singer, I guess."

"I get it. I used to drive my mom crazy on car rides with my singing as a kid."

Alera leaned in. "What about now?"

"Oh, she is my BIGGEST fan – she tells everybody in the neighborhood about my shows and always drags a few people to come see me."

Mai had a wistful look on her face. "Wow. Your mom sounds really supportive."

Victoria nodded. "She's the best."

Cris asked, "What about you, Alera? Any singing?"

Alera shook her head. "Oh, no, you wouldn't want me to sing. I sang happy birthday to someone once, and before I could start the second line, he jumped out the window. And we were on the 17th floor!"

Cris and Victoria laughed.

Alera added, "Seriously, I am tone deaf and rhythm impaired. I can't dance, either. That's why I'm so impressed by someone who can sing."

Jamie, finishing his cereal, "Same here, dude. I got no musical talent at all."

Victoria turned to Mai. "What about you?"

"I guess I can sing. I just don't really enjoy it." Mai managed to look a bit apologetic.

Meryn shook her head. "I sang in church as a kid, but never since."

Cris turned in his armchair to look at Ethan sitting alone at the table. "I feel like we can guess, but how about you, Ethan? Got some pipes on you?"

Ethan responded at first by clearing his throat.

Victoria's eyes widened.

Ethan began to sing a hymn Cris had never heard of. His voice was deep and warbling as he sang of finding strength in belief. While not as trained or precise as Victoria's voice, it was no less beautiful.

As Ethan finished, the room remained in stunned silence for a moment until Victoria breathed, "Wow."

Ethan crossed his arms and sat back in his chair. "Nobody is ever just one thing."

Mai snorted. "Sounded like religious crap to me. Weird that a logician wouldn't reason out that God doesn't exist."

Ethan looked over at Mai. "Logic, like religion, is about trying to find answers to questions, such as the existence of a higher power. While what you're far more familiar with, emotions, are reactions that provide no answers, and can even have disastrous consequences."

Mai stood, walked to the table, and planted her hands on it. "You don't know a fuckin' thing about me. Let's just keep it that way."

As she turned and stalked off, Ethan replied, "Thanks for proving my point."

Without turning around, Mai retorted, "All you're provin' is your ignorance." And she left the room.

After the awkwardness of the moment had passed, Cris remembered something important.

"Hey, Alera, Victoria, did anyone come into your room last night?"

The girls looked at one another briefly before Alera answered. "I hope not!"

Cris leaned in. "When I woke up, my clothes were folded on the chair. Vi confirmed that someone did my laundry last night."

Victoria's eyes widened. "That's creepy. We slept in our clothes, so probably nobody bothered with us?"

Alera added, "But that means whatever sleep agent they're administering to us is strong enough that they're not worried about us waking up and interrupting them."

Cris nodded. "I'd say it also lends credence to the theory that our kidnappers don't want us dead, and this is more of an experiment of some kind. They also have weird ideas about how comfortable we should be, as we're given extremely basic food to eat, hot dogs and cereal, and whoever heard of a kidnapper doing their hostage's laundry?"

Victoria asked, "You think the threat of the third strike might be a bluff?"

"I sure hope so."

Time passed slowly, with small patches of quiet conversation here and there. But the general anxiety rose as the time crept closer to noon. As the deadline grew near, everyone gathered in the comfortable chairs of the common room.

Jamie said for the third time to no one in particular, "Wonder what we're going to have to do?"

Ethan got as irritated as Cris had ever seen him. "Young man, asking that serves no purpose."

Mai, who sat next to Jamie, laid a hand on his shoulder. "Jamie, ignore Ethan. Giving voice to your fears can actually help quiet them."

Jamie threw her a grateful look. Ethan grunted but said nothing.

Cris said, "Regardless, we won't have to wonder much longer."

A moment of silence reigned but was shattered by Vi's klaxon.

Vi happily announced, "It is now time for the day's first task. Please be seated at the table for the task briefing."

Everybody looked at each other before getting up and migrating to the table. Once everyone was seated, Vi continued.

"Your task is to repair a cryomedic chamber."

Meryn scoffed. "What?"

As Vi spoke, a series of pictures and blueprints appeared on the table's surface, depicting a pill-shaped object, large enough to accommodate a person, with a monitor and control panel mounted on its side.

"The cryomedic chamber is defective and appears to be breaking down. You will need to split up into three groups. The chamber and all required spare parts and tools are located behind the blue door. Service manuals with error documentation and possible fixes are located behind the red door. User guides and parts catalogs are behind the yellow door. All participants will be locked in the rooms before access to any materials is granted, and the locks will not release until the task is over."

Mai, confused, reacted, "Oh, so it's a sort of team-building exercise?"

Vi continued chirping, "Cooperation will be required to complete this task.

Cris smiled. "Well, then. This might not be so bad after all."

Vi happily pronounced, "Your time started when you all sat down at the table."

Alera quickly said, "Wait—"

Vi nevertheless continued, "Your time ends when the man in the chamber dies."

Chapter 8

Panic immediately set in as everyone talked over each other.

Meryn overrode the shouting. "WE NEED TO MOVE – NOW!!"

Ethan stood up. "Agreed! Miss Shibata – if there's broken parts on the machine, you're most qualified to replace them, correct?"

Mai reacted a bit slowly. "Yes, you're right. I should go in the blue door."

Cris added, "Meryn, with your medical skills, you should join her. You might be able to keep him alive longer."

Meryn nodded strongly. "I don't know how we'll communicate between rooms."

Jamie raised his hand. "I'm no good at reading manuals and stuff. I'll go with them and do all the communicating."

Victoria said, "The rest of us should split between the other rooms. Ethan, where would a man of logic be most useful?"

Ethan started walking. "The red door – Miss Zeller, you said you're a programmer?"

Alera stammered, "Y-yes, but I—"

"Good, you're with me."

Alera looked confused but followed him to the red door.

Cris looked up at Victoria. "Let's take the yellow door."

"Copy that."

As everyone scurried to their doors, Meryn shouted, "Vi, open the doors!"

Vi remained perky as ever. "Doors will open momentarily for five seconds. Please move quickly into your selected rooms. The doors will shut and lock when the five seconds are up."

As she finished that statement, the doors slid open. Cris and Victoria saw a table with a pair of boxes and a phone on the wall between their room and the blue door room. Cris took a moment to look back at the others, but they were all heading into their rooms, and Cris and Victoria quickly followed suit.

Victoria quickly made her way to the table and tried opening the boxes.

I'm assuming the phone is the only way to contact the others. Looking at the phone, Cris saw just a handset resting in its cradle, no buttons or dialing apparatus of any kind that he could see.

At that moment, the doors slid shut, and Cris heard a click coming from the table. As he turned to look, Victoria removed the box, and underneath was a large book.

"Cryomedic Chamber MX1000 Parts Catalog."

Cris removed the other box and found a book labeled "Cryomedic Chamber MX1000 User Manual". Both books were thin, fifty pages or so.

Victoria sighed. "Fun stuff."

The phone rang. Cris picked it up. "Hello?"

It was Mai's voice on the other end. "Cris! Okay! It is FREEZING in here. Uh, the cryo-thingy is real, and uh—"

Cris heard a garbled shout in the background.

"Okay, there's a middle-aged man in the cryo chamber. Neither of us recognize him, and the screen on the chamber has some error codes on it: E00206 and E00302."

Cris turned to Victoria. "See if you can find anything in those books about error codes."

"Got it!"

Mai added, "Jamie's on the other phone, talking to Alera in the red room, but they don't see any way to call you."

Cris nodded. "Yeah, I figured it would be something like that. You need the info from both of our rooms to fix the chamber, but we can't collaborate with them directly."

"Looks like. Any luck?"

Cris looked at Victoria. "Anything?"

Victoria shook her head. "Just a small blurb in the user manual saying to follow the instructions in the service manual if error codes appear."

Cris turned back to the phone. "User manual says that error code info is in the service manual."

"Yeah, I think...I think Jamie's getting that stuff now."

Some more shouting in the background.

"Jamie says that E00206 is an extruder valve failure, and E00302 is miscalibration in the coolant unit!"

Cris relayed this to Victoria, who continued to rapidly flip pages. Cris shouted, "Vi, how long do we have before the man dies?"

Vi chirped, "I do not have that information."

"Helpful, Vi, thanks."

"You're welcome." Vi appeared to be immune to sarcasm.

Mai said, "Jamie says Ethan found the instructions for replacing the extruder valve, but they're all in text, no pictures or descriptions of the parts."

Cris thought aloud. "Oh, that's where we come in, we can describe the parts and where they are on the machine."

"Alright, I'm up – I'm going to switch with Meryn, okay?"

"Okay!"

There were some noises as the phone was passed over, then, "Cris?"

"Meryn! I'm here."

There was urgency in Meryn's voice. "I don't recognize the man in there, but the cryo-chamber's cooling has failed, and the man is defrosting, for lack of a better word."

Cris' mind reeled. "Wait, shouldn't we go ahead and defrost him? He may be able to tell us more about what's going on."

Before Meryn could, Victoria answered, "It's not that simple. According to this," she held up the user manual, "the revival procedure's very complex and specific. The defrosting has to occur at a certain rate, the oxygen level in the chamber needs to be carefully controlled, and the machine has to inject the body with chemical compounds at specific times to encourage tissue regeneration. If he continues to get warm without all of that, I think he'll just go from being cold and dead to being warm and dead."

Cris relayed that information to Meryn, who replied, "Yeah, that sounds about right to me. His temperature gauge inside the chamber has risen from minus 190 degrees Celsius to minus 184 degrees Celsius since we walked in. Any chance Victoria can figure out how long we've got?"

Cris asked Victoria, "Does it say what temperature he'll die at?"

"Shit, I saw that somewhere..." She flipped rapidly through the pages for several long seconds, then ran her finger down a page. "Got it! It says, in case of coolant problems, any damage to the patient can be reversed as long as the temperature stays below minus 140 degrees Celsius and permanent brain death can be prevented as long as it stays below minus 130!"

Cris asked, "Vi, can you calculate how long it'll take for the temperature in the cryo-chamber to drop to minus 130 Celsius?"

Vi happily answered, "Assuming a stable rate of heat transfer, the chamber will reach minus 130 degrees Celsius in twelve minutes and thirty-nine seconds."

Cris turned to the phone. "Meryn, according to Victoria's info and Vi's calculations, we've got twelve and a half minutes."

"Oh, hell. Mai's taken off the back panel and it looks like there's another cover inside."

More muffled shouting from the phone.

Meryn said, "Mai got the second cover off, but she doesn't know what she's looking at."

Additional garbled shouting could be heard from the blue room.

Meryn added, "Jamie says the next step is to remove the extruder valve, but she has no idea what that is."

Cris said, "That's gotta be in the parts you've got in the room, right?"

"Yeah, but all the boxes just have parts numbers on them, no names."

Cris turned to Victoria, "Can you find the extruder valve part number in the parts catalog?"

Victoria looked up at him, panicked. "I can't read it. It's all diagrams."

Cris' mind raced. "Switch with me. Come take the phone and talk to Meryn!"

Victoria took the phone, and Cris ran over to the table and opened the parts catalog, which was organized by sections of the machine, each displayed in a three-quarters angle exploded view with individual parts labeled with both a reference number and a part number, connected by lines to the rest of the machine and shown in wireframe. He quickly found the section that looked like the rear of the cryo-chamber and, on the next page, found a list of individual parts and a reference number.

Okay, so I find the reference number on the diagram, and that gives me the part number.

Cris found the reference number for the extruder valve and searched the diagram for it. *Come on, where are you—THERE!*

Cris shouted, "Part number XM4-1450! It's a T-shaped pipe with a gauge on the end!"

Victoria quickly relayed the number and description over the phone while Cris tried to find the coolant unit. *Should be nearby, right?*

Before he could locate it, Victoria repeated, "Meryn says Ethan's telling them to stop, should I tell her to ignore him?"

Cris' thoughts whirled at breakneck speed. He stared at the diagram while trying to make sense of the madness. *Wait. So if the coolant unit feeds directly into the extruder valve, then...!*

"HE'S RIGHT! STOP!"

Cris practically ran to the phone, and Victoria held it sideways so they could both hear and speak into it. "The coolant feeds right into the valve, and its at sub-freezing temperatures. If she touches the valve with her bare fingers —"

Meryn said, "I'll tell her, no touching, tools only."

Victoria asked, "Is that what Ethan wanted to warn about?"

There was a moment of conversation they could hear over the line.

"No, Ethan said to pull the power. But if we do that, he will warm up and die even faster."

Cris said, "I don't think we have a choice. If the two parts failed together, seems likely that one of them broke the other. If a miscalibrated coolant unit broke the extruder valve, replacing the valve won't fix it. It'll just break another extruder valve."

Meryn chewed over that a second. "Yeah, I think you're right. We don't have a choice." They could then faintly hear her yell to someone else. "Pull the plug!" There was a muffled reply. Then Meryn said, "Okay, apparently there's a big box it's plugged into, which is then plugged into the wall. Does it matter which one we—" They stood at the phone in silence while someone else talked, and Cris could feel his heart trying to beat its way out of his chest.

"Jamie says to unplug from the box because the box is probably an uninterruptible power supply."

Victoria looked up at Cris and said, "That's basically a big battery, right? If we just unplugged it from the wall, it would keep going, possibly for hours."

Meryn said, "Yeah, we got it. Powered down. Mai's going to try and replace the valve now."

It was probably only a minute, but it felt like an eternity as Cris and Victoria stared at each other, waiting for news. Victoria had a look on her face that Cris couldn't place at first. *She looks helpless, but she's been self-assured and confident since the moment she appeared. I wish I had that much faith in myself, but right now, it's not doing her any good.*

Meryn said, "Temperature's up to minus 160 degrees, but the extruder valve's been replaced. Now Mai's gonna recalibrate the coolant unit."

There was more conversation in the background.

"She's just gotta turn the wheel on top of the coolant unit until she feels a click, but she doesn't want to try using just her fingers, she says her fingers are frozen as it is. She's gonna use...looks like a big pair of forceps."

Cris reached out his hand to Victoria, who grabbed it quickly.

"Come on, come on. Up to minus 150 degrees."

Cris heard only his ridiculously loud heartbeat and Victoria's urgent breathing.

Meryn shouted, "She thinks she got it!" Cris then heard her say, "Quick, plug it back in!"

Cris held his breath.

After a moment passed, Meryn shouted, "It's booting up!"

Cris and Victoria's eyes widened.

"IT SAYS TEMPERATURE STABILIZING! WE DID IT!"

Cris let out an explosive laugh, and Victoria joined him. He hugged her and swung her around in a dance of exuberant joy.

And when he put her down, Victoria grabbed his head and kissed him full on the lips.

Chapter 9

All Cris could say was, "Well, didn't expect that." *And that was the dumbest damn thing to say.*

Victoria looked alarmed. "I'm sorry! I just—I don't know. I'm a very affectionate person."

"You have nothing to be sorry about."

"I'm not apologizing."

"You just said you're sorry."

Victoria looked flustered and said, "I know."

Cris laughed.

Victoria took Cris' hand in both of hers. "Look. This is a crazy situation, and I just feel...safer...with you."

"The feeling is mutual. I just thought you were interested in AI."

"I am."

Cris' momentary confusion lasted long enough for them both to realize there was still a voice coming from the phone. Victoria grabbed it and held it up as both of them put their heads near the handset.

"...are you guys? Hello?" Meryn said plaintively.

Victoria answered, "Sorry! We're here!"

"Something's wrong."

Cris felt something cold forming in his stomach.

"It says it's stabilizing but the temperature in the chamber is still rising. Minus 140."

"I'm on it!" Victoria handed Cris the phone and moved back to the table, grabbing the user manual.

"Minus 139! It says temperature at dangerous levels! What do we do?" Meryn asked.

Cris tried to reason out what was happening. *It probably needs time to spin up the cooling to such a low temperature, but it's not like the machine was unpowered for all that long.*

Victoria kept flipping through the manual.

"Minus 138! Anything?"

Victoria stopped and ran her finger down the page. "I got it!" She ran back to the phone. "The temperature takes some time to stabilize, but it says the process should take no more than a minute."

Meryn sounded like she was on the edge of panic. "How long has it been?! Wait—minus 137 now, but it says temperature stabilized."

Vi cheerily announced, "You have successfully completed your task."

Cris said, "Wait, what?"

Vi repeated, "You have successfully—"

Victoria ignored Vi and spoke into the phone. "Meryn, you have to get the temperature back down to minus 140 degrees, the manual says he'll suffer irreversible damage otherwise!"

Meryn said, "I know, but I don't see—there's just a lock symbol on the screen and it says contact the attending physician. There's nothing I can do. But the temperature still says minus 137. I think he'll live."

Vi continued, "You have each earned one request for food, drink, or entertainment. You may make your request at any time, and if possible, your requested item will be available for the remainder of your time here."

Cris looked at Victoria, and the cold feeling in his stomach refused to go away. *Irreversible damage...and he could be someone's dad.*

Before he could say anything, Vi announced, "The doors will open once all items are returned to their containers. The doors will remain open until the next task requiring these rooms is prepared."

Cris ran to grab one of the boxes Victoria had thrown in a corner. "We need to get to that chamber."

Victoria was reading intently. "Give me just a sec. I'm trying to learn as much as I can here."

Cris covered the parts catalog with a box and headed back for the second. "How old is your father, Vix?"

"Forty-seven. Forty-eight next month."

Cris walked back to her side with the second box. "So, middle-aged then?"

Victoria looked up from the manual, looked into Cris' eyes, then grabbed the box and put it over the user manual. There was a loud click. "Vi, can you open the doors now?"

Vi answered, "Some items have not yet been secured in the blue room."

Cris said, "Mai probably tried to keep a tool or two. I would."

The doors then slid open with a hiss.

Cris and Victoria emerged to find Ethan and Alera coming out of their room. Alera waved excitedly and smiled. Ethan merely said, "Well done, everyone. Shall we?"

The four walked into the blue room to find Meryn, Mai, and Jamie standing next to a long blue pill-shaped cylinder resting at an incline with a two-foot-long window at its front, and a small monitor on what appeared to be a movable arm sticking out the right side. Through the window, Cris could see a man in his late forties or early fifties, with a well-lined face, strong nose, and graying high-and-tight haircut, wearing a navy-blue suit jacket, a smart tie, and a white shirt. There was an American flag pin on his lapel.

Mai asked, "Does anybody recognize him?"

Jamie squinted. "He looks kinda like a geography teacher."

Victoria furrowed her brow. "Never seen him before."

Alera shook her head. "Me either."

Cris stepped right up next to the chamber and stood on tiptoe to see deeper inside. The man was wearing a no-nonsense black leather belt, slacks that matched the jacket, and black wingtips. The suit appeared to be made from finely woven wool with a high thread count and looked like it was tailored to fit. Cris turned his attention to the man's hands. The arms of the jacket ended in very plain polished silver cuff links. *And those hands haven't done an honest day's work in his entire life.*

"My guess? He's a government employee, and not a low level one, either. He's probably somebody high up, like the head of a department or maybe even an entire agency? It's hard to tell."

Meryn tilted her head and gave Cris a look of disbelief. "Where do you get all that?"

"His clothes and his hands, mostly. He's wearing an expensive tailored suit that costs more than I or even Ethan makes in a month, but he's not flashy about it. He wears a very plain set of cuff links, tie, and a belt. He's wearing an American flag pin and his haircut screams ex-military to me, but he's got soft hands, so if he is military, he was likely an officer instead of enlisted. All of that would seem to point to either a government or civilian job that pays very well, but given our current situation, I lean more government."

Ethan folded his arms. "Even I can't argue with that logic."

Alera asked, "So, what should we call him? The President?"

Jamie laughed, but Cris said, "Well, he's obviously NOT the President, or any other public official that I know of..."

Victoria said, "This isn't helpful right now – moreover, while we saved his life, he's likely still going to suffer. The manual said that the temperature rising above minus 140 degrees would result in permanent, irreversible damage."

Ethan asked, "What kind of damage?"

"The manual didn't say."

Meryn said, "With something like this, you could be talking about veins, capillaries, or nerves, but more likely, it means the brain."

Mai's face fell. "So even if we could wake him, he probably couldn't tell us anything."

Meryn glumly shrugged. "Hard to say. Depends on the damage."

Cris put his hands on his hips. "So, you're telling me...we just accidentally brain-damaged the President."

The seven of them slowly filed into the central chamber when Ethan suddenly spoke aloud.

"Vi, can you tell us anything about the gentleman in the cryomedic chamber?"

"I do not have that information."

Jamie asked, "Oh, yeah, weren't we supposed to get something for completing the task? A request or somethin' like that?"

Vi chirped, "Each of you may now request an item of food, drink, or entertainment. Food or drink requests, if approved, will be made available at every appropriate meal for all subjects."

Meryn immediately responded, "I request coffee, cream, and sugar at every meal, please!"

There was a moment of silence, then Vi said, "Request approved."

"YES!! You're welcome, everyone!" Meryn beamed.

Ethan harrumphed. "I, for one, would like to know more about my options before making my one request. What kind of things can we request for entertainment?"

Vi answered, "Entertainment requests will be delivered to your personal dorm room and are not necessarily for everyone unless you wish to share them. Possible choices include but are not limited to books, stereo systems, televisions, computers, tablets, or mp3 players."

Jamie asked, "Vi, what if I wanted to get some weed?"

Vi was silent another moment. "Request approved."

"SWEET! Where is it?"

Cris raised a finger but Vi beat him to it. "Your requests will be delivered to your dorm room when dinner is served."

Ethan asked, "What is the point of asking for computers or televisions? Surely we're not going to be allowed internet access?"

Vi responded, "No device can access the outside world excepting the main computer. However, devices can access a local network including a media server loaded with entertainment options."

Alera's eyes widened. "Including podcasts?"

"There are many podcasts available, along with television shows, movies, and music. If there is something missing from the server, you may use your request to have it added."

There were a few more questions, and then the others began to make requests. Upon learning that requests did not need to be made right away, Ethan headed for his room. Cris requested a laptop from Vi and was approved. *If nothing else, I want to document everything that's been happening here in case I get out alive and can break the story.*

The others gradually split off, and Cris noticed Victoria and Alera having a hushed conversation in the corner. *I'd love to know what they're talking about, but I can't see a way to eavesdrop without being super obvious about it. Also, I really need to bleed off the stress of the last twenty minutes.*

Cris walked into his dorm room, ignored the temptation of just crashing into bed, stripped down and tried the shower. It was very small and a bit cramped, but the water was the perfect temperature, and Cris felt all his muscles relaxing. He tried to focus on that sensation as he momentarily stood motionless in the shower. *You're going to get through this.*

Cris toweled off when he was done and was in the middle of putting his jeans back on when he heard a knock at the door. Without thinking, he walked towards the door, making it open with a steely hiss.

Cris was suddenly extremely aware that he was naked from the waist up as Victoria eyed him up and down.

"Well, hello to you, too." She winked at him.

Chapter 10

Cris quickly spun around and grabbed his t-shirt from the chair as Victoria walked in behind him.

She said, "I wanted to apologize for…I don't know, making things weird. And I wanted to explain." She sat down on Cris' bed while he hastily pulled his t-shirt on.

Cris turned around and sighed. "You don't have to explain yourself to me."

"I want to." She patted the bed next to her.

Cris obediently sat down on the bed and looked into Victoria's brown eyes. *Softer than I've ever seen them.*

Victoria said, "I'm poly."

Cris immediately responded, "I thought your name was Victoria."

Her jaw dropped for a moment before her eyes widened, and she playfully slapped Cris on the arm. "You know exactly what I mean, you big jerk."

Cris chuckled, "I do. Is that why you had the bad breakup? Because you wanted to see more than one person?"

Victoria's face darkened. "Sort of the exact opposite, really." She turned and looked at the wall and sighed. "She knew I was poly, but she wasn't, and asked me to just be with her. And I loved her, so I agreed. And then she saw other people behind my back anyway."

Cris looked at her and noticed she was trembling. Without thinking about it, he put his arm around her shoulders and squeezed. "I'm sorry. I've, uh…I've been cheated on, too. It's not fun."

Even mentioning it brought back memories of Julie. It was his second year in college, and he'd gotten a job at the school library, where he'd met a sweet-looking blonde girl with a lightning-fast wit that won him over completely. Things between them proceeded very quickly, and after a month of basically living with her in her dorm room, Cris gathered up the courage to tell Julie he loved her.

The very next day, he'd left his shift at the college library early, and with a smile on his face, he approached her door, and put his key into the lock. This was always the sharpest part of this memory, for some reason – he could really hear the metallic ring as the key slid into the lock, and the click of turning the key to unlock the door seemed preternaturally loud.

As he pushed the door open, he realized he could hear other noises coming from her room, but he didn't really register what they were, and he took two steps into the entrance alcove before his brain warned him that something was very wrong. The noises he was hearing were human, guttural, and almost violent.

Cris took another step into the room, allowing him to finally see the source of the noises. On her single bed, in the corner of the room, Julie was writhing atop another man. Cris couldn't really remember the other man's face, something he put down to the fact that it wasn't anyone he knew, and as a result, it didn't really matter who he was. What he did remember was the look of shock that suddenly appeared when the man spotted him.

Julie's head whirled around. He recognized her face, sure, but he didn't recognize the look on her face. There was almost no humanity in it. She looked at Cris, almost imperceptibly smiled, and she only said one sentence.

"You might want to grab your things."

For a long time after, Cris regretted not saying anything back, but the experience was so surreal, and his emotions were so out of control, that he just shut his mouth and did as he was told, gathering up his things and leaving without looking back. Julie would attempt to contact him a couple of times in the days following, but whenever he heard her voice, Cris would immediately hang up or delete the voicemail.

Cris shuddered as he cast aside his reverie and looked back at Victoria. *Took a long time to trust anyone again after that.*

Victoria rested her head on Cris' chest and hugged him tightly. "Yeah. Not fun. Anybody ever tell you you've got a way with words, Mr. Reporter?"

"I do words good."

Victoria laughed and let go of her hug to gently take his chin and kiss him on the lips. "You really are incorrigible."

Cris nodded. "Very hard to corrige."

Victoria laughed again. "So, I wanted to talk about Al. Because I don't think I'm alone in liking her."

Cris felt weirdly defensive. "What gives you that idea?"

"You went straight to her door this morning, the day after you met her."

"Only to find you'd beaten me there by quite some margin."

Victoria gave him a coy smile. "Listen. I don't know how you feel about being in a poly relationship, but if you're open to it...I think she might be, too."

This feels...surreal. "Vix, are you telling me...you want to be a throuple?"

Victoria nodded. "Unless you're telling me you don't."

Cris stared at the wall for a second or two. "I'm open to it. But I have some concerns."

Victoria looked at him curiously. "Such as?"

"Well, you've just come off a bad breakup, for one, and I worry this might be some sort of rebound. Also, we're currently in a crazy situation, and I don't know if the heightened emotions might be clouding all of our judgment, and feelings might change when we're out of here."

Victoria nodded. "I think those are valid concerns. I don't know that I can address the rebound theory – all I can really do is assure you that I'm not that kind of person. I may be poly, but relationships aren't disposable to me."

Cris crossed his arms. "I can accept that."

"And when we get out of here, if our feelings change, then we can address that as well. Communication is the answer. As long as we're open in our communication, we can figure it out, or end things with no hard feelings, but for right now, I think...I think I need this."

Just then, there was a knock at the door.

Cris and Victoria looked at each other for a moment, then Cris shrugged and walked to the door. It slid aside to reveal Jamie.

"Yo, dude. I just wanted to ask – oh, Victoria, sorry, am I intruding on somethin' somethin'?"

Victoria stood up. "Nah, we're good. Mind if I get a pull or two when you get your weed?"

Jamie's eyes lit up and his smile split his face. "OH MY GOD, OF COURSE! That's what I was coming to ask this guy. Cris, I know you're not a regular, but you can totally toke up if you want."

Cris just smiled. "I may take you up on that."

Jamie beamed. "Cool, dude! And Vicky, you can—"

Victoria interrupted. "Do NOT call me Vicky."

"Sorry. You can have some, too, you are TOTALLY welcome."

Victoria walked out, squeezing past Jamie in the doorway. "Sweet. Cris, I'll clock you later."

As she left, Jamie looked confused. "She's clocking you? What, like punching you? Are you guys starting a fight club?"

Cris laughed. "No, I think she just means she'll see me later. Like, you can clock something meaning you see it and understand it."

Jamie relaxed. "Cool. But if you start a fight club, I want in."

Cris napped away the remaining stress, knowing that when dinner was brought in, he was going to be knocked out anyway. He awoke and, blearily blinking his eyes into focus, slowly realized there was something new in the room.

On the table next to his lone chair sat a small laptop. It appeared to already be plugged into the wall. *Wait a minute. I could swear there were no outlets in here.* Cris inspected the outlet, but aside from being recessed slightly into the wall, he could find nothing strange or unusual about it, and it did appear to be providing power. *Maybe it was always here and they just uncovered it?*

Cris booted up the laptop, and while waiting for it to boot, he inspected it. The laptop appeared to be new, though it had a brand name he didn't recognize. Once the operating system had started, Cris checked it for any data, but the only files on the hard drive were those required by the OS and a couple of minor apps. Cris brought up the Writer word processing software and was greeted by a blank white sheet. *Where do I even begin? At the beginning, I suppose.*

Cris moved to type, but letters started appearing one by one before his fingers hit any keys. A growing sense of unease filled Cris, followed by utter confusion as the mystery message filled in completely.

It read, "A TOP PURIST FOP NODDED".

Chapter 11

What the actual fuck? Are the bad guys just messing with me?

Cris waited for some time, but nothing new added to the message. Cris deleted it and tried typing. Everything worked. *But for some reason, somebody HAD to give me that message.*

"Vi, is my laptop defective?"

Vi pleasantly answered, "Your laptop is functioning within acceptable parameters."

"Then someone sent me that message deliberately?"

"I do not have that information."

Cris groaned, but then an idea struck him. "Vi, do you have the ability to generate anagrams?"

Vi chirped, "That is not a part of my programming."

Cris scoffed. *Of course, they wouldn't make it easy.* "Thanks anyway."

"You are welcome."

Cris struggled to make anagrams of the message manually for a while. He did manage to come up with "A SODDED PUP FOOTPRINT" and "DAD FOUND POE TRIP STOP" before the growling in his stomach caught his attention. *Not likely to get anywhere on an empty stomach – besides, dinner should've been delivered by now.*

Cris headed for the central room and found everybody else already eating. To his surprise, there were some new options for dinner – a container of warm French fries and a platter of hamburgers had been added to the hot dogs and water from before. There were also some carafes of coffee and Styrofoam cups available, with creamer, milk, and sugar, which Cris gravitated toward immediately.

Mai said, "There you are, doll. The burgers and fries were Al's idea, though somebody needs to ask for ketchup and cheese."

Meryn asked, "Well, what did you ask for, Mai?"

"A computer. Seems to work okay."

Cris turned to the group with his Styrofoam cup in hand. "Did anyone get anything...sinister with their requests?"

Everyone stopped eating.

Victoria asked, "What happened?"

Cris added milk to his coffee. "I asked for a laptop. It works fine, but a message appeared on the screen when I opened Writer. It said, 'a top purist fop nodded'."

Jamie, red-eyed, asked, "Did Cris just have a stroke? Wait, did 'I' just have a stroke?"

Alera repeated, "A top purist fop nodded?"

Ethan cleared his throat. "A nonsense phrase meant to hide a real message through anagram or encryption."

Jamie asked, "What's a fop?"

Ethan answered, "A person who is obsessively concerned with their clothes and appearance. It's another word for a dandy."

"Maybe it means that rich guy in the tube?"

Victoria shook her head. "The President is deliberately dressed in a plain way, so I doubt it."

Cris put a burger and some fries onto a plate and added, "If it is an anagram, the original sentence doesn't have to make sense."

Jamie responded, "Who's this Anna Graham lady?"

After dinner, everyone sat around in the armchairs in the part of the room they'd dubbed "the lounge" and engaged in some light conversation. There was still a sense of unease, as they knew another task was coming soon, but bolstered as they were by the morning's success, everyone's anxiety had been tempered somewhat.

"Yo, I just wanted to apologize, everybody." Jamie said.

Mai snorted. "For what?"

"I don't know. I just feel like I haven't contributed much."

Meryn spoke up. "I can't speak for Mai, but that's definitely not true for me. You kept your cool in a tense situation, and that really helped me not freak out."

Mai nodded in agreement. "Yeah! You got nothing to apologize for, doll."

Jamie sunk even deeper into his chair. "Thanks. I don't know. I guess I'm just worried about this next one. I'm not what you'd call, like, socially gifted."

Cris reached over and put his hand on Jamie's shoulder. "We'll get through it together, man. What say we toke up after this?"

Jamie brightened up immediately. "Oh, hell yes."

Vi interrupted, "It is now time for the second task of the day. Because you succeeded at your first task today, this task will be easier than it would have otherwise been."

Alera whispered, "Here we go..."

Cris winked at her.

Vi continued, "Your task is to confess a sin. You'll take it in turns to tell the group one sin you've committed. If the confession is approved, your collar will glow green. All collars must be turned green before one hour elapses to succeed at this task. Your time starts now."

Huh. Doesn't sound that bad. Cris looked around the circle of armchairs and noticed that while Victoria, Jamie, and Al wore pensive faces, Meryn and Ethan looked decidedly uncomfortable.

Mai, on the other hand, was resolute. "I'll start. I dishonored my mother and father."

She left it at that and waited to see if her collar would change color, but it remained pure white.

Ethan said, "Confession in church usually includes details of the sin. That's probably what they're after. They want to humiliate us."

Mai grimaced, then continued, "They wanted to force me to be a part of their religious cult. I ran away, stole a few things and some money from them, and I haven't seen them since."

Her collar remained white.

Mai looked down at the floor. "And I stabbed my brother."

Even as her collar turned green, Cris asked, "Really? You killed him?"

Mai shook her head vigorously. "He should be fine, I just stabbed him in the shoulder. But I ran away and didn't look back. Ya know what, fuck it, I hope the bastard's dead."

Cris kept his eyes on Mai. *That last part felt like the truth to me. What did they do to her?*

Everyone else looked at each other nervously.

Jamie said, "I don't know if this counts, but, uh...I technically lied when I took the Oath of Enlistment. I have no faith in America, especially its leadership."

With no change to his collar, Ethan asked, "Have you fought against America in any way?"

"No!"

"Then I don't think that qualifies. You're going to have to dig deeper."

"You go then if you're so smart."

Ethan cleared his throat. "Very well. I stole money from my former employer, somewhat in excess of forty thousand dollars."

Multiple people gasped even as Ethan's collar turned green.

Cris asked, "How? Why?"

Ethan responded, "Irrelevant, Mr. Thorpe. May I suggest your own sin as being too nosy?"

Cris found himself getting to his feet. "I'd say it's actually very relevant, given that the people who imprisoned us here are clearly criminals, and you've now also admitted to being a criminal."

"Last I checked, assault with a deadly weapon was also a crime, yet I cannot help but notice you're not giving Miss Shibata the third degree. Sit down and shut up, Mr. Thorpe."

Before Cris could retort, Jamie leaned over and punched Ethan full in the face.

Chapter 12

Everyone stared in shock at what had just happened. Ethan's glasses had come halfway off, and he was now struggling to reseat them with shaking hands. There was an angry red blotch on the side of his face where Jamie had hit him.

Jamie sat back in his chair calmly and said, "I punched a kidnapping victim."

His collar glowed green.

Jamie looked back at Ethan. "I'm sorry, yo. But I needed a sin. And even though you're a college professor, you still never learned how not to be a dick to people."

Ethan's voice wavered for the first time since Cris had met him. "At least... at least I don't go around punching them."

"At least I know how to say I'm sorry."

"Enough." Meryn spoke up as Cris sat back down. "This is getting us nowhere. Four people left to confess a sin, myself, Al, Victoria, and Cris. I...I'll go next."

Meryn took a moment, gathering her thoughts.

"Last year, I was working a shift when a homeless man was brought in, alive but non-responsive. He was rushed to the ICU and hooked up to a ventilator." Meryn took a deep breath. "Later, that same shift, a young girl was brought in, victim of a car crash, also unresponsive. We had no more ICU beds, and we needed a ventilator."

Cris' stomach sank.

"I...a decision had to be made, and there were no doctors available. I...I disconnected him from life support. I killed him."

Meryn's collar turned green, but she gave no sign that she noticed.

"I very nearly lost my job, as taking a ventilator OFF someone, even to save someone else, risks lawsuits for the hospital and myself. Luckily, if he had any family, they didn't sue, and even some doctors said I made the right call.

But the girl passed peacefully in her sleep a couple of days later. I still wonder whether the guy would've lived if he'd stayed on life support. But I'll never know."

Mai hesitantly reached over and put a hand on Meryn's shoulder, and she patted Mai's hand with her own.

Cris looked around at everyone and sighed. "I'll go next, but mine is rather tame in comparison. I...I genuinely hate not knowing what's going on. It's led to learning skills that are incredibly useful to a reporter, as I'm sure you can imagine. Still, it's occasionally made me a toxic person to be around. I've frequently eavesdropped on friends and family. And I've gone to extreme lengths to learn people's secrets. The worst was probably when I hacked my ex-girlfriend's phone to find out if she was cheating on me. She was completely innocent, but when she learned what I'd done...it didn't matter."

Cris looked at Victoria and Alera and thought he saw a bit of fear in their eyes. *It's probably for the best. I'd just end up hurting them.* As he looked down at the floor, he spotted a green glow reflecting off of his shirt. "Total and complete trust is impossible for me."

There was a moment of silence until Victoria spoke up.

"Well, I'm sure plenty of people would say my entire existence is a sin."

Victoria looked down, but her collar remained steadfastly white.

Meryn chuckled. "You didn't REALLY think you'd get off that easy, did you?"

Victoria sighed. "No. So, shortly after I first got hired at the library, we had a sort of open house event, with food and music and all sorts of stuff. It was really fun. About an hour before it was due to end, this girl rocked up and asked if I remember her from middle school, and I didn't recognize her at first, but when she said her name, I realized she was the quiet girl nobody really talked to. She was really nice at first, but when she questioned why we had rainbows everywhere, I said, well, it's a cute sunshiny thing and also, it celebrates diversity. And she went full-blown bigot on me."

Alera muttered, "Oh, no."

"She spewed anti-gay, anti-trans, anti-everything-other-than-straight-and-white rhetoric for a full few minutes, and as she clearly expected me to agree with her, she must not have known that I'm bisexual. So I quietly nodded, asked her if I could get her some punch, and when I got to the table, I put a teeny tiny bit of a nearby cleaning solution in her drink."

Meryn's eyes widened. "You could've killed her."

Victoria nodded. "That was made clear to me when she wrote an angry letter to the library after she'd had to go and get her stomach pumped."

Cris whistled even as Victoria's collar turned green.

She continued, "Thankfully, there really wasn't any way for her to prove either I or the library had done anything wrong, so that was the end of it."

Slowly, one by one, all eyes turned to Alera.

She spent a long time staring at the floor. Victoria reached over and squeezed her hand.

In a tiny voice, Alera finally said, "I had an abortion."

Cris's eyes threatened to fill up with tears until he noticed her collar was still white.

Victoria whispered, "That's not a sin, sweetie."

Alera started crying. Victoria knelt in front of Alera's chair and gently embraced her as she cried into Victoria's shoulder.

The only sound in the room was Alera's sobs. At one point, Ethan cleared his throat as if to say something, but Jamie raised a fist, and Ethan shrunk back down and remained silent.

After the storm of weeping subsided, Alera pulled herself together, taking one long deep breath.

"My ex-boyfriend doesn't know. I told him I'd had a miscarriage, and we broke it off after that."

Her collar turned green.

Vi announced, "You have successfully completed your task."

The room carried a heavy silence as all their collars returned to plain white.

Vi continued, "You have each earned one request for food, drink, or entertainment. As before, you may make your request at any time."

Cris muttered, "Thank heavens for that."

Everyone looked at Cris.

"I was just thinking we're gonna need a lot more weed."

There was little talking after that. The common room had taken on a somber, vulnerable feeling that eventually drove Cris back to his own dorm. *Better to get my thoughts in writing than let them stew inside of me.*

His own confession had brought back memories of Rachel. Cris sighed deeply and felt himself back at Rachel's apartment like it was yesterday. She had just walked in the door and was hanging her coat on the hook.

"Rachel...are you pregnant?"

She turned around, the dark-haired girl's usually-dazzling eyes tired and lifeless. "....what?"

"You've been going to the doctor and not telling me about it, what am I supposed to think?"

She slammed her bag down on the counter. "Have you been following me?"

"Why have you been going to the doctor so much?"

Rachel crossed her arms. "Not until you tell me how you know about that."

"....fine. Last week, I went to the salon, intending to surprise you by taking you to dinner, but you weren't there, and your boss said you'd gone home early, but you weren't at the apartment either. When you did get home, you said absolutely nothing about it, pretending you'd been at work all day....so I cloned your phone."

Rachel gasped in dismay and disgust.

"I needed to know you weren't cheating on me, so, yeah, I went through your messages, and checked out your calendar, where I found several doctor's appointments that you'd said nothing about."

Rachel turned her back to Cris and put both hands on the counter.

"Look, I know it was an invasion of your privacy, and I'm sorry. But I'm not the only one in the wrong here."

Rachel said something quietly that Cris couldn't hear.

"Speak up, I can't hear you."

She spun around, her eyes blazing, and the words erupted from her in a shout. "It's Non-Hodgkin's Lymphoma! Stage 2! Fucking cancer! You piece of shit!"

Cris' face fell as the enormity of it hit him. "Why...why wouldn't you tell me?"

Her face momentarily softened a bit. "The doctors say I have a seventy-seven percent chance of survival. That means a twenty-three percent chance of death. Not really the sort of thing that's easy to bring up to a relatively new boyfriend." Rachel's face hardened again. "But whether I'm living or dying, I'm one-hundred percent doing it without you."

"What?"

"Give me your key. Get your shit and get out."

Cris snapped back to the present. *She deserved better. I am a piece of shit. But enough of the immutable past. Instead, let's deal with the inscrutable present.*

Cris sat and wrote for a long time, recapping the events that had led to the first task, and reached the end of that task and stopped. *I don't know that I need to include Victoria kissing me in this. Genuinely can't tell if she'd be more offended by me leaving it in or leaving it out.*

A knock at his door saved him from having to make that decision.

"One moment!"

Cris saved his work and closed the laptop. He walked to the door and it slid open.

With a smile and a twinkle in her eye, just beyond stood Victoria.

Chapter 13

Victoria launched herself into Cris' arms, holding him fiercely as the door shut behind her.

Cris returned the hug. "Okay. Hi."

"Hi."

Cris went to release her after a few seconds, but Victoria didn't let go.

"Nope. You are getting the full twenty-second hug, my dude."

Cris laughed and put his arms back around her. *She's amazing.* "I didn't think you'd still like me as much after..." He let the thought trail off.

Victoria stroked the back of Cris' head. "I thought about that, but I figure now that I know, and you know that I know, whenever you're feeling like you need to know something about me, you can just ask and we can talk about it."

"Communication is the answer."

"Always." Victoria finally released the hug, and instead took his face with both hands and looked him in the eyes. "My love is in you now. You cannot escape it."

Cris pointedly looked around the room, then back into her eyes.

Victoria said, "Oh, yeah. Kinda can't escape, period."

Cris laughed and kissed her. "Don't really want to at the moment."

"Good. Now that that's settled, we should talk about Al."

Cris' smile vanished as he remembered Alera in tears. "How's she doing?"

Victoria answered, "Not great. I don't want to leave her alone tonight, and I think you should come with me."

Cris hesitated. "Okay."

"If you're unsure, we can—"

"No, I need to know if my confession is a deal-breaker for Al. And besides, I'm worried about her."

Victoria nodded and gestured to the door. "Shall we?"

Cris stopped short. "Actually, there's one more thing. It's a small thing, but...I've been writing a memoir of sorts about my experience here."

"Oh, for an article? Once we're out, I mean?"

"I don't know. If I can break the story, sure, I'm going to cover it, but for now, it's just for me. Anyway, I've gotten to the end of the first task, and I didn't know whether to write about our kiss because I didn't want to offend you."

Victoria smiled. "I appreciate that you asked my consent. I suppose as long as it's just for you, you can write whatever you want."

Cris mimed typing. "Dear Diary: at that moment, Victoria kissed me and completely blew my mind."

Victoria's smile turned sultry. "Oh, I've barely gotten started. But let's go talk to Al before I change my mind."

She took his hand and they left Cris' room and headed to the door opposite, where Victoria knocked three times.

The door slid open, and Alera stood there, the ice blue of her left eye and the warm green of her right eye both muted somewhat by the redness that had accumulated from crying. Wordlessly, Victoria hugged Alera while Cris sort of stood there uselessly.

After a second or so, Victoria opened the hug up but did not let go of Alera's side and pulled Cris with her free hand into a three-person hug. Cris felt awkward at first but leaned into it, stroking Alera's long red hair and rubbing her back.

Alera tried to let go, but Victoria wasn't having it. "Twenty seconds, Al. You are getting all of our love."

Alera laughed. "Okay."

As Cris stood there, holding both of these women he barely knew, he had to admit Victoria was onto something. *I genuinely feel more at peace now than I have in a very long time, since even before getting kidnapped.*

After a moment had passed, the hug broke up, and Victoria said, "Mind if we come in, Al?"

Alera shook her head. "Please."

Victoria walked in and sat on Alera's bed. Cris sat in the chair nearby, and Alera finally sat down next to Victoria as her door shut with a hiss.

Cris leaned forward. "I am so sorry you had to relive that."

Victoria put her hand on top of Alera's. "Me, too. But you don't have to talk about it if you don't want to."

"No, it's okay. It was three years ago or so. Talking about it can only help, right?"

Victoria nodded and sat further back on the bed, putting her back against the wall and her legs up on the bed.

Alera continued, "I was eighteen. I'd been dating this guy, Cody. He was into death metal and he was kind of a goth, but he was genuinely one of the sweetest people. And he wanted to be a dad. More than anything." She took a deep, shuddering breath. "After prom, I found out I was pregnant. I'd never seen him so excited. And I had never been so scared. I mean, I was eighteen! I loved him but I didn't know if I loved him enough to have a child with him. And I had so many dreams, and they were all vanishing in a puff of baby powder."

Alera stared off into the corner of the room. "I knew he'd never agree to it, so I scheduled the appointment, paid the whole thing in cash that I'd saved up over years of summer jobs, and came out physically and emotionally emptier. I told Cody it was a miscarriage, but I could see it on his face. He knew. We broke it off then and there. And since Cody was also planning on going to Castleton State, I took a couple of years off to minimize any chances of running into him. And that's it."

The three of them sat in silence for a moment.

Victoria sat up straight. "It sounds to me like you did the right thing."

In a small voice, Alera asked, "Did I?"

Cris agreed, "Yeah. Vix is right. I mean, you weren't ready to be a mother. And Cody might not be happy about it, but you're not his broodmare. He doesn't get a say if you don't want to have his baby. You really just saved both of you a pointless argument by not telling him."

Victoria looked at Cris, nodded approvingly, and raised a hand, "Up top!"

"Right on." He high-fived her without taking his eyes off Alera.

She laughed, "Did you guys just plan to come in here and double-team me?"

Victoria smiled. "Honestly? Yes."

"Wait, what?"

Victoria's smile grew wider. "We just wanted to talk to you about something, that's all."

Cris nodded. *Here we go. I'll genuinely be amazed if this doesn't blow up in both of our faces.*

Victoria scooted forward on the bed and took Alera's hand in her left hand. "So...I like you. You know that, right?"

Alera reddened but didn't say anything.

Without letting go of Alera's hand, Victoria took Cris' hand in her right hand. "I like Cris, too."

Alera looked mildly confused but remained silent.

Victoria continued implacably. "Cris likes me. But he also likes you, Al."

Alera looked sharply at Cris, who swallowed and nodded but did not look away. "It's true. I've been fascinated by you since we met. But after my confession, I wouldn't blame you at all if you didn't feel the same way."

Victoria nodded slowly, adding, "I think you like me, Al. But I think you like Cris, too. And if I'm right, there's no reason why we couldn't all be together."

Alera seemed incapable of speech and instead looked back and forth between Victoria and Cris.

Cris locked eyes with her. "I get it, you know? It's a lot, especially if you've never done anything like this, which I haven't, and I gather you haven't either?"

Alera shook her head rapidly but didn't break eye contact.

Cris nodded. "On the other hand, we could all be dead tomorrow."

Victoria frowned. "Cris!"

"She likes dark jokes! I'm trying to lighten the mood."

Victoria shook her head but Cris thought he caught a hint of a smile on Alera's lips.

Cris, still holding Victoria's hand in his left, leaned forward. "Vix says she needs this. And with everything going on, I'm starting to think that I do, too. So, Al...I guess the question is...what do you need?" And he punctuated that question by extending his right hand to Alera.

Alera looked at Cris. She looked at Victoria. Then she ripped her hand from Victoria's grasp, grabbed Cris' face and kissed him passionately.

Oh...yes? Oh, no? What is going on?

Alera released Cris and then grabbed Victoria and kissed her deeply.

Oh, thank heavens.

Alera then let go of Victoria and fell backward onto her bed. She sighed, smiled, and said, "My mother's going to kill me."

Chapter 14

Cris let out a breath he did not realize he'd been holding. "I was totally prepared for that to completely go south."

Victoria looked over at him, "I'm a little disappointed we didn't get to do the hand-holding thing."

Alera sat up. "How can you two joke at a time like this?"

Victoria smiled. "Because I was so tense a second ago I thought I might explode." She stroked Alera's hair. "What's your favorite thing to have for breakfast?"

Alera thought about it for a second. "I guess French toast and bacon."

Victoria looked up. "Vi, I'd like to request French toast and bacon for every breakfast. And syrup, please."

As Alera looked at her, mouth agape, Vi replied, "Request approved."

Alera said, "That's so sweet. You didn't have to do that."

That reminds me. Cris looked up. "Vi, I'd like to request an mp3 player and headphones pre-loaded with every episode of the Don't Walk Alone podcast."

Alera's jaw dropped even further as Vi responded, "Request approved. You may access a full library of music and podcasts through the media server."

Alera gaped at Cris. "You remembered—and you're going to listen to—"

He held her face in one hand and kissed her. "You've just made us both very happy. I'm just returning the favor."

Vi interrupted, "Attention. It is now eleven P.M. In five minutes the door to the common room will lock. Please proceed to your dormitories. I would advise being in bed by midnight as that's when your collar will signal your brain to produce the neurotransmitters that will induce sleep."

Alera said, "Oh, no. We just made this huge decision and there's so much to discuss."

Victoria replied, "Oh, we're not going anywhere."

At Alera's puzzled look, Cris told her, "Victoria thinks you shouldn't be alone tonight, and I agree with her. So if it's all right with you, we'll crash here."

Alera brightened. "Oh. Okay. Like a big sleepover."

Cris followed with, "The bed's not big enough for three. I'll take the floor."

Victoria said, "Nonsense. There's room for all of us in the bed if we squeeze, and I, for one, like squeezing. But we have another problem."

Alera asked, "What problem?"

Cris realized what Victoria was referring to. "Laundry. Your clothes only get washed if they're off."

Victoria nodded. "And Al and I have already been wearing our clothes for two days straight."

Cris nodded back as the implications of that hit him. "Got it. Why don't you two stay here, and I'll go back to my room?"

Victoria laughed as she kicked off her shoes and started to unhook her overalls. "Don't be such a silly Billy."

Alera also appeared uncertain. "Isn't this all moving a little fast? Shouldn't we talk before we get into sex stuff?"

Victoria muttered darkly to herself, *"Children."* She shook her head and addressed them both, "You can be naked with people without having sex, you know. It's called intimacy. Maybe you've heard of it?" She punctuated her sarcasm by dropping her overalls to the floor.

Cris couldn't help peeking. *Even her underwear is cute.*

Alera appeared to be steeling herself. "...alright. Okay." She dove under her covers, and Cris didn't realize what she was doing until her hand appeared from the covers, dropping her sneakers to the floor beside the bed.

Victoria removed her t-shirt and looked at Cris. "Well?"

The surreal nature of the situation had completely overwhelmed Cris, so he just said the first thing that came to his mind. "Uh, my clothes were washed yesterday, I can sleep in them."

She fixed Cris with an imperious glare. "Nope. Off."

Cris blanched but did what he was told, removing his clothes while Victoria watched intently. Alera, for her part, had also removed the rest of her clothes, laying them neatly in a folded pile on the floor while never revealing more than her head or hands from under the covers.

When Cris was down to just his underwear, Victoria told Alera, "Now scoot back as far as you can."

Cris removed his underwear and quickly got into bed alongside Alera, whose eyes did not leave his face as she slowly, hesitantly draped her body over his. He nervously smiled at her and she giggled.

Victoria removed her underwear and joined them under the covers, her hand meeting Alera's hand on Cris' chest. "See? This isn't so bad, right?"

Cris reached his arms over and around them both. "This is nice." *Understatement of the century.*

Alera apologized, "I'm sorry for being so anxious."

Victoria reached over to caress Alera's face. "No, sweetie, that's okay. We've all been through the wringer today. But you're safe here with us."

Cris added, "Yeah. I won't let anything happen to either of you." He squeezed Alera even more tightly.

Alera reached up the wall with her free hand and flipped the switch, plunging the room into darkness. "I know. You guys make me feel like we're gonna get out of this. I can't tell you what an incredible gift that is to me." She rested her head on Cris' chest.

They quietly talked the rest of the night away until the collars forced sleep upon them.

When Cris awoke, as his eyes adjusted to the dark, he realized there was a finger in his mouth. Befuddled but remembering where he was and that he was not alone, he quietly looked around until his eyes found Victoria wielding a mischievous grin. She burst into laughter but did not remove her finger.

"Wemm, gomm mommimm."

Victoria laughed harder and pulled her finger from his mouth. "Good morning to you as well, sir." She reached up and kissed him even as Alera began to stir.

Sleepily, Alera said, "Oh. Hi."

Cris leaned down and kissed Alera, followed by Victoria leaning over and doing the same.

Alera purred, "Mmm. I need to wake up like this more often."

Victoria laughed and languorously stretched with a yawn. "You missed it, I was just fingering Cris."

Alera became alert immediately. "Wait, really?" Victoria laughed again.

Cris answered, "It was actually pretty enjoyable."

Victoria pulled back the covers and slowly got out of bed, giving them both a tantalizing view. "What can I say, I aim to please." She walked to the table, which was covered with three small piles of clothes.

Alera still looked uncertain. "You're joking. Right?"

Victoria looked a little forlorn as she started putting on her outfit. "True. Sadly, it was just a little mouth play."

Cris looked at Alera. *I will never grow tired of looking into her gorgeous eyes.* "Ready for French toast and bacon?"

Alera's eyes widened with excitement, and she smiled, but her smile rebounded as something else occurred to her. "Oh. What do we tell the others?"

Victoria pulled on a shirt. "Honestly? I say we don't announce it, but we don't hide it, either. Hiding who you're with is just giving yourself another source of fear, which we don't need in our situation."

Cris turned to Alera as Victoria put on a pair of jeans. "She's got a point. If anybody's got a problem, I'll deal with it."

Victoria walked to the door but stopped when it didn't open. "Oh, yeah. Al, a little help?"

Alera said, "Oh, Vi, can you please open the door?"

The door slid obediently open, and Victoria went out into the hallway. Cris waited for it to shut again before coming out from under the covers to dress, and it was only upon seeing a pair of overalls on top of Alera's sneakers and a tie-dye t-shirt on top of his jeans that he realized what Victoria had done. He picked up the tie-dye shirt and read the tag. As he feared, it was a size Small.

"Well, I hope the others don't mind seeing my belly button."

Cris and Alera could hear Victoria's muffled laughter through the door.

They were a thoroughly mismatched trio as they arrived at the common room; Alera was wearing her flower-pattern top and overalls, Victoria was wearing jeans and a black t-shirt that was clearly a size too big for her, and Cris wearing a tie-dye t-shirt that was a size too small, baring his midriff over his jeans.

Meryn, already seated at the table with a coffee and some French toast, raised an eyebrow. "Quite the fashion show."

As Victoria and Alera giggled, Cris said, "We played laundry roulette. I lost."

Meryn smiled. "Clearly."

They fielded strange looks and a few questions from the others as they arrived for breakfast, and the three of them answered most of them with a wink. *Let them think what they want.*

For her part, Victoria seemed to be thriving. Cris noticed that she didn't let a moment go by without touching either Alera or himself, whether holding hands, touching their faces, or simply resting a hand on his leg. And Alera was speaking up more, actually taking part in conversation instead of just watching and listening. Cris just ate quietly, but you couldn't chisel his grin off with a jackhammer. As he ate, Cris noted that Ethan didn't say a single word to anyone.

As the group finished breakfast and headed over to the armchairs, and the time of the next task grew nigh, the conversation took on a strange turn.

"Does anybody here like to garden?" Jamie had asked with bloodshot eyes.

Mai asked, "Why, doll? Wanna grow more herb?"

"No. Well, yes. But no."

Cris murmured, "Your intellect is truly dizzying."

"Thank you. But seriously, I just like growing things, man. Vegetables, potatoes, you name it, yo."

Meryn laughed. "Potatoes ARE vegetables."

Jamie stared wide-eyed at Meryn like this was an Earth-shaking revelation. "OH. MY. GOD."

Most everyone chuckled.

Mai changed the subject. "I wish there was a gym or something here."

Meryn nodded, "Oh, me too! I've been running in place in my room, but it's not quite the same. I miss going to the park and throwing the Frisbee for my puppy."

Alera perked up. "Any chance you're an Ultimate Frisbee player?"

Meryn shook her head. "I've heard of it, but I've never played."

Cris filed away asking about Ultimate Frisbee for later and instead asked, "Vi, hypothetically, were we to ask for gym equipment as a request, would that get approved?"

Vi responded, "Yes, that request would be approved."

A twinge of uncertainty asserted itself somewhere in the back of Cris' mind. *There's something wrong with that, but I can't quite put my finger on it.*

Mai brightened. "Well, I've already used my requests. But maybe after this task."

Victoria looked over at Ethan. "You've been awfully quiet."

Ethan barked, "Because speaking up is now met with threats of violence."

"It was wrong of Jamie to do that, but you've been dismissive of people's feelings since this all started. Are you really that surprised that someone lashed out?"

Ethan looked troubled but said nothing.

Victoria very slowly put her hand on top of Ethan's. "If you want your feelings to be respected, then you have to respect others. Until we get out of here, we are all we have."

Ethan looked like he was about to cry as he stared at the ceiling for a few moments in silence. Suddenly, he said, "Vi, I would like to request free weights and a treadmill for the common room here."

Mai gasped and a grin could be seen on multiple faces as Vi said, "Request approved."

Victoria smiled wide and clasped Ethan's hand with both of hers. "That is an excellent start. Thank you, Ethan."

Ethan said nothing but looked at Mai and nodded. Mai looked down at the floor for a moment, then her eyes came up to meet his, and she nodded back.

Vi announced, "It is now time for the day's first task."

Chapter 15

Vi continued, "Please be seated at the table for the task briefing."

Meryn stood but didn't walk to the table with the others. "Does our time start when we sit down, like last time?"

Vi answered, "No. Your time starts when the briefing is finished, and all of you are ready to enter the rooms."

They all sat in chairs around the table as Mai removed a few leftover breakfast dishes. Once the table was cleared, Mai also sat down, and Vi started the briefing.

"Your task is to maneuver a spaceship through an asteroid field."

Jamie straightened up in his chair as Meryn said, "Oh, what, we're playing video games now?"

Images of a ship in space surrounded by large rocky asteroids appeared on the table as Vi continued. "Visual screens are non-functioning, but sensors can find and plot the asteroids on the navigation map. However, radiation from the field drains the power systems, meaning thrusters and sensors cannot activate simultaneously."

Jamie paled and said, "I'm not gonna be able to see where I'm flying?!"

Vi continued undisturbed, "The piloting and navigation stations are behind the green door. The power station is behind the orange door. The sensor station is behind the pink door. All participants will be locked in the rooms before access to any materials is granted, and the locks will not release until the task is over. You have five minutes to get the ship clear of the asteroid field before the radiation destroys too many vital ship systems to survive. Your time starts when you have all entered the rooms."

Meryn said, "It's another cooperative exercise. Whoever's in sensors needs to tell navigation where the asteroids are so that they can tell Jamie where it's safe to fly, and whoever's in power needs to switch the power back and forth as needed so both can do their jobs."

Mai shrugged. "I don't think I'm gonna be much use on this one, y'all, but

I'll probably head to the power station."

Victoria nodded. "That makes sense. If anything goes wrong with the power, you're the only one who could fix it." As Mai gave her a look, she added, "Theoretically."

If it's anything like last time we'll need people dedicated to communication between the rooms, and as the power room is in the center... "Two more people should go with Mai." Cris said.

Ethan raised his hand. "I'll volunteer. I don't know that I'd be very useful in the sensor room, and I'm uncomfortable working alone with Mr. Gamble."

Jamie looked like he was going to argue but then backed down. "That's fair."

Alera added, "I'll join Ethan and Mai in the power room."

Cris looked expectantly at Victoria, but to his surprise, she said, "I'll help Jamie with navigation."

Meryn nodded. "That leaves Cris and myself on sensor duty."

Cris reminded everyone, "We have just five minutes, not a lot of time, so let's be very clear on what everybody is going to be doing before we head in. Jamie, you're our pilot. Victoria, you're on navigation and the phone, correct?"

Victoria nodded while Jamie swallowed, stone-faced.

Cris continued, "Mai handles the power station and Ethan and Alera handle the phones for the power room, while Meryn – do you want to be on the sensor or on the phone?"

Meryn looked pensive. "I think I'll try the sensors. It might be like some of the scanning equipment at the hospital. But we can switch if need be."

Cris nodded. "Then that's the plan. If everybody knows what they're doing – ", he looked around quickly, saw no confusion, " – then let's do this."

Everybody got up and headed to their respective doors. Victoria shouted, "We've got this, everybody!" And Cris noticed she had her hand on Jamie's shoulder as they stopped in front of the green door.

When everyone was in place, Vi announced, "Doors will open momentarily for five seconds. Please move quickly into your selected rooms. The doors will shut and lock when the five seconds are up."

The doors hissed open, and Cris walked forward into the dark room beyond. Thanks to the light from outside, he could make out the outline of a phone on the wall and a large desk-like protrusion from the wall opposite the door.

Meryn said, "I can't see shit in here." As the door behind them hissed shut, enveloping them in complete darkness, she asked, "Can you reach the others through the phone?"

Cris felt for the phone on the wall, knocked the receiver off the phone, and swore when it collided with the ground. He felt the phone cord on the bottom of the phone and followed it to find the receiver, pulling it to his ear, but he heard nothing. He hung it up and picked it up again, but still the phone was silent.

"Damn. Nothing. I guess even the phones are out if our power is down."

Just then, a bright light filled the room, and Cris blinked a few times as he heard Alera's voice in the receiver. " – should do it. Hey, Cris?"

"Hey, Al. Did you guys get the power going here? We didn't even have lights."

"Yeah, but it's more complicated than flipping a switch. Mai has to route the power through specific areas or something, I don't really get it. How's it going over there with the sensors?"

Cris turned back to look at Meryn who was poring over the desk built into the wall. Now that they had light, Cris could see a large screen built into the center of the desk, which Meryn was poking and swiping with her fingers. "How's it look?"

Meryn didn't turn around. "It's a pretty standard touchscreen interface. There's a pulse that reveals the asteroids around us momentarily. If I understand right, I just have to highlight the asteroids when I see them to send the info to navigation." She tapped the screen several more times. "Alright, that covers this area. Tell them to flip power to Jamie. He's gotta move on to reveal more."

Cris said into the phone, "Al, flip power back to piloting!"

He heard Alera say "Got it! Mai, power to piloting!"

And after a moment, the phone went dead, and all of the lights went out.

Cris said, "This is going to be a charming few minutes."

Meryn snickered. "Well, stay ready. It could all come back in a flash."

Another second or two passed before the lights came back up, and Meryn went back to work on the sensor screen.

"Okay, gotcha. You, you, you, and you. Wait. The ship can't fit through these rocks. This looks like a dead end." Meryn turned back to Cris. "Send it back to Jamie. It's a dead end." She then turned back to the screen.

Cris told Alera, "Flip it over to Jamie, please!"

As Cris could hear Alera and Mai talking, Meryn suddenly shouted, "No, wait! That button rotates – tell them to stop!!"

Before Cris could say anything, the lights went dead.

Out of the darkness, "SHIT! FUCK! Oh, I just fucked everything up."

Cris said, "What the hell happened?"

Meryn sounded defeated. "I didn't check what all the buttons on the screen did. And it didn't occur to me that the ship would be traveling in three-dimensional space, so now the only way forward is either up or down, and

Jamie has no idea what he's going to fly into."

Cris thought for a second. "Well, every task so far has been solvable, and assuming they're not changing that now, that means there's roughly a fifty/fifty shot of Jamie getting it right."

Just then, a klaxon went off, and Vi announced, "Warning. Structural and hull damage to the ship. Power conduits to sensor room damaged. Repairs commencing."

Meryn's voice emerged from the darkness, filled with self-flagellation. "Tails. We lose."

Damn. And there's nothing we can do.

Cris slid down the wall beside the phone until he was sitting on the floor. "Well, by my calculations, the rest still have three minutes to get us out of this. Who knows, maybe Mai can do something to restore our power."

Meryn didn't sound optimistic. "Maybe."

Cris struggled for something to say upon realizing he didn't know Meryn that well, but then he remembered something. "I'm sure your pets are alright."

There was a sound of something hitting the floor and Cris assumed Meryn had also sat down. "Hope so."

"You said you had no family or friends? How is that possible?"

There was a quizzical silence. "How do you mean?"

"I just mean, you seem very likable. I would be your friend."

Meryn sighed. "That's kind of you to say, but you wouldn't." And before Cris could stammer a denial, she continued. "I just push people away, you know? I jump out in front, take the lead, and do what I like, and that just rubs people the wrong way."

Cris snorted. "Stupid people, maybe."

"Too bad the world's full of them."

"And as a reporter, I can actually attest to that."

There was a sly silence for a moment. "So what's going on with you, Victoria, and Alera?"

"And I thought I was supposed to be the nosy one."

Meryn laughed. "Listen, I'll take good news where I can get it."

Cris scratched the back of his head. "Well, I don't know how much I'm allowed to say, but I feel calling it good news is appropriate."

"That's nice. I've been thinking a lot about Jamie."

Wait, what? "Really?"

"Yeah, I keep catching him looking at me when he thinks I'm not paying attention. Well, if he gets us through this, I am going to rock his little world."

If Cris had a mouthful of anything he would have spit it out. Instead, he blew something of a dry raspberry. "Are...are you serious?"

"Yeah, why not? I do like a man in uniform, and he's so small, I could absolutely wreck him."

Cris stifled another astonished laugh.

Suddenly, the lights came back on, and Vi announced, "Attention. The ship has been destroyed."

Cris stood up. "Oh, no!"

Meryn sadly repeated, "Tails. We lose."

Vi continued, "The task has been failed. All subjects will now receive one strike."

Meryn lay down on the floor. "Trust me. You're gonna want to lay down for this."

As Cris tried to reconcile this in his brain, he was suddenly wracked with the most intense pain he'd ever experienced in his life. It was as if each individual part of his body had been set on fire all at once. He barely noticed collapsing to the floor and spasming wildly as he instinctively tried to find a painless body position, but nothing he did alleviated it. And it just carried on and on.

And then it was gone.

Cris curled into the fetal position as he struggled to breathe. His throat felt hoarse, and he suddenly realized he'd been screaming the entire time.

And as his brain resolved the identity of the sound he'd been hearing, Cris realized he wasn't the only one.

Cris looked up to see Meryn still screaming and thrashing wildly.

MERYN HAS TWO STRIKES!!

Cris crawled on his hands and knees and lunged at her, trying to bind her arms and legs with his own, and he earned a couple of bumps for his trouble, including a particularly nasty headbutt. Meryn was immensely strong but he did eventually succeed at holding her still. This did nothing to stop the screams, which now included gibbering, mindless sobbing between them.

Cris' eyes filled with tears as he held her tightly. "I got you. You're gonna be okay. You hear me? I got you." The tears flowed.

Cris was still weeping when the screams died down, and her body stopped shaking.

He was still weeping when the door slid open, and the others found them.

Chapter 16

After some discussion, Meryn was moved to her room to sleep it off. Jamie stayed with her, saying "I don't want her to wake up alone." Nobody argued with him.

Cris sat in an armchair in the common room, his mind whirling and raging. *I let myself lose sight of the fact that we're trapped here by monsters. One more strike, and Meryn is dead. The pain was indescribable, and I felt it for only one second. Meryn suffered so much more. These people are fucking MONSTERS.*

Victoria wordlessly crossed to Cris, sat on his lap, and embraced him. His eyes filled with tears again.

He said, "I couldn't help her. I just couldn't do anything at all."

She whispered into his ear. "That's not true. You kept her from injuring herself, and you reminded her she wasn't alone, and that you cared. I can't speak for Meryn, but that would mean the world to me, and it means the world to me that you did it for her."

He squeezed her tightly and said, "We are getting the fuck out of this hellhole."

"Hell yeah."

Victoria suddenly let go and got up, and Cris was momentarily confused until he was embraced from behind. Alera's sweet scent filled his nostrils. Neither of them said anything, and after a moment, without releasing the embrace, Alera walked her body around and squeezed into the chair.

Victoria shouted, "Dogpile!", and got on top of both of them as they all embraced each other.

Cris said, "Thanks, Al, Vix." He paused a moment. "It is insane that we all met just two days ago, because I feel so comfortable with you both. It just feels...right." He squeezed them both tightly as they did the same.

Mai, the only other person in the room, shouted from the table, "Oh, my God, you three, get a room already."

Victoria opened the group hug up and gave Mai an arch look. "There's room for one more."

Mai walked over to the armchairs but remained standing. "Thanks for the offer, doll face, but I don't even like to be touched, so that would be a no-go for me, y'all."

Cris remembered something. "Would that be your parents' doing?"

Mai froze for a moment, then relaxed. "I guess that's right, in a manner of speaking."

"They didn't—"

"No, no. Nothing like that." Mai shrugged, then plopped down in an armchair next to the dogpiled Cris. "My family was hyper-religious. And I mean super-hyper-omega-ultimate-class-S religious. If they weren't workin' or sleepin', they were prayin'. We went to church twice a week, and I've since come to learn that it was not a normal church. And we were a super huggy family. I genuinely loved huggin' my mom, my dad, and even my stupid brother. And then one day I had doubts, and I expressed I had doubts, and they tied me to a chair and locked me in a closet."

Cris' jaw dropped while Alera and Victoria gasped.

Mai continued, "This went on for years. If I acted up, into the closet. If I did anything ungodly, a.k.a. anything they didn't like, into the closet. If I told anyone that they tied me up and put me in a closet, into the closet."

Cris asked, "When did you run away?"

Mai looked down at the floor. "As I was approachin' my sixteenth birthday, they informed me that I had been 'promised' to the deacon's brother – a man in his early forties who'd always given me the absolute creeps when he was around. So one day, when I'd got home from school, and nobody was there, I stole anything of value that wasn't nailed down, threw it in my bag and just high-tailed it. And I guess you know the rest."

Victoria said, "I'm so sorry, Mai. You didn't do anything to deserve that, and I'm sorry they ruined hugs for you. Do you mind if I give you a word hug?"

Mai looked uncertain. "Sure, I guess."

Victoria sat up. "Mai, I love that you always just jump in to do what needs to be done in the tasks, and I love that you had the strength of will to save yourself from an awful situation, and between those two things, you make me feel like we're all going to get out of here alive."

Mai blushed. "Wow. That was lovely. You know what? I'm a convert. Give me all the word hugs you want." She paused a moment. "Well, I'm not getting much accomplished here. I'm gonna go keep an eye on Meryn, let everybody know when she's awake."

As Mai returned to the dorms, the reminder of what had happened to Meryn caused Cris to squeeze Alera and Victoria even more tightly.

There were still a couple of hours before dinner would be brought out. Cris spent the time listening to Don't Walk Alone while he continued to type up the story. As Alera's voice vividly described to him the events surrounding the unsolved murder of a co-ed, he couldn't help but admire her passion.

"Sonia took a shortcut on her walk home that day, a path through some back alleys that avoided the foot traffic at the busier intersections. And she had no reason to be afraid. Between being a Krav Maga instructor and carrying her own personal firearm, she had every reason to be confident she could handle herself. So the police were baffled when her body was found in that alley, with her torso virtually shredded, her gun still in its holster, unfired – and no defensive wounds whatsoever on her arms or hands."

This is literally more words than she's spoken since I've met her, and she's very good at painting a word portrait. But I have enough mysteries on my hands at the moment. Such as, what is the purpose of our imprisonment? Why are the physical tasks so far so science-fiction-ish? What sort of practical result could any of this produce? Cris sighed. And why am I already feeling this strongly for a pair of women I just met?

Cris stared at his laptop screen for a long time, but the answers to his questions never materialized. He sighed, saved his work, closed the laptop, and hopped into bed, hoping to get a decent nap before the mandatory sleep period arrived.

Just as he was getting comfortable, there was a rapid knock at his door. Cris grumbled a bit, but he got out of bed and walked to the door. When it slid open, Mai was standing there.

"It's Meryn. She's awake."

She looked haunted, dark circles under her bloodshot eyes, but she wore a wan smile all the same. Meryn said, "Party in my room, huh?" Her voice was hoarse.

Victoria, who sat at the end of Meryn's bed, said, "Sorry we forgot to get balloons."

Cris added, "Yeah, the store only had cereal, French toast, and bacon for some reason."

Meryn laughed. "Worst store ever."

Cris softly said, "I'm super glad you're okay."

Meryn looked at Cris. "If there is a hell, that's what it's like." She smiled at Cris. "But I heard you. I couldn't really register what you said, but the fact that I knew you were there was my only comfort. Thank you."

Cris' eyes welled up as he nodded.

Jamie sat in the chair across from the bed and his eyes were full of tears. "I'm so sorry, Meryn."

She looked at him fondly. "Nothing to be sorry for."

"I was the one flying. I have one skill, one thing I can do for this team, and I screwed it up." Jamie's tears streaked down his cheeks.

Meryn shook her head mutely.

Victoria assured him, "The assholes who set all this up deserve the blame, not you."

Meryn reached across to rest her hand on Jamie's. "I was controlling the scanner and I didn't know what I was doing until it was too late. And that forced you to fly blind. None of this is your fault."

Jamie asserted, "I could've flown slower. I should've been more careful. If I'd been at the top of my game—"

Standing in the doorway, Ethan remarked, "Then you would have been hit by something else. Looking at all the elements, I can't help but conclude that that task was designed to fail from the beginning."

Mai turned to him. "What makes you say that?"

"The impossibility of it. A five-minute time limit in a task where one mistake results in sensor failure, which takes over two minutes to repair? If I had to guess, I'd say our captors didn't like the fact that we were doing so well and decided to take us down a peg."

Cris couldn't help but agree. *We literally sat in the dark for the majority of the task. That feels deliberate.*

Alera then spoke up. "It's getting pretty close to dinner time. Maybe we should let Meryn rest?"

Mai said, "Yeah, that seems like a good idea."

As everyone stood up, Meryn said, "Wait, Jamie."

He turned and looked with wet eyes at Meryn.

She said, "I'd really like you to stay."

He sat back down, but his haunted look remained as the others filed out, offering Meryn well-wishes. Cris was the last one out, and as he looked back, before the door slid closed, Jamie fell to his knees at Meryn's side as she embraced him.

Chapter 17

Dinner was a somber affair. Meryn and Jamie sat next to each other, and occasionally she would clasp his hand or stroke his back, gently reassuring Jamie. Victoria and Alera did the same for Cris, but everyone ate in gloomy silence.

The social tasks supposedly get easier when we succeed. What on Earth will a hard social task be like?

Victoria spoke up first. "I feel like I should sing something to keep our spirits up, but I don't know what everyone will like."

Mai asked, "I don't suppose you know any Within Desires?"

Victoria shook her head. "Never heard of them."

Mai smiled. "They're a sort of symphonic goth metal band, but I suppose that'd be outside your lane, being Miss Broadway and all."

Victoria smiled right back. "If you think I don't enjoy Nightdream, you're sorely mistaken."

Mai's jaw fell. "I saw them in concert! They were amazing!"

"Emilia's voice is INCREDIBLE. She's an absolute legend—"

Jamie interrupted, "Guys, I'm not trying to be a jerk or anything – " Jamie judiciously avoided looking at Ethan as he said that, " – but we've gotta stay focused on doing these tasks and getting out of here."

Cris looked at Jamie and saw almost no trace of the super-friendly stoner he'd come to know. Instead there was a man struggling with equal amounts of determination and fear. *I think I can upset that balance.*

Cris stood up and put both hands on the table. "I know you're scared, Jamie. We all are. Because we know what's at stake. And I'm going to say it out loud. If we fail one more time, Meryn dies."

Everyone looked at Meryn, but her expression showed no fear, shock, or anxiety, instead there was just a calm curiosity.

Cris continued with as much resolve in his voice as he could muster, "But I'll tell you right now that that doesn't matter because we are NOT going to fail. We are going to crush each new task, and we are going to get the hell out of this place. And then we're going to kick the ass of every son of a bitch responsible for putting us in here!" Cris punctuated this by standing up straight and stepping away from the table.

The reaction was mixed. Jamie seemed somewhere between resolute and grateful, and Meryn smiled sweetly at him. However, Ethan and Mai just stared at him with bemused expressions while Victoria and Alera wore mirthful faces. It was about then that Cris remembered what he was wearing and glanced down at his exposed belly button.

He said wryly, "That speech probably would've been more inspiring if I wasn't wearing a tie-dye t-shirt two sizes too small for me."

They gathered after dinner in the 'lounge' area, as was nearly habit now. Their conversation was still a little subdued, but energized as they were by Cris' speech, the group enjoyed some amiable small talk until the next task's time grew near. Meryn and Jamie didn't say much, but they held each other's hands.

Mai wondered aloud, "It's still a social task, right? Even if it's harder, doesn't that just mean we have to say worse stuff?"

Alera looked down at the floor. "I don't have anything worse than..."

Victoria jumped in, "It might be something else. Don't worry, Al."

Alera gave her a wan smile as Ethan harrumphed.

"It's the 'something else' we should be worried about."

Vi interrupted, "It is now time for the second task of the day. Because you failed at your first task today, this task will be more difficult."

Cris sarcastically muttered, "Can't wait for this." He looked at Meryn, as if to remind himself how important this was. Despite her generally positive attitude, she looked more and more lost as the time of the task got closer.

Vi continued, "Kill one person."

While he and the others gasped, Cris noticed Meryn just looking at the floor.

Mai shouted, "WHAT?!"

Vi merely repeated, "Your task is to kill one person."

Mai growled, "We heard you, jackass."

Vi blissfully continued, "You have one hour. Your time starts now."

Cris said to Meryn, "You knew what the task was going to be, didn't you?"

She didn't look up. "I guessed."

Victoria said, "What do they—they expect us to trade another life for yours?"

Ethan replied, "Maybe they expect Miss Sarovitch to sacrifice herself for us."

Jamie stood up, "NO!"

Ethan said placatingly, "That's not what I'm suggesting, mind you. I'm merely saying that might be what our captors expect her to do."

Meryn looked up suddenly, and her eyes widened. She then stood up and walked away from the armchairs.

Jamie said with a strong hint of worry, "Hey, where are you going?"

Cris watched as Meryn strode through the blue door. A wild hope grasped his heart. *OF COURSE!*

Cris got up and ran to the blue door alongside Jamie while the others followed more slowly. When he reached the door, he saw Meryn standing in front of the cryomedic chamber.

Jamie yelled, "Meryn, that's brilliant! We can kill the President!" He stopped and looked perturbed. "I cannot *believe* I just said that."

As the others filed into the blue room behind them, Meryn said, "We still don't know anything about him. Who he is, if he has any family..."

Cris added, "How he relates to all of this..."

Victoria said, "One thing we do know is that he's going to suffer brain damage, or maybe already has, that can't be repaired. I hate to say it, but you might be doing him a favor."

Meryn almost shouted, "No! Death is not a favor!" There was a long pause. "It's giving up."

Ethan moved towards the front of the group. "You can't do it, can you?"

Meryn turned to face everyone, her eyes full of tears. "I...I can't. Not again."

"Not even to save yourself?"

She looked at Jamie, tears streaming down her cheeks. "I'm sorry."

Ethan gave Meryn a fatherly sort of look. "Your selflessness, misplaced though it may be in this instance, does you credit, Meryn. You impress me, young lady, and I do not say that lightly."

Meryn had a questioning look. "...what are you—"

"I'm a bit more selfish."

And he walked towards the rear of the machine.

Meryn shouted, "NO!" and lunged towards Ethan.

Ethan pulled his arm out of her reach even as he pulled the plug from the back of the chamber.

There was a loud click, and the screen attached to the chamber darkened.

Meryn yelled, "PLUG THAT BACK IN!" She attempted to wrest the plug from Ethan's grasp, who was struggling to hold her back with one hand whilst holding the plug behind his back.

Ethan growled with effort, "You will have to harm me to take it from me, and I don't think you'll do that."

Jamie said softly, "Meryn, it's too late."

Meryn, her voice breaking, screamed, "NO!!" and continued to try to grab the plug from Ethan.

Jamie said, "Meryn, *please...*"

Meryn broke down in tears but kept weakly fighting. "I can't..."

Vi announced, "You have successfully completed your task."

Meryn fell to her knees and sobbed. Jamie knelt in front of her and embraced her as Ethan dropped the plug to the floor. The rest were silent as they took in what had just happened.

Vi continued, "You have each earned one request for food, drink, or entertainment. As before, you may make your request at any time."

Ethan looked at Meryn with an emotion Cris couldn't quite read on his face. *Empathy? Pity?*

"I'm sorry I had to do that. Logically, it was the best move to keep us all alive. I know that's poor consolation, but it's all I have to give you."

Ethan brushed past Cris as he headed back to the common room. Cris continued to watch Ethan as he walked through the door to the dorms, and while Jamie hugged an inconsolable Meryn behind him, he wondered just what else Ethan would do to survive.

Chapter 18

Jamie escorted Meryn back to her dorm room and stayed there. Ethan was apparently in his own dorm, and the rest retired back to the 'lounge.'

After a long silence, Alera said, "That was fucked up."

Mai nodded, "Absolutely twisted."

Victoria added, "What is the point of all this? Repairing cryo-whatever machines we've never seen before, flying a spaceship through an asteroid belt, confessing our sins, and just straight up killing people?"

Alera sniffed, "It's a game."

Cris suddenly sat up straight. "You're right. To our captors, this is a game. We're not doing actual important tasks that need doing. This feels like some kind of big simulation. Like there's no way that that cryo-chamber just happened to fail right when it was time for the first task, and moreover, how do we know the President hasn't been dead this whole time? Remember, the only reason we thought he was alive was because the cryo-chamber said so."

Victoria shuddered. "You mean, they want to see who lives and who dies?"

"That might be part of it. I don't know, it feels like it's bigger than that."

Victoria tilted her head. "How do you mean?"

Cris sat forward in his armchair. "Well, let me ask you this – why do you play a game?"

Mai leaned forward and spoke somewhat conspiratorially in a low volume. "You think this is all for someone's entertainment?"

Alera sat back, horrified. "That's just sick."

Cris added, "And there's more. We've only had two practical tasks, but they're both futuristic science-y sort of things. That can't be a coincidence."

Victoria straightened in her seat. "I think I know how we might be able to get an answer or two." She got up and walked back towards the blue room, and the others slowly followed.

Victoria strode up to the cryomedic chamber and appeared to be searching for something under the lip of it. "In the first task, in the user manual, I recall seeing something—a-ha!" She pulled down a lever, and the lid of the cryomedic chamber popped open, blasting everyone with a jolt of cold air.

Alera jumped. "Ah! Cold! Cold cold!"

Cris enfolded her in a big bear hug to warm them both up and said, shivering, "Brr. Be careful touching the body, he's probably still really cold. Wrap your hands in something."

All the girls looked at themselves and then back at Cris. Mai asked, "With what?"

Cris couldn't come up with anything else, so despite the freezing cold, he took off Victoria's tie-dye shirt and handed it to Mai. "Just be careful with it, it's my new favorite top."

The women all laughed as Mai wrapped her hands in the t-shirt and began to probe the man's body. "This is creepy, y'all. I keep expectin' him to wake up and grab me," she said.

After a minute or so, she removed a small card from inside the man's jacket pocket, holding it up for everyone to see. Without even getting up close, Cris could see the logo on the corner.

"NASA?!"

Victoria said, "Looks like you were dead on the money with that government employee guess. How high up is he?"

Mai answered, "The card just says Administrator."

Cris got close enough to see the card in its entirety.

National Aeronautics and Space Administration
Office of the Administrator
NASA Headquarters
300 E Street S.W.
Washington, DC

James Arnold
Administrator of the National Aeronautics and Space Administration

He asked, "Anyone recognize the name, James Arnold?"

The women all shook their heads.

Mai asked, "Do we know that this is legit? They could've printed any old thing, and I wouldn't know if it was NASA or nonsense, y'all."

Cris looked at the body, which he now assumed to be James Arnold. "I can't be certain. If it IS a fake, they went to a lot of effort to convince us it's not."

Alera crossed her arms. "Alright, let's assume that our captors are faking things – what else do we think is fake? Like, are cryo-chambers a real thing, or is this all some sort of simulation?"

Victoria frowned. "The manuals were complex, and they lined up with the actual machine, so, again, if that was faked, it would've taken a lot of effort. I suppose it's not impossible, but given how cold it was when we opened the chamber, I'd say it's real."

Cris asked, "What about the spaceship? I never got to see either of the other rooms."

Mai shook her head. "It was all touchscreens, and the power rerouting screen looked and played like a video game. Also, I know our captors did –" Mai looked around, "– all this, but buildin' an actual spaceship that has now been destroyed seems like a bit much. I'd say it wasn't real."

Alera looked pointedly at the body. "So what about him? He's an Administrator for NASA? Is that, like, the head of NASA or is he more like an office worker?"

Cris looked again at the man's face. "I'd say he's the leader."

Mai asked, "What makes you say that, doll?"

"Physiognomy. Reading a person's facial features to determine personal characteristics or ethnic background. He's just got a face that appears stern, but fair, and that screams leadership to me. I could be way off about all of this, mind you."

"But you were dead right about him bein' a government employee."

Cris was troubled. "Yeah." *And if he really is or was the head of NASA – this is so much bigger than us. And our lives are in very real danger.*

Victoria was staring at Cris. "You know what this means?"

Alera raised her hand. "Um, is it possible that we're in space right now?"

Cris still did not look up. "I doubt it, but I can't discount it. The lack of windows means they don't want us to know where we are, so we could be in space, but there's gravity here. Artificial gravity, as far as I know, is still fictional. It doesn't exist outside of science fiction."

Alera shook her head. "Gravity, or at least the semblance of it, could still be created if the station we're on is spinning fast enough."

Victoria stepped forward, "Oh, yeah! Loads of books and movies feature space stations with a wheel and spoke design, so they imitate gravity through centrifugal force?"

"Exactly."

Mai stared at Cris. "We're in space? For real?"

Cris answered, "Maybe."

"Well, if the head of NASA is dead in space...how boned are we?"

Cris followed Victoria as she led him and Alera to the dorms. Victoria had taken both of their hands and had not let go since their conversation in the blue room. If he had been more alert, he would have realized she was taking them to her room, but he could not take his mind off the severity of their situation. *If our captors have the capability of kidnapping a high-ranking government official and launching him into space along with seven total strangers without anyone being the wiser...*

Cris was vaguely aware of entering Victoria's room and the lights going out. Then he could feel hands on him, caressing his face, and sliding down his chest.

I can't save them.

Someone was lifting the tie-dye t-shirt, attempting to remove it. Cris obligingly lifted his arms, and the garment was removed.

I can't save myself.

Lips pressed against his lips, then on his chest, then down on his stomach. *We have no future.*

Someone undid the button on his jeans and pulled down the zipper. His pants and underwear were pulled down to his ankles. Cris absentmindedly kicked them away.

At least we have now.

As despair exploded through him, Cris wanted to surrender himself to it. *No. Not like this.*

Cris heard himself say, "Um...can we...can we just stop?"

There was an alarmed silence, and then suddenly, the lights came back on. Cris could barely see Victoria at the wall switch through the tears in his eyes.

"I...I think maybe...I'm not alright..." he said.

Chapter 19

Victoria crossed to Cris, but Alera got there first, and they both embraced him tightly. Victoria stroked the back of his head and whispered, "Shh. It's okay. It's okay."

Cris felt the tears release from his eyes and stream heavily down his face.

Alera gently rubbed his back and asked, "What's wrong, sweetheart?"

Victoria pulled back slightly so she could look into his eyes. "I know it's a bit scary and strange if you're not used to poly relationships, but I won't hurt you, I promise, okay?"

Cris shook his head slightly, so as not to disturb Alera, whose head was in the crook of his neck. "That's not it."

"What is it? You can tell us."

He just stared at Victoria, completely lost in his own fears.

She arched an eyebrow. "You remember my motto, right?"

Communication is the answer.

Something about that thought snapped Cris from his reverie. "Yes, you're right. I..."

Alera said, "Here, let's sit down," and gently guided him to sit on the edge of Victoria's bed.

As the ladies sat on either side of him, Cris took a long, shuddering breath. "I don't think I've ever been this scared in my entire life." He paused, and took another, steadier breath. "When Meryn got her second strike...when I saw that guy's body...I've been thinking this whole thing has to be just an experiment, but if these people could get to the head of NASA...then we're all in such terrible danger." He took Alera and Victoria's hands and squeezed them together. "And I *just* found this."

Alera pulled her hair back from her face. "I've been thinking about this – Cris, I wonder if your problem isn't that you don't trust people, I think maybe you just jump to conclusions. We don't know for sure that man is the head of NASA. At best, all we know is our kidnappers want us to THINK that's who he is."

Victoria looked down at their hands clasped together. "I screwed up, guys." Cris quickly shook his head no, but she continued, "I just thought we all needed some comfort, and...and I wanted to provide it."

Cris held up a hand. "I'm the one who should apologize for killing the mood."

Alera stroked his back. "No, Cris, if you're not up to it, you have to say something."

Victoria nodded. "I'll have you know that emotional maturity is very sexy. You're worth waiting for."

The two of them...they're like a dream in the middle of a nightmare.

Cris could feel himself relaxing, but he was suddenly extremely aware that he was completely naked. "Uh...so now what?"

"Well," Victoria looked across to Alera, "the best way to deal with fear is to face it, so...what can we do to help?"

"Yeah," Alera arrested Cris with her gorgeous multicolored eyes, "whatever you need."

He looked at both women for a moment. "You got any more of that 'intimacy'?"

In the morning, they emerged from the dorms into the common room in their own clothes this time. Cris was surprised to discover they weren't the last to arrive. Only Mai and Ethan sat at the table.

Victoria asked, "Did we miss Meryn and Jamie?"

Mai said, "Nah. I think they're still canoodling."

Ethan glanced over at Mai. "I still think emotional attachments are a distraction."

Cris threw Ethan a look. "Says the man who killed someone to save Meryn."

"That was a logical choice, not an emotional one. Of the two of them, Miss Sarovitch is more useful, plus completing the task saved all of us another strike."

Cris scoffed as he moved to fill up a plate. "Man, every time I think you might be human, you beep at me, and I remember."

Ethan scowled. "Denying my humanity is beneath you, Mr. Thorpe. I'm just trying to get us all out alive."

Cris instinctively prepared a retort, but then he saw Alera's mismatched eyes in his peripheral vision. *Maybe I've been jumping to conclusions with Ethan, too.*

"Ethan, you're right. You didn't deserve that, and I'm sorry."

A look of delighted surprise appeared on Ethan's face. "Apology accepted, Mr. Thorpe."

Cris looked up at Victoria and Alera to see warm smiles. He mouthed the words "Thank you" to Alera, who responded by blushing.

Aloud, he said, "Ladies, let's eat."

They sat down to breakfast while Mai got in some time on the treadmill, and Ethan sat quietly in the lounge. As they were finishing up, Meryn and Jamie finally showed up, Meryn looking far better and happier than Cris had seen her in some time, but Jamie appeared to be having some minor difficulty walking.

Cris muttered just loud enough for Meryn to hear, "Atta girl."

She flashed him a smile and a wink before grabbing a carafe and pouring some coffee. Jamie hobbled over to her side, where she handed him the steaming mug. Jamie sat down with some care.

"Yo!" Despite his obvious discomfort, Jamie sported a wide grin.

Cris smiled. "Good morning. Did you sleep well?"

Jamie nodded. "And I woke up even better."

Meryn snorted loudly while pouring a bowl of cereal.

As was now their custom, as the time for the task grew near, the group gathered in the armchairs, though this time, nobody was relaxed.

Jamie leaned forward. "Does everybody have everything they need? Any last drinks or runs to the bathroom?"

Meryn laid a hand on his arm. "We've been through this twice now. Everybody knows what they're doing."

"I just wanna be sure. We all gotta be on top of our game, or else..."

"I know. But you also don't want to get too wound up."

Jamie sat back. "You're right."

Victoria turned to Jamie. "I feel safe in saying I'm speaking for everyone when I say we're going to do everything we can to beat this task."

Cris nodded. "Damn right."

Meryn interjected, "I would have one more promise from everyone, if you don't mind."

There was a quick chorus of assent.

"If things go sideways, and the threat of death is not a bluff, and I am killed – I want your promise that you will not blame each other – or yourselves."

Mai said, "Trust me, doll face, the only people gettin' blamed are the people who put us here."

Ethan vehemently added, "They will pay for what they have done. I give you my word."

Meryn gave Ethan a look, but then simply nodded.

Vi announced, "It is now time for the day's first task. Please note: today is the final day of tasks."

Everyone's eyes widened as Jamie said, "Does that mean—"

Vi continued, "After the completion or failure of the social task tonight, all remaining subjects will be able to leave via the white doors."

Cris looked again at the white doors, cold and impenetrable, and was still not entirely certain that freedom lay on the other side.

Vi chirped, "Please be seated at the table for the task briefing."

As the group slowly migrated to the table, Cris found his eyes drawn to Meryn's face. She smiled as if to reassure him.

Once the last person had sat down, Vi continued, "Your task is to answer the following question: what is your purpose?"

Jamie repeated, "Our purpose?!"

"You must submit your answer before your time lapses, and you may only answer once."

Ethan asked, "How long do we have?"

"You have twenty minutes. Your time starts now."

Chapter 20

Meryn once again took charge. "Okay, everybody, let's break this down – I'm assuming that by 'our purpose' they want us to guess why we've been brought here to do these tasks, right?"

Ethan nodded, "I would agree."

Victoria looked around the table. "We were talking about it last night, Cris, Mai, Al, and myself, and we think we might be in space."

Meryn's jaw dropped. "What?!"

Mai pulled James Arnold's business card from a pocket on her sundress. "The President had this on him." She tossed the card into the center of the table.

Jamie leaned over to read the card. "Administrator of NASA? Never heard of him."

Ethan added, "It's possible this card belongs to someone else, and the President just collected it from him."

Cris nodded, "It's also worth remembering that everything we have is because our captors want us to have it."

Jamie scoffed. "They're probably just trying to throw us off, so we fail."

Cris shook his head. "I've got this feeling our captors don't want us to fail. I mean, think about it, if they wanted us dead, they could've just killed us. They took us from our homes without any of us being the wiser. It would be incredibly easy to just wipe us out."

Ethan looked pensive. "By that logic, we should have everything we need to determine 'our purpose'."

"That's right."

Jamie looked perplexed. "But Ethan, didn't you say yourself that the last task was impossible?"

Ethan shrugged. "It was extremely difficult, for certain, but that does not imply that our captors wanted us to fail. Perhaps this is all intended to train us to work effectively together under high stress."

Meryn asked, "In space? Are they training us to be astronauts?"

Ethan coughed, "I doubt it's that simple, Miss Sarovitch – there's already an effective training program for astronauts, but if NASA is involved, I don't think it can be completely disproven."

Alera raised her hand. "I also wanted to point out – we also have that weird phrase that showed up on Cris' computer."

Mai said, "I forgot all about that one, y'all. Did anyone ever figure it out?"

Cris shook his head. "Everything I came up with made no sense."

Alera said, "I might be able to help with that." She pulled out a folded piece of paper from her jeans pocket and unfolded it. "I asked for a pen and paper for one of my requests, and I've been trying to figure out as many anagrams for 'A TOP PURIST FOP NODDED' as I could. I circled the ones that made the most sense to me."

As Alera placed the page in the center of the table, Cris craned his neck to read it. Among the nonsense ones like "DIPPED AD UPROOTS FONT" and "ADD POOP FRONT DISPUTE", Alera had circled "DAD OP POP TRUSTED INFO" and "ODD FIT TRAP UNOPPOSED".

Ethan looked back at Alera. "Miss Zeller, how are these any more useful than the others?"

Alera shrank a little. "Well, I thought that first one might apply to Mr. Arnold. Maybe his son or daughter is involved with our captors, and he was involved with an operation that he trusted info on and it got him captured."

"That seems a bit of a stretch."

"And the other one, well, we are caught in a trap, so to speak, and the police haven't come for us as far as we know. And the seven of us are kind of an odd fit." Alera lost confidence and volume with every word until the last were nearly silent.

Cris smiled at her. "Well, you still did better than I did, and I write things for a living."

Alera smiled back at him and sat up a little.

Ethan looked up suddenly. "Have you tried making anagrams using the word 'PURPOSE'?"

Alera's eyes widened, and she looked down at her sheet. "That fits! I'll start right away!" She grabbed the paper, flipped it over, and started writing.

Jamie asked, "Vi, how much time is left?"

Vi announced, "You have twelve minutes and thirty-seven seconds remaining."

"Alright, gang, we got anything else?"

Cris shook his head. "Just the tasks themselves. A cryomedic chamber and flying a spaceship through an asteroid field. Which would seem to back up the idea that we're currently in space."

"Couldn't all that be fake?"

"It could, but if we accept that our captors actually want us to figure this out, then everything they've given us that we haven't asked for is probably a clue."

Jamie's eyes narrowed. "I'm still not buying it. That pain was unreal. I'm having a hard time believing that people who could do that to a human being until they pass out are in ANY way on our side."

Cris leaned in. "I'm not saying they're on our side. I'm saying they want us to complete their tasks. Not the same thing."

Jamie leaned back. "I don't get it. What are you trying to say?"

Ethan crossed his arms. "I believe Mr. Thorpe is implying that our succeeding helps our captors in some way and doesn't necessarily help us."

Meryn looked at Cris. "What, you think the white door leads to something bad?"

Cris shrugged. "We were told it leads to freedom. But we have no evidence of that. There could be a firing squad, hungry tigers, hell, if we're in space, those doors opening might just blow us out into cold vacuum."

Victoria shuddered and asked, "So what could they possibly get from us succeeding at these tasks?"

"The only thing that makes any sense at all is that this is some kind of experiment."

Mai said, "Didn't we also say it could be a game? Like some sick entertainment?"

Meryn held up a finger. "Remember, Vi referred to us as subjects. That kind of terminology suggests an experiment."

Ethan said, "We cannot rule out entertainment based solely on terminology."

Jamie looked exasperated. "Have we made *any* progress? I feel like we're just spinning our wheels."

Alera raised her hand again. "What about 'DAD OP PURPOSE: FIND TOT'?"

Victoria frowned. "Some dad is looking for his kid?"

Cris said, "Again, no evidence that James Arnold has a child, and I'm guessing you don't either, Ethan?"

Ethan raised an eyebrow. "Not on your life."

Vi announced, "Warning, you have five minutes remaining."

Jamie shouted, "We need more time!"

Cris remembered something. "Vi, I'd like to use my request to ask for more time for this task!"

There was a moment of silence, then, "Request denied."

"On what grounds?"

"I do not have that information."

Cris growled with frustration while Jamie said, "Appreciate you tryin', man."

Meryn sighed. "Alright. I don't see any other option but to go with what we've got."

Ethan leaned forward. "It's hardly conclusive—"

"Do you have anything else?"

Ethan backed down but remained quiet.

Meryn looked around the table and challenged, "Anyone? Any other clues?"

Most of the others looked down. Alera ignored Meryn and kept furiously writing.

Meryn asked one last time. "Al, you got anything?"

Alera froze and finally put the pen down, her voice gloomy. "No, nothing concrete."

Cris caught Meryn's eye, sighed, and nodded.

Meryn returned the nod. "Vi, we would like to answer the question."

Jamie quietly said, "Oh, God..."

Victoria grabbed Cris' hand and put her other hand on Alera's shoulder.

Vi pleasantly commanded, "State your answer."

Meryn stood up. "Our purpose is...to take part in an experiment."

Mai had clutched a hand to her chest. Ethan crossed himself and appeared to be rapidly praying. Jamie held Meryn's hand in both of his.

There was a silence that felt like an eternity.

Vi pronounced, "Your answer is incorrect."

Jamie stood up, "NO!!"

Meryn ignored him. "Everybody lay down on the floor!"

While Cris quickly complied, pulling Victoria away from the table, and gesturing for Alera and the others to do the same, Vi announced, "The task has been failed. All subjects will now receive one strike."

Jamie screamed, "DO IT TO US, NOT HER!!"

Meryn said, "Jamie, I—"

A giant wave of pain rolled into Cris and stayed there. He'd thought, having felt it before, he'd be ready this time. He was not.

One of the few sensory events he'd be able to recall afterward was that he'd opened his eyes whilst writhing on the floor, and the image of Meryn kneeling over Jamie burned itself into a receptor of Cris' brain.

Otherwise, all he knew was pain.

Cris opened his eyes reluctantly. His throat hurt quite a bit, along with his right elbow and both of his knees.

He looked around, most everybody else appeared to be unconscious, save two.

Jamie sat propped up against the back of an armchair, weakly crying, while clutching the body of Meryn, whose vacant eyes stared blankly at the ceiling.

Chapter 21

The girls all cried. Alera in particular was openly weeping. Cris found himself unable to cry, he just stared blankly at Jamie, still weakly sobbing and holding Meryn.

Finally, Cris stood up and walked over to Jamie. "Let's get her back to her room, man."

Jamie looked up at Cris like he was going to argue, but then he lowered his head and nodded.

Cris grabbed her legs while Jamie held her arms, and between the two of them, they successfully got to her room, and once her body was close enough, the door opened. Cris idly wondered what they would've done if it hadn't. He pulled the chair over with his foot to keep the door open, then they carried her in and put her into her bed, whereupon Jamie crawled into bed with her and pulled up the covers.

Cris opened his mouth to say something, but instead, his eyes welled up with tears, and he turned and walked out of Meryn's room, leaving Jamie to grieve alone.

Cris and Victoria consoled Alera as best they could, but eventually Victoria decided to take Alera back to her room. Nobody was really interested in talking, and the prevailing mood was bleak. For his part, Cris was furious with himself.

I should've gotten to the bottom of this by now. I let myself get distracted, and now Meryn's dead. And if I don't do something, the rest of us could be dead in a few hours.

Cris went to his room to type on his laptop but seized by the impulse to remain accessible to Victoria or Alera, Cris picked up his laptop and mp3 player and took them to the lounge area. As Alera's voice soothed him with the tale of another grisly unsolved murder, he rapidly typed out the last day's events. Once his chronicle of the events that had befallen him was complete, he went back and reread it, searching for any clue he might have missed. Cris also frequently fired off any questions he had to Vi.

"Vi, why is everything made out of this ceramic?"

"Where, physically, is the main computer?"

"Is anyone watching the recordings of us?"

"How does James Arnold fit into what's happening here?"

"Are you based on a real person?"

"Can you tell me what everyone asked for as a request?"

"Why was killing Meryn necessary?"

Vi answered every single question with "I do not have that information."

I don't know why I bothered.

Cris typed his speculations and theories into the laptop until the collar forced him to sleep.

Neither Mai nor Ethan showed up for dinner, and Cris waited for a while, but when Victoria and Alera didn't show, he piled a couple of plates with food and carried them to Alera's door, where he knocked with his foot. After a few seconds of no response, he shouted, "Food delivery!"

The door finally slid open to reveal Victoria and Alera sitting on Alera's bed, with their backs against the wall, and Victoria had an arm around Alera's shoulders. From the redness in both of their eyes, Cris discerned that both had been crying for some time. Cris put the plates of hamburgers and hot dogs on the chair and joined them on the bed.

"Hey. Dinner's here."

Alera said, "I can't even fathom how you can be hungry at a time like this."

Cris nodded. "I get that. Look, maybe we were kidding ourselves that this was something we could defeat, or maybe the rest of us are going to make it out just fine, but there's a very real chance that this is going to be my last meal, and I just thought, who else would I want to have it with?"

Alera's eyes filled again.

Victoria whispered, "I can't get over how even knowing she was going to die, Meryn's primary concern was Jamie and the rest of us."

Cris' eyes welled up again. "Yeah. That's who she was, though. I didn't get a lot of one-on-one time with her, but she was a good soul."

Victoria sang quietly, "Early one morning, just as the sun was rising, I heard a maiden sing, in the valley below. Oh, don't deceive me, oh, never leave me, how could you use a poor maiden so?"

Cris really wanted to close his eyes and fully immerse himself in the warmth of her voice, but he angrily shook it off. "I can't give up yet. I won't."

Alera lightly pawed at Cris and cried, "What are we gonna do?"

Cris kissed her on the lips and said quietly, "We're gonna eat, then we're going to cuddle and take as much comfort in each other as we can, then we're going to beat that final task and walk out together."

Alera's warm green eye and her ice cold blue eye had fully captured both of Cris' eyes. "You promise?"

"I promise." He looked at Victoria and beheld her perfect face. "To both of you." He leaned over and grabbed a plate from the chair. "Now, who wants a burger?"

The announcement stirred Cris from his reverie.

"The second task of the day is imminent. Please congregate in the common room."

Cris groaned along with Victoria and Alera. They had piled into bed together, just holding one another close, and Cris had thought he was just about to fall asleep, but no longer. Being closest to the edge, he tumbled out of bed and stood up, stretching. As he did so, on the floor, he caught a glimpse of the piece of paper Alera had been using to try and decipher Cris' secret message, so he picked it up.

It was mostly a jumble of words and letters, but Cris noticed down near the lower left corner, Alera had removed the letters in "PURPOSE" to try and determine what the rest could be. Like most of the rest of Alera's attempts, most were silly, like "DAFT ODD POINT" or "TAD FOND DO TIP".

One option had been circled twice. "FIND TOP TO ADD"

Alera had just stumbled out of bed after him. "Something wrong?"

Cris looked back at her. "Did you make any headway with that anagram? You've got this one circled twice."

She scoffed. "Not that it matters. It's the only thing that makes any sense at all, and it still doesn't make any sense. Find what top? How does a top add purpose?"

Cris struggled with it. "I...don't know. I feel like this has got to be close, though."

Victoria had joined them. "Do you think this could still help us with the final task?"

Alera shrugged. "I don't know, but I feel like we should bring it with us anyway."

Cris folded the page and put it in his pocket as he strode out into the common room. Ethan and Mai were already seated in the lounge area, so the trio joined them, Cris moving his laptop and mp3 player from the seat of his armchair to the floor beside it.

Nobody said a word for over a minute.

Finally, Ethan said, "Should somebody go and get Jamie?"

Cris answered, "Just leave him be. If we need him for the task we can go get him, but I don't think he'll leave Meryn right now, even for the task."

Vi pleasantly announced, "It is now time for your final task."

Cris steeled himself for the worst. *Last time we failed the first task of the day, the evening task was to kill someone.* He looked around at the others. *Who would we sacrifice now?*

Vi continued, "After this task is complete, the white door will open, and all remaining subjects will be able to leave."

Hope began to blossom in Cris' heart.

"Kill all but two subjects."

Cris' jaw dropped as that hope withered and died.

Vi carried on, "You have one hour. At the end of that hour, the task will be complete if exactly two subjects remain alive."

Alera stared dead-eyed straight ahead, and Victoria began to cry.

"Your time starts now."

Chapter 22

Without a word, Mai stood up and walked towards the dorms.

Cris shouted, "Mai! Where are you going? We have to figure this out!"

As Mai ignored him and disappeared into the dorms, Ethan leaned forward. "I believe she's already accepted the reality that eludes you, Mr. Thorpe. Everybody left alive has two strikes. If we fail this task, all of us die. So we must complete it, meaning only two of us may survive."

Cris spluttered, "But...but..."

"Four of us need to die within the next hour, whether by self-sacrifice or murder. I don't know what you all intend, but I've had an interesting life." Ethan stood up. "See you all in the next." He followed Mai towards the dorms.

As the door slid shut behind Ethan, Cris said, "There has to be another way!"

Alera numbly said, "There isn't."

Victoria, a split-second later, said, "Like what?"

Cris cast about, uncertain. "Well, maybe we can trick the system, or maybe it's worded in a weird way that we can take advantage of?"

Alera's voice broke. "It was pretty clear."

Victoria added, "God, I don't want to die."

Cris looked at Alera, who stared blankly into space, and Victoria, who had completely fallen apart and was sobbing openly. *I can't save all three of us. There has to be SOMETHING I can do! Think, goddammit, THINK!*

Cris' mind raced as his eyes flew and landed on several objects in the room. The dining table, still carrying uneaten hot dogs and hamburgers. His laptop. Alera's face. The blue door. A dumbbell. The treadmill. The dumbbell.

The dumbbell.

Something is bothering me about that dumbbell, but what? Ethan requested free weights and a treadmill for the common room to make peace with the group, and it was a nice gesture, but something's wrong.

Someone could use that dumbbell to hurt someone else. Or even kill them.

Our captors had to know that was a possibility.

And requests can be made and granted in secret.

Cris' eyes widened and his head came up as the implications of that revelation hit him.

Just then, the sound of an explosion coming from the dorms hit the trio.

As the girls gasped, Cris stood up. *Oh, God, no!*

Victoria asked, "What the hell was that?!"

A few seconds later, another explosion was heard.

Cris ran towards the dormitory door, convinced he was about to die any second.

The door slid open with its customary efficiency, revealing Ethan standing just beyond, blood-spattered, holding a shotgun in his hands.

A shotgun he now aimed in Cris' direction.

Cris grabbed the barrel and yanked up and to the left—

BAROOM! The shotgun belched fire and buckshot, and Cris felt a kick to his left shoulder and the upper-left part of his torso, followed by a stabbing, burning pain. He released the shotgun barrel from his grasp and staggered back a step, his ears ringing and his left arm hanging uselessly by his side.

Ethan pumped the shotgun, loading another shell into the chamber, and took another step forward.

Cris reached for the barrel with his right hand, forcing it toward the ceiling, and if Cris had the use of both arms, he'd easily be able to overpower the older gentleman. But he only had one good arm, and Ethan was slowly forcing the barrel back down towards Cris' face—

Which is when a flying object roughly the size of a deck of cards struck Ethan in the side of the head.

Ethan recoiled backward and released enough of his grip on the shotgun for Cris to wrest it from him. As Ethan collapsed to the floor, Cris looked and saw the object, his mp3 player, on the floor by the door, and he risked a look back to see Alera's arm outstretched and a look of grim satisfaction on her face.

Cris turned back to Ethan and admired the angry red welt on the side of his head as the older man gasped with pain on the floor. "So much for noble self-sacrifice, eh, Ethan?"

Ethan weakly asserted, "It...was...logical..."

Cris looked up into the hallway, catching sight of Mai and Meryn's dorm rooms, and the doors of both were open. Instantly, Cris knew what had happened.

Cris leveled the shotgun at Ethan's head. "So is this. Get up. MOVE!"

As Ethan struggled to get on his hands and knees, Cris started wetly coughing, and he spit what had come up on the floor.

It was blood.

Ethan looked up at Cris with a grim smile. "It's too late, Mr. Thorpe. The shot pierced your lung. Without immediate medical attention, you're as dead as I am, and I don't think our kidnappers will be too helpful in that regard."

Cris heard the sounds of footsteps behind him, and he risked a look back to see Victoria and Alera at the hallway entrance. He extended the shotgun's handle towards Victoria, saying, "Hold this for a second." She complied, though she held the gun awkwardly.

Cris carefully walked to Ethan's side so he could see inside Mai's room, and even though he fully expected it, he wasn't prepared for what he saw.

Mai's body was just past the doorway, a look of surprise forever caught on her face and a bloody crater in her chest. She was not breathing.

With a sudden rush of rage, Cris roared, grabbing the back of Ethan's shirt and throwing Ethan into Mai's room. As Ethan awkwardly collapsed just past the bed, Cris dragged Mai's body out of the room by her foot and pushed her clear of the door while standing in the doorway. He then extended his hand towards Victoria, who wordlessly handed him the shotgun.

Ethan, still clutching his head, was clambering to his feet. "What the hell are you doing?"

"You're a math guy." Cris slid the shotgun along the floor, coming to a rest in the far corner of Mai's room. "What's this add up to, Ethan?" And he stepped clear of the doorway into the hall.

The door slid closed with a deathly hiss.

Victoria stared at Cris in horror. "What?! He's just going to come after us again!"

Alera shook her head. "He can't. He's trapped in there without Mai. Even if enough people die and he passes the task, he can't leave through the white doors without her. So-"

The sound of a slightly muted gunshot from Mai's room made everybody jump. They stood in silence for a moment. Then Cris turned to look in Meryn's room.

He found an unrecognizable bloody mess lying next to Meryn. Cris started crying. "I'm so sorry, Jamie. I am so sorry." He slowly backed out of the room, kicking the chair holding the door open into the room, and the door shut behind him.

He turned around to see Victoria and Alera staring at Mai's body and holding each other. When Alera looked up at him, he said, "Nice throw, by the way."

"I play Ultimate Frisbee. I meant to tell Meryn about it, but...well..."

Victoria and Alera began lightly stepping around the remains of Mai to join him but he waved them off. "No, don't bother. They're all dead!" His voice had become ragged, and he coughed wetly, pulling his hand from his mouth to find more blood on it. *That's it, then.*

Victoria ran to his right side, "We have to get you to a hospital!"

Cris groaned as the adrenaline of the last minute started to wear off and his entire left side started to burn. He risked a look at his shoulder and had to restrain himself from throwing up. His arm was in tatters and his shoulder looked like bloody hamburger meat.

He held back the nausea and looked instead at the faces of the women he loved. "I'm so glad you're okay." He held the back of Victoria's head in his right hand and kissed her passionately. He then reached over to Alera and kissed her as well, and as he pulled away from her, Cris spotted her collar. The final part of his plan fell into place.

Alera asked, "Where the hell did Ethan get a shotgun?"

Cris laughed ruefully. "He requested one."

"What?!"

"It only occurred to me when I looked at the dumbbells. There was no restriction on us requesting dangerous items, was there, Vi?"

Vi answered, "That is correct."

Cris told Victoria and Alera, "Our captors probably wanted us to kill each other at some point, but none of that matters now – we have to get to the white doors."

Alera asked, "Do you have a plan?"

Cris nodded. *At least I don't have to lie.*

Cris let Alera lead them to the door to the common room as Victoria supported him under his right arm. When it slid open, with his right hand, he shoved Victoria towards Alera, and as they collided, Cris ran to his own room, got inside, and moved far enough in for the door to close.

Cris breathed a sigh of relief even as they pounded on his dorm door. *At least they will survive.*

He took a deep breath, getting ready to shout, but it caused him to have an extended coughing fit, and he coughed up even more blood. Cris sat down, hard, on the edge of the bed.

He could hear Victoria yelling and Alera crying beyond the door. He did his best to raise his voice without shouting. "Ladies!"

The pounding and yelling quieted.

"I think...I think some of the buckshot pierced my lung. In about an hour, I'm going to drown in my own blood."

He heard Alera faintly crying.

"The task won't end in time for medical help to save me. I'm already dead.

At least this way, you two will survive."

He heard Victoria shout something muffled through the door, but it sounded like she said, "That's not enough!"

He ignored her. "Vix, my laptop is in the common room. Take it to the authorities if you can. And find my sister. Tell her I love her." His eyes welled up with tears and his throat tightened up. "And I love you both very, very much."

Alera shouted, "No! Wait! Please!"

Cris had another coughing fit, this one more painful than the last. And the whole of his left side still burned. He fixed their faces as firmly in his mind as he could.

"Go!"

Cris grabbed his collar with his right hand, pretending to try and yank it off.

Almost immediately, a klaxon blared.

Vi announced, "Tampering with your collar is against the rules."

Cris kept focusing on Victoria and Alera's faces in his mind.

Vi continued, "You will now receive one strike."

Cris sat back and waited for oblivion. Unbidden, he suddenly remembered he was carrying Alera's attempts to anagram his secret message in his pocket.

The words "FIND TOP TO ADD" flashed in his mind like a neon sign.

Wait a min—

Interlogue

Suddenly, the door to her lab opened, prompting Trina to jump with a little yelp. She spun around from the papers on the table that she'd been furiously writing on to see Samantha standing there in a navy-blue blazer, cream-colored blouse, and navy-blue pants, one hand on her hip, smiling.

Oh, hell. Trina straightened her glasses and ruefully said, "I don't know what gives with you government folks and your complete failure to knock. It's real easy. You just ball your hand into a fist and—"

Samantha waved that off. "Knocking wastes time. Time we don't have. How's it coming?"

"And then you take your fist and you hit the door with it, three times or so."

"If I knock on your head, will I get a status update?"

"I mean, if you want your update to be 'ow ow ow', sure."

Samantha smiled sweetly. "I can make the rest of your life incredibly miserable if that's what you want."

Trina smiled just as sweetly. "The whole three weeks? Wow. Or was that intended to threaten to shorten my lifespan even further?"

Samantha dropped the smile. "How's. It. Coming?"

Trina likewise assumed a neutral expression. "Slower than if you weren't here."

"Details, Trina. What's happening? How are they responding? Is it as your projections predicted?"

The faster I give her what she wants, the faster she leaves. Trina sighed and slipped her pen back into her lab coat pocket. "It's going according to spec. There are some slight issues with consistency, and a weird memory bug, but otherwise, behavior is exactly as I outlined."

Samantha turned to look at the back of the room, and Trina followed her gaze to what she'd come to call "the farm". Separated from them by a glass wall running the width of the room and only accessible via a single glass door were eight boxy black machines, each eight feet tall, three feet wide and three feet deep, evenly spaced. "The farm" was kept chilled and poorly lit.

Samantha stared at the machines for a long moment. "Any security issues?"

Trina smiled. "None. They're all snug as a..." Her smile faded, replaced with a look of consternation. "...well, something that's very snug."

Samantha laughed. "You didn't tell me you were taking up poetry in addition to your many other pursuits." She turned to face Trina. "Speaking of, I'm still getting flak for the morbid game you're playing. I don't like it, either. We need these people."

"Do you think I'm enjoying this?!" Trina grimaced and turned back to her notes on the table. "I explained why it was necessary in the outline. And you saw the results. Not my fault Senator Keller doesn't have the reading comprehension of your average sixth grader."

Samantha chuckled. "And he's not remotely as pleasant." Samantha gave Trina a contemplative look, then took a step forward to stand beside her at the table. She glanced at Trina's notes, then looked up at Trina herself. "I'm sorry. I don't mean to put more pressure on you. You've done absolutely outstanding work so far, and I know it's hard on you. I'll deal with the scoundrels and naysayers on the Hill. You just keep doing what you do best." Samantha paused for a second. "Is there anything at all I can do? Are your agent escorts treating you well?"

Trina threw a look towards the front door of her lab before loudly stating, "You mean the ARMED GUARDS who follow me EVERYWHERE I go, giving me NOT EVEN ONE MOMENT'S PRIVACY?" Trina leaned conspiratorially towards Samantha and whispered. "They're alright."

Samantha nodded, then loudly said, "Any other complaints?"

Trina practically shouted, "Justin shit his pants yesterday!"

A plaintive voice could be heard through the lab door. "I did NOT!"

Trina and Samantha laughed together.

Samantha said, "You know why they're absolutely necessary. Word has by some miracle not gotten out yet, but if it does, that could literally doom everything."

Trina turned and looked at Samantha with a calculating look. "Why are you really here, Sam? You didn't come all this way for some witty banter and to tell me things I already know."

"Those things are the cornerstone of our relationship."

Trina glared silently.

Samantha wrung her hands. "Your appeal was denied."

Trina's glare got angrier. "What?! Why?!"

"The deal was for you and you alone. No one else."

Trina stepped into Samantha's personal space and pointed a finger at her face. "No, the deal was, if Alera doesn't go, then I don't go, and the deal's off."

Samantha stepped back and nodded with her hands up. "I know, I know – I'll talk to them, okay? I'll get everything straightened out."

"Goddamn it, Sam, it was supposed to be straightened out *already.*"

"I know! What can I say? I didn't expect them to push back this hard."

Trina scoffed. "Well, push back harder, then. Alera's non-negotiable."

Samantha said, "Believe me, I read you loud and clear."

"You'd better." Trina turned away from Samantha for a moment. "Also, for what it's worth, I'm sorry about Jim."

Samantha nodded and took a moment before speaking. "He was honestly the best man I've ever known. I just hope I can live up to his memory."

Trina turned back around. "I'm sure you will, Madam Administrator."

Samantha threw Trina a look. "It's Sam, Trina. Just Sam. Keep up the good work, keep me posted, and send me an email if you need anything, day or night. You understand me?" She started walking towards the door.

Trina loudly said, "I don't need anything, but could we maybe get some diapers for Justin?"

A plaintive, muffled voice could be heard through the lab door. "Oh, ha, ha."

Chapter 23

Cris was awakened by the vague sensation of pain. He'd narrowed it down to his right leg and was starting to open his eyes when he was struck with a massive charley horse in his calf. Cris let out a little yelp and immediately started clutching his leg. Over the next few seconds, he just breathed heavily and endured the pain until he remembered to flex his foot, pulling his toes towards his body for some relief until the pain subsided, and he could start massaging his calf muscle.

Why does this keep happening to me? Wait. Keep...happening...? WAIT—

Cris was so startled, he fell out of his bed and onto the cold, wooden-tiled floor.

I'M NOT DEAD!! HOW AM I NOT DEAD?!?

Cris shouted, "Vi, are you there?"

A klaxon went off, and after a second or two, some words appeared on the white ceramic wall (a wall that seemed oddly further away than Cris remembered) in blue.

LOADING, PLEASE WAIT

"Loading?! What the fuck?" Cris realized his left side wasn't hurting, and where he'd previously been perforated with buckshot was now completely undamaged skin and clothes. "Vi, how the hell am I still alive?! Did you give me medical care?"

The words vanished, another klaxon went off, and more blue words appeared.

LOADING, PLEASE WAIT

Cris growled in frustration. *The last thing I remember is thinking about the words Alera had circled, "FIND TOP TO ADD" and then...nothing. I should be dead. Why am I still here? Did Alera and Victoria make it out okay?*

Cris got up from the floor and suddenly realized that things had changed. The room was approximately twice as wide as it had been. The bed, which had previously been roughly twin-sized and had a thin mattress on it, had been replaced with a double bed with a much thicker mattress. The floor and the doorways were now tiled in wood grain. *Instead of a prison cell, it's a little larger than my college dorm room was.*

Cris walked to the door, but it didn't budge.

"Vi, open the door, please!"

A klaxon went off.

PLEASE BE PATIENT
YOU WILL BE RELEASED SHORTLY

"Well, hurry up, damn it! I've done your stupid tasks and played this stupid game already and I want out!" He impotently punched the door, hurting his hand, but Cris didn't care. *I have had ENOUGH.*

Finally, after what felt like several minutes of standing there angrily tapping his foot, the door slid open with a familiar hiss, and Cris looked across the way to see another open door, and a familiar person just beyond.

She wore an orange top with a purple flower-pattern and jeans, and she had long red hair in a ponytail that reached the middle of her back. She had a small pointed nose and a mouth like a small pink bow.

She also had different-colored eyes, her right a warm green, her left an icy blue.

Cris breathed, "Alera..."

His gratitude upon seeing her collided with his frustration that she was still trapped in this place, and that caused him to fail to register the fear in her eyes. He said sadly, "How the hell are you still here? You should've gone through the white doors. You should be free!"

Her voice shook. "H...how...do you know my name?"

WHAT?!

Cris shook his head, trying to clear his confusion, and in so doing, spotted the corridor floor, which was now tiled in wood, just like his dorm, and Mai's corpse was gone, along with any sign of blood stains. "How, what... you don't remember? We've been trapped here for four days together."

Alera backed away a step. "N...no. I just woke up here a few minutes ago. Last night I was in my bed."

"It's the truth!" Desperation fueled inspiration. "Your name's Alera Zeller, you're a 21-year-old college student at Castleton State College in Vermont, where your major is undecided, but you're thinking of majoring in Computer Sciences because you enjoy programming so much – you also have a podcast called Don't Walk Alone in which you discuss unsolved murders that fascinate you, and honestly, episode 7 about that Krav Maga teacher was absolutely brilliant."

Alera stared at him in stunned silence.

"You're not a senior in college because you took two years off to avoid your ex-boyfriend, Cody, who you described as a goth who was into death metal and was really sweet, but something happened that you didn't want, and when you did something about it, you lied to him, and also honestly, fuck that guy, you made the right call."

Her eyes filled with tears, but her confusion did not dissipate. "How do you know this? I didn't even tell my friends about this."

Cris looked down at the floor. "We...uh, we were more than friends."

Alera continued to stare at him.

"Actually – and I'll completely understand if you refuse to believe it because I could hardly believe it myself when it happened – we were in a throuple with a girl named Victoria."

Alera's eyes widened even further.

"I was in a throuple? Neat."

Cris and Alera turned to see, at the end of the hallway (which Cris noted was longer now), a young woman with shoulder-length brown hair, glasses, a tie-dye t-shirt and overalls, big brown doe eyes, and a sunny-but-confused expression approach them.

"Victoria! Please tell me you remember being trapped here with us for four days!"

Victoria shook her head. "Sorry, my guy. I just woke up here and I've got no idea what's going on."

Cris sighed. "Victoria Latimer, a librarian from Carlsbad, California, you're a culture expert who loves books, TV, movies, video games, theatre, everything. You once poisoned an old classmate bigot who came to your open house, and you're poly, and you just got out of a bad relationship where she cheated on you, which you absolutely did not deserve, because you're one of the sweetest, most supportive people I've ever met. You've also got a killer voice and can belt the hell out of Funny Face."

Victoria stared at Cris open-mouthed.

Alera asked, "Is he right? He knew a LOT of stuff about me."

Victoria nodded. "Yeah, how...you say we've been here for four days?"

"At least. Five days now, assuming today's a different day."

Victoria held up her hands. "Whoa, whoa, whoa. Maybe you'd better tell us the whole story. What happened to you that we're not remembering?"

Cris looked down at the floor, then back up. "Okay. We've been trapped here in this facility, being forced to do these crazy tasks to avoid getting strikes. There were seven of us, but Meryn, Jamie, Mai, and Ethan are all dead."

"Wait, I'm what?!"

Cris turned in amazement at hearing Meryn's voice. Just past Victoria stood Meryn, Jamie, Mai, and Ethan, all very much alive and staring at him in bewilderment.

Chapter 24

Cris' brain was rapidly unraveling. "You...I...you were all dead. I—" He looked at Mai. Unlike the others, she looked very different from before. She had the right side of her head buzzed low and a spiral line shaved into it, while the rest of her black hair fell loosely over her left shoulder. Instead of a sundress, she now wore a black baseball jacket with white stripes on the collar and cuffs and a pink floral design interspersed every now and then with open-mouthed skulls. The jacket was unzipped, revealing a black tank top underneath, and she wore dark jeans and bright pink trainers.

Her face hadn't changed. Cris was very familiar with the suspicious glower she aimed at him. "What? What the hell is your problem?"

"You've changed. Everyone here looks the same as they did before, except your hair and clothes."

"Dude, if you're on drugs, you should share." Mai folded her arms. "I went to bed last night and woke up here wearing the same clothes I was wearing yesterday."

Cris shook his head and turned to Ethan. "And you...I killed you myself."

Everyone took a step back, and Victoria stood in front of Alera as if to protect her.

That was a mistake. "Not literally. He killed Jamie and Mai, and shot me in the shoulder before I locked him in a room with a shotgun, where he killed himself."

Ethan stared at Cris in astonishment. "I highly doubt your story, sir, as your shoulder appears undamaged, and I remain comfortably un-killed."

Jamie said, "Are you sure, like, you didn't just have a really bad dream?"

Cris' eyes were wild. "I am not hallucinating or imagining things. We've all been trapped in this place together for four days, why the hell am I the only one who remembers?!"

Meryn rubbed her face and said, "I don't like this. Maybe he's with whoever kidnapped us."

Mai pointed out, "He knew our names."

Victoria said, "Uh, he knew a lot more than that."

Jamie cocked an eyebrow. "Like what?"

Cris sighed and turned to Meryn. "Meryn Sarovitch, registered nurse from Buffalo, cat and dog mom but claimed to me that she had no real friends despite her being a perfectly lovely human being – she also took a homeless man off life support to attempt to save a young girl and lost them both, and that still haunts her to this day."

Meryn stared at him open-mouthed.

Mai's turn. "Mai Shibata, mechanic from Jonesborough, Tennessee, knows a lot about science and tech despite being raised in a cult by her hyper-religious family who repeatedly punished her by sticking her in a closet. She only escaped when she was 16, though she had to stab her brother to get away, all of which contributed to her not wanting to be touched."

Mai swallowed hard.

Jamie was already cringing a little bit as if not looking forward to what Cris had to say. "Jamie Gamble, Air Force pilot stationed at Wellens Air Force Base in Wayland, Massachusetts, but originally from Niagara Falls. Weed enthusiast. Claims he doesn't have a sin to confess during a social task."

Jamie was confused. "I mean, I guess that's true...? Wait. How do you know all that stuff?"

"You told me." Cris turned at last to Ethan. "Ethan Winters I know the least about, but he's a professor of applied mathematics at the University of Cambridge in Massachusetts, and he stole over forty thousand dollars from a former employer, and on the final day of our tasks in this miserable place, he killed Jamie and Mai, and mortally wounded me."

Ethan crossed his arms. "Again, all of this has not happened. If it wasn't for the specifics, I'd put you down as a lunatic, Mr..."

"Thorpe. Cris Thorpe, I'm a reporter from Arlington, Virginia. I had just submitted the biggest story of my life for editorial approval when I woke up here four days ago and met all of you for the first time. And since it's only fair, my dirty laundry is that my need to know everything that's going on has cost me several friendships as well as my most recent girlfriend, when I accused her of cheating on me, and in fact, she had been seeing a doctor about her cancer diagnosis."

Cris looked at everyone staring at him in a mix of horror and disgust. *The hell with it.* "Yes, I'm a shitheel. Victoria and Alera were helping me to be better, and then all hell broke loose. But somehow, instead of being over, it's started all over again, and the women I love don't remember me at all. So you'll forgive me if I don't give a shit what you think."

Meryn regarded him icily. "Maybe you'd better tell the story from the top."

The door behind Cris slid open. Cris spun around to see the common room behind him, as pristine as everything else, but now also with a wooden-tiled floor. "More wooden tile."

Victoria asked, "Something wrong with that?"

"Mai's outfit and hair aren't the only things that have changed. Our dorm rooms are twice the size they used to be, and the flooring used to be the same ceramic as the walls, but now it's this wood tile."

"What does that mean?"

Cris shrugged. "I don't know. But there's no point standing around gawking at the floor. Maybe we should make ourselves comfortable."

He walked into the common room and sat easily in his usual armchair. The others slowly entered behind him, looking around at everything, and Cris couldn't help but notice the last two armchairs filled were the ones on either side of him.

Meryn sat to his left but didn't take her eyes off him. Mai stood a little ways off instead of sitting down.

Cris extended a hand to the empty chair, but she waved him off. "I'm fine, thanks, doll."

"Your choice, doll."

Her eyes flared.

Cris ignored Mai and addressed the group. "Any second now, Vi will make her presence known, unless – you're not loaded up yet, are you, Vi?"

A klaxon went off and the wall behind Ethan lit up with blue lettering.

LOADING, PLEASE WAIT

Cris tsked. "My, my, she sure does take a while to load."

Meryn said, "What the hell are you talking about?"

"Vi is short for Virtual Instructor, she's some sort of artificial intelligence who corrals us through the tasks, takes our requests, and answers questions."

Jamie was still confused. "Wait, what tasks?"

Cris gave off a long-suffering sigh.

After ten minutes or so, Cris had explained all the rules and summarized most of the events of the past four days.

"So, let me see if I've got this story straight." Meryn still had a hard look in her eyes. "We don't know where we are, who kidnapped us, or why, and all you managed to put together in four days was that we *might* be in space?"

Cris opened his mouth to speak, then, hesitating, closed it again. "Well, when you put it like that, it seems kinda silly, but trust me, getting information out of Vi is like pulling your nose hairs out with your fingers."

Ethan harrumphed. "Seems to me there are two possibilities. Either Mr. Thorpe is working for our captors, which would explain how he knows what he knows, and this is a clumsy attempt to blind us to that possibility – or, he's telling the truth, and we've all somehow lost our memory of the past four days. Personally, I'm inclined toward the first possibility."

"You SON of a—"

"To my knowledge, specific memory manipulation is impossible. I also cannot see the point of removing our memories and keeping his."

Cris stared incredulously at Ethan. "They didn't just erase your memories, they brought you back to LIFE! But it's the memory thing you have a problem with. Sure." Cris scoffed and folded his arms.

Jamie spoke up then. "But if he's with the bad guys, why tell us all this stuff? Wouldn't it be smarter just to blend in and pretend you don't know what's going on?"

Ethan snorted. "The fact that you would even make that argument proves it's not a bad idea."

Meryn shook her head, "This is giving me a headache."

Cris snapped his fingers. "Meryn, do you already have a strike?"

"What?"

He leaned forward. "When we all woke up here the first time, you tried to get your collar off and got an early strike. Did you do that this time as well?"

She looked at him strangely. "I...I got the warning not to meddle with the collar, and I thought it was a bluff. I was going to ignore it and keep trying to break it anyway, but something told me not to."

Cris shook his head. "It sounds like you don't remember the past four days consciously, but maybe some part of you subconsciously remembers?"

She stared at him for a moment before her hard eyes softened a little. "....maybe."

A familiar voice emanated from the middle of the room. "Hello!"

The others looked startled, but Cris merely smiled. "Vi! Welcome back. Now our party is complete."

Vi cheerfully continued, "Forgive me if I startled you. No, I'm not actually here. I'm a virtual instructor, or V.I. for short, but—"

Cris interrupted, "We know, we know, we're here to do some tasks, if we complete them, we get to make requests. If we fail we get strikes. The first two strikes are pain, third strike is death, all correct, yes?"

Vi chirped, "Yes, that is correct. Do you wish to skip the tutorial?"

Everyone looked at Cris. *Well, this is new.* "I don't want to speak for the group. What do you all want to do?"

Mai asked, "Well, that depends on the tutorial."

Cris shrugged. "Vi just tells you all the stuff I already told you – and that Vi has already verified to be correct."

Alera spoke up. "Well, I mean, we might want to ask questions."

He nodded. "You can ask questions any time, even from the privacy of your own room if you want."

Meryn looked around at the group. Alera was mollified, and Ethan just shrugged helplessly. Everyone else was looking at her or Cris.

She looked him in the eyes one more time. "Well, if that's the case, I see no reason why not."

Cris nodded. "Vi, we'd like to skip the tutorial, please."

Vi cheerfully said, "Very well. It is now time for the first task of the day."

"WHAT?!"

Cris' stunned shout froze everyone else in place.

Vi, as usual, carried on. "Please be seated at the table for the task briefing."

Everyone was looking at Cris. "This didn't happen last time! The tasks didn't start until the second day!"

Mai had an edge in her voice. "Well, it sure sounds like they've started to me."

Vi repeated, "Please be seated at the table for the task briefing."

Cris stood up and gestured for the others to follow. "Let's go. You DON'T want to get a strike for not following instructions."

Everybody seated themselves at the table.

Vi announced, "Your task is to properly dispose of this body."

A chill ran down Cris' spine as an image appeared on the surface of the table. As Cris surmised he would, he recognized it.

It was the naked body of James Arnold.

Chapter 25

Cris stared in disbelief. "The President?!"

Jamie raised an eyebrow. "Uh, dude, that ain't the President. That's a geography teacher."

"No, ugh, we called him the President because he looked like he worked for the government. His name is James Arnold, and he's the Administrator for NASA."

Eyes widened all around the table.

Victoria asked, "Are you for real?"

Cris groaned. "Yes. Mai found a business card on his body after...after we killed him."

Vi carried on, "The blue room contains the body, surgical tools, and two receptacles, Recyclables and Incineration. The red room contains the receptacle rules and regulations, and the yellow room contains medical records. You have one hour. Your time starts when you've entered your chosen rooms, at which point the doors will be closed and locked until the task is completed."

Victoria said, "There has to be a way to communicate between rooms," to which Cris nodded.

Alera stuttered, "S-so it's a sort of macabre group exercise? We gotta work together to figure out what body parts go where?"

Ethan said, "Awfully kind of our captors to let us destroy all the evidence of our alleged murder."

Cris shook his head, "I wouldn't be so sure about that. We are being recorded."

Mai looked around. "Cameras?"

"Not that we ever found, but Vi admitted we were under surveillance under questioning. And you theorized that this may all be for someone's entertainment."

Mai bit her thumb.

Meryn stood up. "I should be the one to handle the body. Does anyone else have a preference?"

Cris said, "We should have three people in the blue room, and two people each in the red and yellow rooms." When everyone stared at him, he added, "That way there's one person at each phone and one person working on each problem."

Meryn nodded. "Then that's how we'll do it."

"Considering my...unique situation, I'll go wherever I'll be tolerated."

Ethan harrumphed. "In that case, Mr. Thorpe can come with me to the yellow room."

Cris' jaw dropped. "Are you sure?"

Ethan crossed his arms. "As I said, it's not often one gets to confront their killer. Also, I'm certain that one way or another, you're the key to what's going on here."

Cris considered this, then simply nodded.

Meryn said, "Then that's settled. Does anyone else want to volunteer for the blue or red rooms?"

Cris raised a hand. "Victoria's pretty good with manuals. She should probably go to the red room."

Victoria gave him an odd look. "I was just about to suggest the same thing."

Alera raised her hand. "I'll go with her."

Meryn looked at the remaining two. "Jamie, Mai, you okay to come with me?"

Jamie said, "Of course!" while Mai merely shrugged.

"Let's go!"

Everyone grouped up in front of their chosen doors, and Cris loudly announced, "Vi, we're ready! Open the doors!"

Vi replied, "Doors will open momentarily for five seconds. Please move quickly into your selected rooms. The doors will shut and lock when the five seconds are up."

The doors slid open with a hiss, and Cris entered the yellow room with Ethan. Inside was the usual phone on the wall as well as a simple desk with some file folders on it. Ethan went straight to the desk, and once the doors closed, Cris picked up the phone and stared balefully at Ethan.

He didn't have to wait long until Jamie's voice came through the receiver. "Hello? Uh, anybody there?"

"Yeah, Cris here. Ethan's looking through the medical records now."

Ethan did not look up from the papers he was perusing. "Yes, but it would help to know what we should be looking for – the more we know about this recycling process, the better."

Cris passed that on to Jamie, who asked, "Hey, wait, Cris, you've been through this, so you should know, right?"

"No, this is an entirely new task. I'm just as clueless as everyone else on this."

"Right." There was an uncertainty to Jamie's reply that Cris didn't enjoy.

While Cris waited for Jamie to come back with information, he kept his eyes firmly fixed on Ethan, who momentarily looked up, caught Cris glaring at him, and looked back down at his papers without any sign of disturbance. "My executioner appears to be angry with me."

"Damn right I'm angry. Yesterday, you took a shotgun and killed two of my friends before nearly killing me."

Ethan still did not look up. "And yet, your friends are alive, and you're completely undamaged. Excepting, perhaps, mental damage."

"The point is, you can't be trusted, Ethan."

"And I suppose you can be?"

Cris was ready to retort, but Jamie's voice interrupted, "Okay, so apparently, we have to surgically remove and recycle as many organs as we can. Victoria's got a list of the organs that can be recycled and what can't. Meryn's already started cutting the President open."

Cris passed that on, but Ethan appeared confused. "That doesn't explain why the medical records are necessary. Can Victoria give us any details about what makes an organ eligible or ineligible for recycling?"

There was about a minute of silence, then Jamie returned, "Yo, she says there are a couple of things that disqualify organs from being recycled, like if the liver is damaged from alcohol-related liver disease, or if anything's contaminated by radioactivity or metal."

Ethan looked up sharply as Cris relayed this. "Metal, are you sure?"

"Yeah, why?"

"Mr. Arnold didn't drink, and as far as I can tell, hasn't been near radioactive materials, but he did serve in the Iraq War, during which he apparently was hit with shrapnel from an IED. The shrapnel perforated his stomach and left kidney."

"Got it – I'll tell the others." Cris passed that on to Jamie.

Ethan did not take his eyes off Cris. "And I am not a killer."

"The hell you're not – there was nothing recognizable left of Jamie's head and a huge hole in Mai's chest thanks to you."

"Or you're a liar. Did you forget that is also a possibility?"

Cris shrugged. "You can think what you want. I lived through it all."

"I'd be willing to believe you except for one thing – as a Catholic, I cannot accept that I would have just started taking lives. Unless there was some mitigating factor you're leaving out?"

Cris continued to glare at him. "The task was to leave only two survivors. We all had two strikes. It was either two of us survive, or all of us die, and you did say at the end that it was logical."

"And I agree – better that four die instead of six, but why not myself? I'm the oldest, and I've had a full life. If it came down to it, it makes absolute logical sense to sacrifice myself for someone younger, so why didn't that happen?"

Cris' glare softened a little. "I know you might scoff at this, but is it possible there was an emotional reason?"

Ethan looked confused. "What possible emotional reason could I have for committing murder? I have no family, and I don't know any of you."

Cris cast his mind back and had a minor epiphany. "Meryn."

"What?"

"She was special to you, I think. You told her that she'd impressed you, and that wasn't something you said lightly."

"Very few people do. I still don't see why—"

"Meryn died mere hours before the task."

Ethan looked sharply at Cris. "And you...you think..."

"I think you had a fatherly pride in her. And I think you were heartbroken when she died. We all were. But give a man who runs on logic one of the strongest emotions there is, grief, and...well, maybe he snaps."

Ethan scoffed and looked back down at the papers on the desk. But he remained silent for a long time.

"Susie Q."

Cris' eyes darted to the older gentleman and stayed there until Ethan's gaze slowly rose to meet his.

"My old job. First, I want it understood this is off the record. Breathe a word of this to anyone and I'll deny it." He sighed. "You are aware of those AI programs people use to make art or chat, things like that?" Cris nodded. "We were coders working on an artificial intelligence program that would assist doctors and nurses in diagnosing and treating comatose patients. The goal was to eventually figure out how to bring patients out of comas at will."

Even as Cris whistled, Ethan sighed heavily. "Susie Q was incredibly intelligent, strong-willed, and also extraordinarily kind. She was the closest thing to a best friend that I've ever had."

Cris' jaw dropped open. "You say was – she didn't...?"

He let out a humorless chuckle. "No, as far as I know, she's still alive. At least, I certainly hope so. But when some executive came down from on high screaming about some money that had gone missing from our department's budget, which I was technically in charge of, Susie defended us, defended me. Said we were programmers, not accountants, and it was no business of ours if he'd lost money. He told her to pack her things and be off the premises within an hour."

Ethan's volume dropped. "As she was packing, she started to cry, and I tried to tell her that with her skill set, she'd land on her feet or even find something better, and that's when she told me that her daughter was pregnant. Her sixteen-year-old daughter who wanted to keep the baby."

Cris turned his gaze to the floor.

"In an instant, I realized that Susie had placed her family's livelihood in danger in order to protect me, and I just had to do something. I found the missing money the very next day – some months prior, the same jackass executive had earmarked forty-thousand dollars for his pet project. Since the AI we were working on was supposed to be adept at tracking minute or involuntary muscle contractions, the jackass thought it might be possible to adapt it to improve a golfer's swing."

Cris looked back up in amazement. "You're joking!"

"As God is my witness. We'd already transferred the money, in cash, to a new account per company policy, and the paperwork that was supposed to go to accounts had apparently gone down the back of my mailbox and got trapped between it and the wall. Long story short, I had the only record proving where the money was."

Ethan looked back down at the President's records and cleared his throat. "About a week later, Susie Q received a hand-delivered package containing forty thousand dollars in laundered, untraceable twenties and tens. That same day, the C.E.O. of our company received my resignation. I hear the project stalled until a few weeks later, when the primary medical consultant, one of the top coma experts in the world, also quit, effectively killing the project for good."

He looked back up at Cris. "So, if your story is genuine, I committed a crime to help a woman I respect and admire, and in doing so, killed a project that could have prevented another woman I respect and admire from having to make an awful choice that haunts her to this day."

Cris shook his head. "You can't blame yourself for that."

Ethan looked back down at the medical files and said nothing.

There was some more back-and-forth over the phone when Meryn had questions about James Arnold's medical history, but no more discussion about anything other than the task at hand.

After what Cris guessed to be about 40 minutes or so, there was an announcement.

Vi cheerily informed them, "You have successfully completed your task."

Cris breathed a sigh of relief. "Well? What do you think? You still think I'm a liar?"

Ethan organized the papers back into their respective folders. "I think the possibility cannot be thoroughly squashed as there's literally no way to prove anything you've said is true."

Cris looked down at the floor as Vi announced, "You have each earned one request for food, drink, or entertainment. You may make your request at any time."

Ethan walked up to Cris and adjusted his glasses. "But I'd call it statistically anomalous. If you are telling the truth, I want you and I to be very clear on one thing."

Cris looked back up to meet Ethan's gaze as their door slid open with a hiss.

"I can't say for sure why that...alternate Ethan did what he did, but I can say with some certainty that after killing you, he'd have turned the gun on himself. I would never kill anyone and be able to live with the guilt. End of discussion."

Ethan abruptly turned and walked through the door as Cris watched him leave, his eyes full of mystery.

Chapter 26

They congregated in the common room, abuzz with their recent victory.

Jamie was telling Victoria, "I don't know how she did it. Meryn was an absolute girlboss in there, slicing that dude up like a ninja doctor."

Meryn replied with a dazzling smile as Ethan walked up to her.

"Well done, young lady."

"Thank you. I couldn't have done it without everybody's help."

Mai raised a hand, "So what's up with these requests, y'all?"

Cris answered, "We can ask for any foodstuff, and it'll be available for every appropriate meal we have afterward. For example, Vi, I'd like to request French toast, bacon, and maple syrup for every breakfast, please."

Vi replied, "Request approved."

Alera turned to Cris. "That's my favorite breakfast!"

"Yes," Cris said sadly, "I know."

Her exuberance dimmed, and she returned to looking uncertain.

He added, "And if someone wants to request coffee at every meal, I know Meryn would appreciate that."

Immediately, Ethan said, "Vi, I'd like to request coffee and several cream and sugar options at every meal, please."

Vi chirped, "Request approved."

Jamie muttered, "Damn it. I wanted to do it."

Meryn turned and looked at Ethan. "You didn't have to do that."

Ethan crossed his arms. "That is correct."

Mai asked, "But what about entertainment – Vi said that was an option, what, like magazines and such?"

Before Cris could answer, Vi responded, "Entertainment requests will be delivered to your personal dorm room and are not necessarily for everyone unless you wish to share them. Possible choices include but are not limited to books, stereo systems, televisions, computers, tablets, or mp3 players."

Cris added, "And there's a media server somewhere hosting a ton of TV shows, movies, and podcasts, apparently. But before we get too far into it, fair warning, dangerous items aren't off-limits. That's how Ethan got his hands on a shotgun."

Meryn nodded and said, "Then perhaps we should make an unofficial rule that you have to tell everybody what you request. And we can keep track somehow, so if somebody's got a request they haven't used, we'll know that person might be dangerous."

Victoria crossed her arms. "That seems reasonable. Can everyone agree to that? And who do we put in charge of keeping track, they could be fudging their own records, right?"

Meryn shook her head. "We'll make it public. I'll request a whiteboard and a set of markers, and we can keep track of all the requests right here in the common room. Does that work for everyone?"

There was a chorus of assent.

Meryn looked up. "Vi, I'd like to request a whiteboard and a set of colored markers for the common room, please."

Vi responded, "Request approved."

The rest of the day passed quickly, especially as nobody was particularly interested in spending any time with Cris, who, feeling rather aggrieved by the whole situation, was weirdly resentful of the rest of them for losing their memories. So that's just fine by me.

The mandatory sleep period came and went, and Cris realized, *I should have asked for a laptop instead of showing off. Now I'll have to wait for another task before I can record what's happened to me.*

Instead, Cris spent his time at the new whiteboard. They'd created a graph with everyone's names on rows and task numbers on columns, and filled in their requests for the first task. Jamie's read "WEED" in big capital letters, Cris had scribbled down "French toast, bacon, syrup", Mai's box simply read "PC", while Ethan had requested "Coffee, cream, sugar". Meryn wrote "this whiteboard and markers", and once she'd been informed what dinner would be, Alera added "hamburgers, ketchup and mustard". Victoria's box remained empty.

There was some free space at the bottom of the whiteboard, and while everybody else talked quietly after dinner, Cris had written "FIND TOP TO ADD PURPOSE" and was staring at it, trying to puzzle out its meaning, right up until Vi announced the evening task.

"It is now time for the second task of the day. Because you succeeded at your first task today, this task will be easier than it would have otherwise been."

As the others quieted down, Cris took his seat.

Vi continued, "Your task is to hurt each other's feelings."

Mai said, "What if we don't have feelings?"

Vi ignored her. "You'll take it in turns saying something hurtful to the person whose name comes alphabetically before yours. If that person becomes genuinely upset, your collar will glow green. All collars must be turned green before one hour elapses to succeed at this task. Your time starts now."

Meryn said, "This just sounds cruel."

Cris nodded. "Agreed, but trust me, all of us getting a strike is worse."

Vi announced, "Victoria will go first. Your target is Meryn."

Victoria's face fell. "Why me? I don't want to hurt anybody."

Meryn stood up. "Don't worry, I won't take it personally."

"You have to take it personally. Vi said you have to be genuinely upset."

Meryn's face took on a distressed look and she immediately burst into tears. "How could you say something so hurtful?"

Victoria raised an eyebrow as her collar remained pristine white.

Meryn straightened and wiped her eyes. "Worth a shot. Alright. I guess we've gotta do this for real. Don't hold back. I can take it."

"Who gives a fuck what you think, you piece of shit?"

Meryn's eyes widened and her mouth opened in shock even as Victoria put a hand to her mouth but her collar remained unchanged.

After a moment, Victoria dropped her hand and her eyes moistened. "Meryn, I didn't mean it, I am so sorry!"

Meryn sighed. "I know. But it wasn't enough."

Victoria looked up suddenly as inspiration struck. "Meryn, if Cris is telling the truth, we've been trapped here for five days. What if nobody's been taking care of your pets?"

Meryn's eyes went glassy as Victoria's collar glowed a sickly green.

Victoria quickly hugged Meryn. "I'm so sorry. I'm sure they're fine. We're gonna get you back to them, I promise."

Meryn took in a shuddering breath. "Thanks."

Vi pronounced, "Meryn, your target is Mai."

Mai stood up even as Victoria let go of Meryn and sat down. "Well, thanks to Cris, everybody knows about my family, so I'd suggest pushin' those buttons if y'all want me to crack."

Meryn looked at Mai with sadness in her eyes. "I don't suppose your parents ever really loved you."

Mai nodded as Meryn's collar remained white. "Anybody could tell ya that."

"And I know you think it's because you're unlovable."

Mai froze.

"It's why you keep running. You're not just avoiding your old family, you're deathly afraid of making a new one."

Mai's lip quivered.

"Because deep down, you know they'll eventually realize they don't love you. And your heart'll get broken all over again."

A tear streaked down Mai's face even as Meryn's collar glowed green. "H-How...?"

Meryn clasped Mai's arms. "You're wrong. You are lovable, Mai. I hope one day you understand that."

Mai stood there, stunned, as Meryn released her.

"And I love your hair. That swirl and the notch in your eyebrow are super cool." Meryn smiled as she sat down.

The task came to a screeching halt when Mai had to hurt Jamie's feelings. For several minutes, Mai berated Jamie with blistering vituperation, insulting everything from his baldness to his tiny size and everything that implied.

Mai threw her hands up. "This is impossible, y'all, how do ya hurt a stoner's feelings? He's too chill."

Jamie scratched his head. "I'm sorry. I am trying to take this personally, but I know it's all bullshit for the task, so it's hard to get upset."

I think I know what would get him to react emotionally, but how can I get Mai to do it without embarrassing him? Cris snapped his fingers. "I've got an idea. Can I ask everyone to leave the room except Mai and Jamie?"

As everyone complied, Cris crossed to Mai and whispered, "You need to insult Meryn."

"Wait, what? Why would—" Mai looked at Jamie. "Oh. OH. I get it."

Jamie looked at both of them with uncertainty. "What? What is it?"

"Meryn sure is a dumb loser, ain't she?"

For the first time, Cris saw anger on Jamie's face. "Hey, hey, you leave her alone!" Then Jamie noticed Mai's collar had turned green and his face reddened. "Oh. Right. Good call, good call. Um, we can keep this to ourselves, right?"

Mai smiled and said, "No worries. I think y'all'd be cute together," as Cris went to the dorm hallway to retrieve the others.

Vi announced, "Jamie, your target is Ethan."

Jamie looked at Ethan returning to the lounge. "Oh, fuck me. I don't even know where to start."

Ethan walked up to Jamie and whispered as everyone else sat down.

Jamie's looked surprised, then sad. "Really? You're sure?"

Ethan nodded.

Jamie sighed sadly. "You've never fit in anywhere, and you never will."

Ethan let out a shaky exhalation as Jamie's collar turned green.

Meryn held up a finger. "I hope you know that's not true."

"If I did, it wouldn't have worked. Thank you, Mr. Gamble."

As Jamie sat down, Vi announced, "Ethan, your target is Cris."

Cris stood up and approached Ethan. "Well, this should be easy for you."

Ethan remained silent for a long moment. "If I'd successfully killed you yesterday, that would've meant one more had to die. Which would you have preferred me to kill, Miss Latimer or Miss Zeller?"

Cris could only stare at Ethan with agonized acrimony as his mouth worked wordlessly and his heart raced.

Ethan's collar turned green as his eyes widened slightly, and he took a step closer to Cris and said quietly, "You really believe all that actually happened."

Cris gulped in air and tried to calm down. "It did."

Vi announced, "Cris, your target is Alera." *Oh, no.*

Alera slowly stood up as Ethan took his seat. "It's okay. You have to do it. I forgive you."

Cris took a deep breath. "You absolutely did the right thing. If you weren't ready, then you weren't ready, period." *But I can't lie to her.* "What bothers me is that you didn't tell Cody. He didn't even have a chance to do the right thing. Maybe he would've gone with you so you didn't have to be alone during the procedure. Now you'll never know."

Alera's tears burned holes in Cris' heart, and he was only distracted by a green glow coming from his neck. He quickly said, "I'm so sorry, and I don't believe that," as he sat down.

Victoria stood up before Vi could say, "Alera, your target is Victoria."

"Al, you've got this. I'm a big girl, I can take it. Don't be afraid, okay?"

Alera looked at Victoria, and her mouth worked for a moment. "I...I can't."

Victoria clasped Alera's hands with her own. "Yes, you can. You HAVE to, we're so close!"

"I-I-I can't!" Alera cried harder. "I can't hurt you!"

Victoria hugged Alera and gently stroked her hair. "Shh. It's okay. You know I'll forgive you."

Alera stopped crying and deadpanned, "No, dipshit, I mean I'm not coming up with anything hurtful to say."

Victoria froze for a second before she busted out laughing.

To everyone's surprise, Alera's collar turned green.

Vi announced, "The task has been completed."

There was some slight cheering muted by confusion as their collars turned back to plain white.

Ethan posited, "Brilliant, Alera. I think the collars were measuring our vital stats to detect a combination of shock or surprise with a heightened emotional state, so the same outcome could be achieved by making her worry about you and then making her laugh."

Meryn nodded. "There's no actual way to measure emotional pain, but a heightened emotional state does influence measurable physiological factors, so that would seem to explain it."

Vi announced, "You have each earned one request for food, drink, or entertainment. You may make your request at any time."

Cris muttered, "Two down, four to go."

Cris had returned to staring at the whiteboard. So intent was he on his puzzle that he didn't notice someone walking up behind him.

"Whatcha doing?"

Cris spun to see Victoria, wearing a smile on her face that was like a balm for his soul. She wrote in her first request box "a variety of fruits for breakfast".

"Oh, just trying to figure this stupid thing out."

Victoria put the marker back in the tray and leaned over. "FIND TOP TO ADD PURPOSE. Are you sure this is what it's supposed to say?"

"Well, the first task of the third day was to guess our 'purpose' and this was as close to something that made sense as AI could get."

"Does it have to be that order?"

Cris turned to look at her and was struck once again by the kindness in her eyes. "Uh, what do you mean?"

Victoria picked up the eraser and wiped away 'FIND' and 'ADD' and rewrote them in each other's positions, forming the phrase 'ADD TOP TO FIND PURPOSE'.

Cris gasped, his eyes then drawn to the request graph where Jamie had written in all capital letters, 'WEED'. He then took the eraser and marker from Victoria, erased the 'T' and 'P' from 'TOP', and wrote 'POT' instead.

'ADD POT TO FIND PURPOSE'

Could it REALLY be that simple?!

Cris excitedly put the eraser and marker back on the whiteboard tray. "Vix, you're a genius!"

Victoria leaned back, a look of mild disgust on her face. "Vix? Eww, no. Don't call me that, please."

Cris' exhilaration faded to confusion and dismay. "What? I call you that all the time." Reality crashed back down on Cris, and his tone turned acidic. "Oh. Right. You're not her."

As he walked away, Victoria blurted out, "What do you want from me?!"

He spun and shouted, "Something I can't have!" He swallowed, calmed himself, and started walking back towards her. "The Vix I knew was kind, caring, strong, and brilliant, and miraculously, she loved me. I know this because she did her best to stop me from killing myself to save her life. Now, somehow, I'm still alive, and a complete stranger is wearing her face. And every time I see her, I'm reminded of just how much I've lost." Cris' eyes filled with tears.

Victoria's eyes were also misty, but they still carried anger. "So by all means, carry on shouting at me, blaming me, and making me feel bad. Because that's the smart plan to get her back."

Victoria wiped her eyes and stalked off, and Cris couldn't bear to turn and watch her go.

Chapter 27

Cris stood in front of the dormitory door with some trepidation but eventually summoned the courage to knock.

After a moment, the door slid open, revealing a red-eyed Jamie, who immediately broke into a big smile. "Hey, man, how are you?"

Cris relaxed and smiled. "I've been better. My heart's a little sore, and I want to get the hell out of here, but otherwise, I'm doing alright."

"Yeah, today was rough. You want to come in?"

"Sure. Actually, I was hoping I might be able to toke up with you."

As Jamie stood clear of the doorway, his eyes lit up. "For real, man? I didn't know you were a traveler of the green! THIS IS GONNA BE AWESOME!!"

Cris walked in and sat in the chair opposite the bed as Jamie giggled, and he couldn't help but laugh himself. "I'm not usually. Haven't smoked since college, but I just got a hint that it might be the key to getting out of here."

Jamie sat down on the bed and pulled a vape pen and cartridges from under his pillow. "Yeah, I find it to be the key to a lot of things."

Cris picked up the vape pen and inspected it carefully. "Did you receive any kind of message with this stuff?"

"Message? Nah. Nothing like that."

Cris unscrewed the cartridge from the pen and looked inside the pen.

"Uh, dude? What are you—"

"Oh, sorry. Just making sure there wasn't anything hidden inside it." He screwed the cartridge back on.

"Am I missing something here?"

Cris sheepishly handed the pen back to Jamie. "My, uh, coded message. Victoria pointed out it could say 'ADD POT TO FIND PURPOSE'."

Jamie laughed. "Yeah, I got that message in high school." He held up the pen. "Just press that button and breathe it in, man."

Cris awkwardly took the pen and took a drag from it. "It actually tastes kinda good."

Jamie nodded and held his hand out. "Weed's changed a bit since you were in college. They got flavors now and gummy bears, all sorts of stuff, it's crazy."

Cris handed the pen back. "I don't really know how this is supposed to help me find our purpose."

Jamie took a long, smooth drag from the pen. "Well, I find it helps me think about stuff. Helps me realize when I'm being stupid about something, and I need to be better."

Cris threw Jamie a look even as he accepted the pen back from him. "That little morsel of advice feels a teeny bit pointed."

Jamie laughed as Cris took another drag. "Yeah, well, I know you're unhappy about how things with your ladies went, and I get it. If even one of those two loved me and I lost her, I'd be heartbroken about it."

Cris handed back the pen. "Heartbroken is a funny word for it. They're still alive. I still love them."

Jamie interrupted his drag, and as a result, started coughing, holding up a hand. "Maybe that's it."

"What's it?"

"Just love them. Be the guy you were when they loved you before. It sucks that you have to start over, but instead of being sad that you have to, maybe you should be grateful that you can."

Cris sat back in his chair and held up a hand to Jamie's proffered vape pen. "Jamie the Love Therapist."

Jamie took one last drag between giggles. "The Doctor is in."

"Speaking of which, Jamie, how's things with Meryn?"

Jamie immediately started spluttering and coughing. "What?"

"Come on. It's obvious. And you ended up getting together a few days ago, sadly, it was right before she died."

Jamie just stared at Cris.

Cris said, "My advice? Don't wait. There's so little time."

As much as Cris hoped getting high would bring answers, he and Jamie spent most of their time telling each other stories from their respective childhoods and laughing with glee, and he would admit to himself later that it was still totally worth it.

Jamie asked, "So what do you think, man? Why is all this happening? And why is it happening to you twice?"

Cris shook his head. "I don't know, man. I should be dead. It's like...it's like an alternate universe or something."

Jamie's eyes widened and he exploded, "WHAT IF YOU TIME TRAVELED?! OH MY GOD?!"

Cris couldn't help but laugh, and Jamie joined in. When the laughter wound down, Cris answered, "I don't think so, because some things are different this time, like that first task. And the President was already dead."

Jamie said, "So, what, they just saved your life, let your body heal for however many months, keeping all of us under wraps, and just started over?"

"Nah, you took a shotgun blast to the face at close range. There's no coming back from that."

"Clones."

Cris leaned back. "What?"

"They just cloned us. Our personalities and our histories are all exactly the same, right? We just don't have the memories you do."

Try as he might, Cris couldn't dismiss the idea. "Maybe."

"Hey, man, were you serious about before?"

"You're gonna have to be a little more specific."

Jamie looked somber. "Meryn."

Cris smiled at him. "Yeah, man. I'm serious. In fact, what are you doing hanging out with me? Go knock on her door."

Jamie looked confused as Cris stood up. "Huh?"

"No time like the present." Cris pointed a hand at Jamie's door. "Lead the way."

Jamie didn't move. "Are you coming with?"

Cris scoffed. "And be a third wheel? Nah, fam. But maybe wear your camo jacket. She likes a man in uniform."

Jamie slowly got up and grabbed his jacket. "Okay. But what do I do?"

"Just talk to her, dude. Get to know her. She's lonely, and she doesn't deserve to be, and she likes you." Cris gently guided Jamie towards the door and it opened.

"But what do I talk about?"

Frustrated, Cris shoved Jamie out the door and followed him out. "Dude, you just spent an hour telling me about times you snuck out of your house and slept on the porch. I'm sure you'll come up with something."

"Alright, yeah. I got this."

"You got this."

Jamie looked at Cris and hugged him. "Thanks, man."

Cris hugged him back. "Now go forth and kick ass."

Jamie released the hug and smiled. "You got it, dude." And he walked off in the direction of Meryn's dorm room.

Cris headed to his dorm but stopped upon realizing he was hearing something. *Sounds like voices...coming from Alera's room. I'd give a lot to listen in, but with Jamie right there...wait, what am I thinking?*

Cris shook his head and walked to his door, even as Jamie knocked on Meryn's door. As much as he wanted to see how that turned out, he quickly walked into his room once his door opened, and he sat heavily on the bed with a sigh.

He's right. I've just gotta relax and not let it get to me.

Cris disrobed and got into bed. Despite attempting to stay relaxed, Cris tossed and turned for some time before finally drifting off to sleep.

Cris awoke feeling like he'd spent the night as someone's punching bag. He groaned out loud. *Apparently, even a more comfortable bed can't stop me from pretzelizing myself while I sleep.*

He rolled over and caught a glimpse of an object resting atop his cleaned laundry. *Oh, right, the laptop I requested is here.* Cris forgot all about his aches and pains and pulled back the covers while he swung his legs out from under them and sat upright. He swiftly picked up his laptop and turned it on. *Can't believe I'm going to have to start all over.*

Once the machine had booted up, Cris opened up Writer, and to his amazement, it loaded the most recent document, which was his perfectly intact report on all the events since his imprisonment, exactly as it was before he "died".

Okay, not that I'm ungrateful, but why the hell is this still here?!

"Vi, how...why does my computer have my old files on it?"

Vi chirped, "I do not have that information."

Cris scoffed. "Why did I even bother asking you?" He looked down at the laptop, and said in a self-mocking tone, "Might as well ask you – hey, computer, why do you have my old files still?"

To Cris' surprise, black lettering appeared on his wall.

COMMAND UNRECOGNIZED
PLEASE RESTATE QUERY

Chapter 28

Cris set his laptop down and stared at the words on the wall.

"Vi, where did these words on my wall come from?"

Vi answered, "You are currently interfacing with the main computer."

Cris stared for a moment until the words vanished as the revelations started to hit him. *Of course! Just because the main computer isn't physically here doesn't mean there's no way to interact with it, like a terminal miles away from a server. And if I'd bothered to check my assumptions, I might've realized that Vi wasn't the only thing that responded to speech.*

Cris thought for a moment. "Computer, list commands."

VIDEO - AUDIO - MESSAGE

Cris furrowed his brow. "Computer, video, please."

1 - 2 - 3 - 4 - 5 - 6 - 7 - MAIN

"Computer, one, please."

Cris jumped when an image of himself standing in his dorm room appeared, and simultaneously the image of himself started as well. Cris waved an arm and watched as the image performed his movements exactly.

It's a live feed.

Cris looked up to where the camera was supposed to be, the upper right corner by the door, and saw nothing. He pulled the bed over to the corner, and stood on it, reaching up towards where the camera would be, and felt nothing, but the corner was rounded. *Is the camera literally built into the corner?*

Cris pressed his finger to the corner, trying to block the camera. However, as he watched the feed, the moment his body was covered, the image switched to a new angle, and the shot seemed to be in the opposite corner. When he moved his finger, it returned to its original position and angle. *Who knows how many cameras there are?*

"Computer, video two, please."

To Cris' surprise, the video switched to Alera's room, where Victoria and Alera appeared to be quietly talking, though no noise of any kind could be heard.

"Computer, audio two, please."

"—eally think so?"

Cris jumped again as Alera's voice seemed to be coming from right beside him.

Victoria's rich voice rang out next. "I do. I know what loss looks like. What it feels like. I think Cris is in real pain, which indicates to me that he's telling the truth."

Cris sat down on his bed, leaning back against the corner. Alarm bells were ringing like crazy in the back of his mind, but his need drowned them out.

Alera sat down on the bed. "I...there's something that I need to tell you, but you've gotta promise me that you won't think I'm crazy or working with the bad guys or anything."

Victoria quickly sat down next to her. "Of course, anything."

Alera looked down at the floor. "I...I've been noticing that I'm having trouble remembering things. Like when you were talking about your mom, I realized I...I can't remember certain things about my mom, like her favorite music or what she smells like. And when we talked about middle school? I can't remember my best friend's face. I remember her name, but why can't I remember her face? I can't even remember the name of the middle school. I should be able to remember that, shouldn't I?"

Victoria shrugged. "I'd personally like to forget middle school, but I get what you're saying. You think your memories have been messed with."

Alera's voice wavered. "What if Cris was telling the truth? What if we've been through all kinds of awful things, and we don't remember because those memories were erased?" She looked down at the floor. "And then there's you."

Victoria leaned back in surprise. "Me?"

"Even if Cris is telling the truth, we've only known each other for five days. So," She looked up at Victoria with her eyes brimming, "how am I already so in love with you?"

Victoria touched her forehead to Alera's head. "I know what you mean. I move fast when I know what I want, but when it comes to love, it usually takes me a while to get there. Not with you." She kissed Alera, and sighed. "And then there's Cris. My heart hurts for him, and I admit, the idea of being in a throuple with the two of you is really enticing."

Alera nodded. "I do kind of have a thing for sad boys. And he did use one of his requests to get my favorite breakfast. I just..."

The silence was deafening. *You just what?!*

Victoria asked, "Do you want to go talk to him?"

Cris' heart was in his throat.

Alera looked at the wall for a moment and then looked back at Victoria. "No. Not just yet. Let's see what happens today."

Cris' heart returned to its normal position.

Alera lifted Victoria's head from her shoulder with two fingers. "We don't have to go to breakfast right away. If you don't mind." They began to kiss.

Cris said, "Computer, stop video and audio, please."

The wall became blank, featureless, and silent. The exact opposite of Cris' brain.

The door to the common room slid open, and only Mai was sitting at the table, eating some cereal. She looked up as Cris approached. "You look like hell."

Cris snorted. "I assure you that I feel much, MUCH worse than I look."

"You're not getting sick, are ya?"

"Just didn't sleep too well. I feel like someone beat me with a wiffle ball bat."

Mai ate another spoonful and chewed for a moment. "Guilty conscience?"

"Yes, you're right, I couldn't stop thinking about that time I helped to kidnap a bunch of strangers and made them do weird tasks with me."

Mai's face darkened. "You're not funny."

Cris finished piling his plate up with French toast and bacon. "That makes two of us."

Mai sneered at him, but he ignored her and simply sat down in a lounge chair to eat. Ethan entered shortly after, and then Meryn and Jamie entered together, nearly prompting Cris to cheer, but he merely threw Jamie a questioning look and a thumbs up, which Jamie returned with a smile. *And I can't help but notice he's having some difficulty walking, too.*

Victoria and Alera soon followed, and they had swapped shirts, which brought Cris right back down. *That stings a bit.*

Further compounding Cris' bad mood was the fact that no one came to sit in the lounge area with him, instead choosing to sit together at the table. The previous task of trying to hurt each other may have been intended to break the group apart, but it appeared to have the opposite effect. They smiled and laughed occasionally while talking in hushed voices, and Cris felt his isolation most keenly.

To his surprise, Ethan came over and stood in front of him. "Would you mind joining us at the table, sir?"

"Mai's made it pretty clear that I'm persona non grata." Cris put the last forkful of breakfast into his mouth.

"Miss Shibata doesn't speak for all of us, Mr. Thorpe. Please." Ethan extended a hand to take Cris' dishes.

Cris shrugged, handed him the plate, and stood up, walking over and taking a seat between Ethan and Jamie, who smiled at him.

Meryn asked, "Do we know when the next task takes place?"

Cris nodded. "Noon. We've got some time."

"Is there anything we can do to prepare?"

Cris shook his head. "Not without knowing what the task is going to be, and Vi won't tell us." *The computer might, though. But I...I can't tell them about that. Not until I've had a chance to check everyone out, make sure nobody's doing anything suspicious when they're alone in their room.*

Alera said, "You've been through this before, and we haven't, or at least, we don't remember it. Um...what do we do?"

"I mean, we usually just sit and talk. We'd become friends in that alternate timeline or whatever, and you can't really prepare for these tasks, so we just kept each other company and stayed ready and alert." He punctuated this statement by getting up and making himself a cup of coffee.

Jamie slumped in his seat. "Aww. I was hoping I could toke up."

Cris returned to his chair. "Afterwards, dude, definitely."

Jamie brightened. "Heck yeah, in fact, after this next task, I say we all get stoned together."

Ethan muttered, "Preposterous."

Mai said, "No, thank you."

Ethan followed up, "Absolutely not."

Jamie shrank back a little. "Alright. Just the cool people then."

The group engaged in some light conversation of no real substance, but at least the atmosphere was a good deal more friendly than it had been.

Inevitably, Vi interrupted, "It is now time for the first task of the day."

Cris looked up. "We're ready, Vi. What is the task?"

"Your task is to successfully maneuver a spaceship through an asteroid field."

Dread washed over Cris. "Here we go again."

Chapter 29

Meryn asked, "Again? Is this a repeat?"

Cris nodded. "Yes, and a bad one at that, we failed this task last time."

Familiar images of a ship in space surrounded by large rocky asteroids appeared on the table as Vi continued. "Visual screens are non-functioning, but sensors can find and plot the asteroids on the navigation map. However, radiation from the field is draining the power systems, meaning thrusters and sensors cannot activate at the same time."

Jamie paled, "I'm not gonna be able to see where I'm flying?!"

Cris got a severe case of déjà vu. "In a manner of speaking, you will. Whoever's on sensors will send their locations to navigation, and you'll then have to avoid them."

Vi continued undisturbed, "The piloting and navigation stations are behind the green door. The power station is behind the orange door. The sensor station is behind the pink door. All participants will be locked in the rooms before access to any materials is granted, and the locks will not release until the task is over. You have five minutes to get the ship clear of the asteroid field before the radiation destroys too many vital ship systems to survive. Your time starts when you have all entered the rooms."

Jamie asked, "How did we fail last time?"

Cris looked at Meryn. "Uh, Meryn made a mistake."

Meryn did not appear offended but curious. "What kind of mistake?"

"The sensor station has controls to move along the X and Y axis, and you knew about those, but you realized too late that there were also controls for the Z axis, and Jamie wound up hitting too many asteroids."

Ethan asked, "Should we assign someone else to the sensors?"

Cris shook his head. "I don't think so. If it weren't for that one mistake, Meryn was doing really well. I think she said the scanner reminded her of medical equipment she knew."

Meryn looked at Jamie, and he returned her look and nodded, saying,

"You've got this."

"So do you."

Cris continued, "Mai should handle the power, but she said it was sort of like a puzzle, so Ethan should probably still go with her. I'll go with Meryn like before. Vix, sorry, Victoria should go with Jamie, and Alera with Ethan and Mai."

Meryn asked, "Does anyone have a problem with this?" She was met with silence. "Then let's get to work."

Everybody lined up in front of their respective doors, and Meryn said, "Vi, we're ready. Open the doors."

Vi answered, "Doors will open momentarily for five seconds. Please move quickly into your selected rooms. The doors will shut and lock when the five seconds are up."

As the doors hissed open, Cris and Meryn were already moving. Wordlessly, Cris pointed to the desk at the back of the dark room while he moved towards the phone. "Remember, once the power comes up, give yourself a few seconds to familiarize yourself with all of the controls before you get started, and remember to check in all directions."

"Got it."

The power came back on. Over the handset's speaker, Cris could hear Alera's voice. "—should be on now, can you hear me?"

"Loud and clear, Alera." He looked over at Meryn, who had both hands on the sensor station's controls and was deep in concentration. "Meryn's already working on marking the asteroids for navigation."

"Got it." There was a pause. "How are you doing?"

Cris ignored the lump that threatened to form in his throat. "I'm good. Really. You don't have to worry about me, but it's appreciated all the same."

After a moment, Alera responded, "For what it's worth, I believe you."

The lump followed through on its threat. "Th-thank you. I...thank you."

Meryn shouted, "Got 'em all, send power over to Jamie!"

Cris said into the phone, "Alera, Meryn's done, switch power to Jamie!"

He listened as she relayed that to Mai, and after a moment, the phone went silent and the room was dark once again.

Cris said aloud in Meryn's direction. "You'll have to get used to this, I'm afraid, but stay ready."

Meryn answered. "I'm all set." After a moment, she added, "Thanks."

"You're welcome."

"Not for this. For Jamie."

"What?"

"He said you encouraged him to come talk to me."

"Oh, I did, yeah."

Meryn started to speak again, but Cris was distracted by the lights coming back on and Alera's voice in his ear. "—says he's moved the ship as far as he can!"

"We're on it." Cris waited patiently as Meryn pressed buttons and rapidly tapped the touchscreen monitor built into the desk.

After a moment, Meryn shouted, "Send power to Jamie!"

Cris asked, "This is where things went wrong last time. Are you sure you checked in all directions in 3D space?"

For a second Meryn looked like she was going to argue, but then went back to the monitor and checked things over. "Yeah, all asteroids marked. Switch to Jamie!

Cris said into the phone, "Switch power to Jamie, please!"

Alera said, "Got it!" once again, and after a moment, the phone was dead, and the room was covered in darkness once more.

Meryn's voice came out of the dark. "Why'd you tell him to talk to me?"

Cris thought for a second before speaking. "Two reasons, first, the two of you had hooked up in that alternate timeline, and it made both of you happy, and," Cris let some bitterness into his tone, "somebody ought to be."

"And the second reason?"

"Because the last time we did this task, you told me that you had no friends. And that seems like an injustice to me."

Silence reigned.

The lights suddenly came back on. "—says we should be clear, but the task hasn't ended."

Cris looked at Meryn. "Jamie says we're clear?"

She shook her head. "I don't believe it. We might be clear of that clump, but we're not out yet." She wore a look of determination that Cris thought suited her. "Yeah, there's an asteroid at the extreme edge of my scanning range. Tell Jamie to get right up close to it."

Cris looked sharply at Meryn, then smiled and said into the phone. "Alera, tell Mai to switch power, and tell Jamie to get right up close to the asteroid at the edge of scanning range."

"O-Okay." Alera relayed the information, and the room was dark again.

It was a statement instead of a question. "You think they set up a trap."

Meryn answered, "Exactly. It's what I'd do: leave some open space so the pilot thinks he's free to blast away and then WHAM – a wall of rocks. Lucky for us, my Jamie's smarter than that."

"Your Jamie?" Cris couldn't help but smirk.

Meryn sighed. "I don't know. Maybe I've been getting by on animal companionship for so long that I've forgotten how good human companionship can be. And you can't really blame anyone else for me having no friends."

The power came back on. "—ow what? Vi says there's two minutes left."

Cris did his best to calm Alera. "That's okay, I think we might be at the final hurdle. Meryn's scanning and plotting our way out as we speak."

Meryn affirmed, "Yeah, there's a wall of asteroids blocking the way, but there's a hole in the wall just large enough for our ship, I think. Tell Jamie—" A rare look of consternation appeared on her face. "—what's a cool piloting thing to say?"

Cris told Alera, "Meryn's found a way out – switch the power and tell Jamie Meryn said 'turn and burn, baby!'"

Alera and Meryn both laughed, and Alera said, "On it!" And once again, after a moment, they were in darkness.

Meryn's voice came to Cris from the dark. "I've always been pushy. I like to take charge and I like to get my own way and that pushes people away."

"Yeah, I think you said something like that last time."

"Did I say that maybe I do it deliberately?"

Cris' tone softened. "No, you left that part out."

"For the longest time, it was just me and my Dad, and he was in the military, so we moved around a lot. And then the world took him away from me, and all I had was myself. Maybe...maybe I got a little too used to that."

Just then, a klaxon went off and Vi announced, "Warning. Structural and hull damage to the ship. Power conduits to sensor room damaged. Repairs commencing."

Cris said, "Oh, no."

Meryn said, "Wait for it..."

Cris didn't understand what she meant until the lights came back on and Vi had a new announcement. "You have successfully completed your task."

Meryn nodded and stood up. "I had a feeling that gap in the wall was a bit small. But Jamie got us through."

Cris said, "Well, last time you said that if Jamie completed the task, you would, and I quote, 'absolutely wreck him.'"

Showing zero signs of embarrassment, Meryn looked Cris in the eye and said, "Pretty sure I did that last night."

Vi continued, "You have each earned one request for food, drink, or entertainment. As before, you may make your request at any time."

Cris awkwardly laughed and said, "W-Well, now I suppose you're going to have to top that."

Meryn smiled and folded her arms. "I guess I'll just have to grind him into a fine powder."

Cris' jaw dropped and he turned beet red as the doors hissed open. "Uh..."

Meryn put her hand to her mouth. "Oh, I'm sorry. What part of me pounding Jamie into a sticky paste makes you uncomfortable?"

Cris fled, chased only by Meryn's laughter.

Chapter 30

They were a jubilant group in the lounge, Jamie telling the story of flying the ship between the rocks and how he just barely clipped an asteroid while squeezing through the wall, Meryn sitting at his side, squeezing his arm, and every now and then giving Cris a wink, making his ears get hot all over again.

After a few minutes, Cris got up and walked over to where Victoria and Alera were quietly talking. They stopped when they noticed him, and Alera gave him a smile.

Cris said, "I'm sorry for interrupting. I just wanted to say something that you, Victoria, said to me some time ago. Communication is the answer."

With the barest hint of a smile, Victoria replied, "Always."

"You were right, and I was wrong. I was wallowing in self-pity when I should have just been grateful you were both still alive."

Victoria's smile became full. "Where did this come from?"

"As much as I would like to take credit, Jamie pointed out that I've been given a second chance, and I should just be the man you loved in the first place."

Victoria nodded. "Should've expected that level of wisdom from a guy who giggles at his own jokes."

On cue, Jamie giggled. "I'm funny A.F., yo. That's right, funny as falafels." He giggled again.

Victoria laughed.

Cris said, "So I'm going to try to be less mopey," he smiled at Alera, "though I know you have a thing for sad boys."

Alera gave him a weird, confused look for a second but reverted to her dazzling smile.

Cris grinned and whispered, "To that end – how many dead orphans can you fit in a dumpster?"

Victoria's mouth dropped open in dismay, but Alera leaned forward and whispered, "How many?"

"I was hoping you could tell me, they're starting to smell."

Victoria turned bright red while Alera erupted with laughter.

The group split off, with a few hours before dinner, everyone decided to find their own way to spend the time. Mai pumped iron in the lounge and spent twenty minutes on the treadmill. Meryn and Jamie disappeared into her dorm, as did Ethan, but Victoria and Alera quietly chatted at the table.

Cris sat quietly in his dorm, using the camera feed to keep an eye on all of them while he updated his record of the events thus far in his laptop. *Though I don't know who the hell this chronicle's for – as far as I can tell, neither this laptop nor any of us are ever leaving this place.*

Cris tried to shake the gloominess of that thought by switching his attention back to the feed. The main feed showed Mai finishing up on the treadmill, while Alera and Victoria sat quietly talking in the lounge.

"Computer, video 3, please."

The image on the wall changed to a room identical to Cris', and he could see just an unmade bed.

Jamie's probably in Meryn's room. "Computer, video 5, please."

Cris could now see Ethan sitting on his bed with his back against the wall, calmly reading a book. There was a small bookshelf next to the bed loaded with books, Ethan's only non-food request.

7 is Victoria's room, but I don't know if I should peek in Meryn's room. After a moment, he shrugged and said, "Computer, video 6, please."

The image changed to show Meryn and Jamie sitting side-by-side on Meryn's bed. They were kissing, and Meryn's hand was undoing Jamie's belt buckle.

Quickly, Cris said, "Computer, video 4, please!"

The image changed to Mai's empty room.

Phew. I'd better give them some time before I go back.

Cris was about to change the video feed again when the door in the image slid open, and Mai walked into her room. She walked past the bed and out of camera range, and the view angle changed to show her entering her bathroom, closing the door behind her.

The camera stayed focused on the back of the room and did not change. *There are no cameras in the bathrooms. That's good to know.*

Despite nothing happening for several minutes, Cris let the feed stay in Mai's room. *She's on the top of my list. Everyone else more or less trusts me now, but Mai is still hostile for some reason, and I still don't know why she got to change clothes and the rest of us didn't. If she is working for the bad guys, I need proof.*

After a few more minutes, Mai exited the bathroom wearing a towel. She sat down at the computer desk she'd requested, and Cris leaned in to see more clearly what she was doing, but Mai merely loaded up a video on her PC's monitor and started watching.

Cris could taste his disappointment. *Well, looks like I'm not going to prove it just this second. Still, it's worth keeping an eye on her.*

After another moment, Mai walked into the bathroom and retrieved her clothes, and sensing she was going to get dressed, Cris said, "Computer, video 2, please."

The feed switched to Alera's room, and as he'd hoped, Victoria and Alera were there.

"Computer, audio 2, please."

"—thing special for dinner?" Victoria asked.

"I'm okay, thanks. We've got so many options now."

"It's just that I literally don't know what to do with my request. It's not like they're gonna get me a salad bowl from my favorite restaurant."

Alera shrugged. "Only one way to find out."

"Is there anything you miss from home?"

Alera thought it over for a second. "One of my favorite things about my mom – that I can remember – she used to make this raspberry jam. It was the absolute BEST. I'd put it on everything."

Victoria smiled. "My mom made a really good spaghetti with meat sauce. I won—I wonder if we'll ever see them again."

Alera stood up and took Victoria's hands in hers. "We will. We've got just three tasks left if Cris' information is good, and none of us have any strikes. We're all going to make it out of here."

Even at the angle the camera was facing, Cris could see Victoria's eyes filling with tears, and he had to fight to suppress the urge to run to her. "You promise?"

"Trust me." Alera gently kissed Victoria on the lips, then hugged her tightly. "I'm not letting go."

Cris watched them hug for a few seconds. "Computer, video and audio off, please." The image vanished from the wall.

Neither am I.

Dinner was uneventful. If anything, the conversation was more jovial than before. Mai continued to give Cris the cold shoulder, but otherwise, there was a camaraderie that hadn't been present until now. *More than ever, I am convinced that what our kidnappers actually want is for us to succeed. Now if only I could figure out why…and we're running out of time.*

On that thought, Cris decided to speak up. "I apologize for bringing down the mood a little bit, but I think it's important to point out that, assuming things have not changed since the previous cycle, tomorrow will be the final day of tasks, and our first task tomorrow will likely be to guess what our purpose is."

Meryn asked, "We got it wrong last time, I'm guessing?"

Cris nodded, spearing a piece of steak with his fork. "We guessed it was to take part in an experiment, and that was incorrect, so we failed."

Alera asked, "Did you get anywhere with that anagram?"

Cris snorted as he swallowed. "While smoking brought me a certain clarity of mind, I didn't come away with any more purpose than before."

Jamie said, "Speak for yourself. I get all the purpose I need."

Cris smiled. "Well, I didn't have any epiphanies, and there didn't appear to be any hidden messages in his vape, so I'd say we're back to square one with that."

Mai said, "What if it didn't apply to you?"

Cris looked up and saw no hostility or malice in her eyes.

"You think that message might have been for somebody else?"

Mai nodded rapidly. "Think about it, doll – if I wanted to pass a secret message to someone without making it obvious that I sent a secret message to someone, coding the message in a weird way and sending it to someone ELSE, wouldn't that almost guarantee that person would tell everyone else, including the person it was meant for?"

Jamie nodded sagely. "That could work. Heck, it DID work, you told everybody about that anagram thingy, it's even written on our board!"

Cris shook his head. "I'm fairly certain that our kidnappers would have a better way of getting messages to a secret collaborator." *Like the main computer's message function.* Not wanting to give offense, Cris quickly added, "That's smart thinking, though, Mai. Any other ideas?"

"Nothing solid. I've been watching space shows on my PC to try and get some inspiration."

As dinner wound down, the group moved to the lounge area of the common room as they waited for Vi's inevitable announcement.

"It is now time for the second task of the day. Because you succeeded at your first task today, this task will be easier than it would have otherwise been."

Meryn asked Cris, "Do you know what this will be?"

He shook his head, "We failed last time, and that task became to kill one person."

Vi announced, "Your task is to find the traitor."

Chapter 31

Cris' eyes widened, but he wasn't as quick to react as Mai, who pointed a finger at Cris and yelled, "I KNEW IT!"

Cris shouted back, "I am NOT a traitor!"

Vi continued, "You will all go back to your dormitories. Once inside and alone, a word will flash on the wall indicating whether you are an Innocent or the Traitor. You will have one hour to investigate and discuss. The Innocents' goal is to correctly vote on who the traitor is before time expires. The Traitor's goal is to avoid detection. Anyone can call for a vote at any time, but a player must receive at least four votes for it to be accepted, and once a vote is accepted, the task is over. If the Innocents successfully vote for the Traitor, the Traitor will receive a strike. If anyone else is chosen, or no vote is accepted before time expires, the Innocents will receive a strike."

Alera said, "It's a hidden identity game."

Cris filled his voice with scorn. "Yes. Turns out we're not looking for an actual traitor to the group." He glared at Mai, who stared back at him coolly.

Meryn added, "But now someone HAS to get a strike."

Ethan said, "I'm guessing our captors are tiring of our success."

Vi continued, "You have one hour. Your time starts when all subjects learn their roles. Please head to your individual dormitories."

Jamie stood up, "If I'm the traitor, yo, I'm telling you. Better one strike than six."

Cris walked next to him. "Hopefully, everyone else feels the same way."

There were some sounds of assent, but Cris couldn't help but notice that none were as fervent as Jamie.

Cris walked into his dorm room and let the door close behind him. He sat down, waiting for his fate to be spelled out on the wall in front of him. *But then I already know what's going to appear.*

Sure enough, after a moment, red lettering appeared on the wall.

* * *

TRAITOR

Cris sighed. *These assholes are really determined to drive a wedge between me and the others, letting me keep my memories but removing theirs, and now making me the Traitor in their stupid game. But I already know what I'm going to do.*

The lettering vanished, and Vi said, "You may now return to the common room."

Cris got up and walked to his door, and as it slid open, he heard several other doors slide open, and in a moment, they were all in the hallway together.

Cris raised his hand and said, "Mai got her wish. For the next hour at least, I am the Traitor."

Alera said, "Well, that's it, then."

Mai narrowed her eyes. "What if he's lyin'?"

Cris exploded, "Why the hell would I lie about that?! If I'm actually an Innocent, voting me the Traitor just gets me a strike anyway!"

She remained unfazed. "If you're workin' with our captors, as I believe you are, gettin' more strikes on all of us might be what yer after, even if it means gettin' one yerself."

Cris sighed angrily. "May I remind you, all of you, that a strike is one step closer to death? I've already watched most of you die once. I've no desire to see it again." With that, he turned and walked to the common room door, which obediently opened and allowed him through.

As he walked to the lounge, he heard the others following in after him.

Ethan said, "We can't entirely discount Miss Shibata's concerns. No matter how eloquently Mr. Thorpe defends himself, there is no evidence to support his innocence."

Cris sat down and cocked an eyebrow at Ethan. "The logician expects me to prove a negative?"

"I'm merely saying we must take the possibility under consideration, Mr. Thorpe." Ethan sat down in an armchair next to Cris.

As the others took their seats, Jamie remained standing. "Well, I believe him. He did exactly what I would've done, spilled it out, and nobody else is saying that they're the real Traitor."

Victoria shook her head. "You're assuming everybody else would do what you'd do. Can we really say that nobody here would be selfish enough to hide being the Traitor just so they wouldn't get a strike?"

Everyone looked at each other.

To Cris' surprise, Alera was first to respond. "Well, I wouldn't. The goal is to get all of us out alive, not just me, and if Cris is right, we'd have to fail BOTH of tomorrow's tasks to get a full three strikes anyway."

Cris caught Alera's eye and nodded. "Exactly. I can take the strike. What I'm not looking forward to is the second one."

Meryn cleared her throat. "Should we call a vote, then?"

Mai said, "Wait! Y'all ain't gonna just play into his hands, are ya?"

Cris growled, "For the last time, I'm volunteering to take a strike so none of you have to, what part of that do you not understand, Mai?!"

"The part where your mouth opens and lies come out."

"I'm not a member of your parents' cult, Mai."

Her eyes widened and her mouth worked for a second before she spoke. "That's true. At least with them, I knew they meant what they said." Mai sat back in her chair, crossed her legs, and glared daggers at Cris.

Cris looked over at Meryn. "Call the vote."

Meryn looked up. "Vi, we'd like to call a vote."

Vi cheerfully informed, "I will call the subjects by name one by one. When you hear your name, please say the name of the subject you would like to vote for. If you fail to say a name within three seconds of your name being called, you will be considered abstaining from the vote. Four votes are required."

After a second's pause, Vi said, "Cris Thorpe."

Cris looked up. "Cris."

Vi said, "Alera Zeller."

Alera looked at Cris. "Cris." Cris gave her a faint smile.

Vi said, "Jamie Gamble."

Jamie looked over at Cris and pointed finger guns at him. "Cris!" Cris couldn't help but chuckle.

Vi said, "Mai Shibata."

Mai remained silent but stared resolutely straight ahead at the wall.

Vi said, "Abstained. Ethan Winters."

Ethan cleared his throat but said nothing.

Vi said, "Abstained. Meryn Serovitch."

Meryn looked Cris in the eye. "Cris." He nodded.

Vi said, "Victoria Latimer."

Victoria looked at the floor. "Cris."

Vi announced, "The vote has been accepted. The task is complete. The Innocents have won, and the Traitor has lost."

The group gave a minor cheer of jubilation at the announcement, but Mai remained steadfast. *Not that it feels like a loss to me, anyway. Which reminds me—*

Cris got down on the floor. "Meryn, Jamie, quick, hold me down, please."

Despite their apparent confusion and concern, they did as they were told while Vi announced, "The Traitor will now receive one strike."

Cris grit his teeth. "Here we go."

The pain was once again instantaneous, extreme, and all encompassing. Cris was only vaguely aware that he was screaming, but he did register shouts of alarm from others in the room, particularly from Meryn and Jamie.

And then it was over. Cris weakly coughed and looked gratefully at Meryn, who stared back at him in shock. "Thanks. You don't need to hold me down any more, it's over. But maybe help me up?"

Jamie said, "Jesus, man. You didn't say it would be like that."

Victoria asked, "Are you sure you're okay?"

As Meryn pulled Cris up to his feet, he said, "Yeah. I'm fine. Getting a strike is like having every inch of your body on fire, inside and out, all at the same time," at this he noted looks of horror from Victoria, Alera, and to his surprise, Mai, "but the first one only lasts a second. I'll be okay in a minute." He attempted to prove this by taking a step, but he clipped the leg of the armchair and immediately stumbled. Luckily, Meryn caught him.

Cris lopsidedly smiled at Meryn. "Maybe we should take me back to my room instead."

Meryn had walked Cris back to his dorm, supporting him the whole way until he got into bed. He looked up at her gratefully. "Please assure everyone that I'll be okay in a bit. I just need to get my sea legs under me." He paused a moment. "Do you think they'll believe that?"

Meryn looked down at him. "I'm not convinced that I do. But ask Vi to page one of us if you need anything. We can do that, right Vi?"

Cris was nodding before Vi announced, "That is correct. I can carry messages of up to twenty-five words to any subject you'd like."

Meryn nodded. "Okay. Rest up, Cris. Hopefully, this all ends tomorrow, and we might all make it out, and at least partially thanks to you."

"You're gonna make me blush. Vi, open the door, please."

Meryn smiled and left, the door shutting behind her.

Cris tried to rest, but he just rolled around on the bed for a while. He briefly considered turning on the common room feed to see if they were talking about him. But honestly, it feels more and more wrong every time I use it. Instead, Cris leaned over and grabbed his laptop from the chair, opened the lid, and pressed the power button. When the operating system had loaded, he pulled up the Writer app.

And before his astonished eyes, two words typed themselves on the next line of his report.

They read, "MORAL PRIG."

Chapter 32

Cris stared at his laptop screen. *Another secret message? Or are our captors just making fun of me? I don't THINK I've been a moral prig...*

Cris took a few minutes to attempt to anagram those words, but the best possibility he was able to come up with was RIP GLAMOR. *And I don't think they're trying to make a statement about the fashion industry. I need Alera's help.*

He disconnected the power cable from his laptop and walked to the door, which slid open to reveal Mai with a look of surprise on her face and her fist raised like she was about to knock.

Cris said, "Oh! Mai. What are you doing here?"

Mai looked at the floor. "I need a word. You got a minute?"

"If you're going to keep accusing me you can save your breath."

She looked up at him. "No. It's kinda the opposite, really. I owe ya an apology."

Cris looked at his laptop. "I suppose this can wait." He threw the laptop on the bed. "Come on in."

They walked into his room. Cris sat cross-legged on the bed while Mai sat in the chair. He waited for her to start but she said nothing.

After several seconds of silence, Cris said. "Good apology. Thanks."

Mai retorted, "Oh, shut up, dumb-ass. This ain't easy." Mai took another moment to gather her thoughts. "You know about my family and what they did to me."

Cris nodded. "Your parents locked you in a closet when you questioned their religion and for many other things besides. Then they tried to marry you to the church elder's brother or something like that."

Mai nodded. "Did I tell you what happened after that?"

"You ran away. I know that at some point your brother found you, and you stabbed him. That's all I know."

"First time I ran away, I tried to make somethin' of a normal life. I got a job cleaning and waxing cars for a local dealership, and then they taught me how to fix mechanical things, and I found I had a knack for it. I had a small apartment that I loved. I made friends. I even went on a date with a boy I liked. And then my brother found me."

Mai leaned forward, putting her hands on her knees. "I knew, as soon as I saw his face, that I'd lost everything. Again. I could handle or escape him, but if the cult sent more people – and they could – I realized there would be very little stoppin' 'em from draggin' me back and doin' God knows what."

She leaned back and sighed. "As soon as my brother was down, I went back to my apartment, put the things I needed into a bag and lit the hell out of there without saying a word to the people who knew me and cared about me. For all I know, they might still be looking for me, but I couldn't take the chance that they'd tell the cult where I was goin', so..."

Cris leaned forward. "So that's why you haven't gotten close to anyone."

Mai nodded. "I don't know, maybe Meryn was right and I'm scared of getting my heart broken again. Either way, I ain't stayed anywhere longer than a couple months since. Good mechanics are pretty scarce these days, so I can find a job anywhere, but I don't get attached to anything I can't drop in two seconds flat if I need to bolt."

She leaned forward and pressed her palms together. "And I don't trust anybody. Three people knew I was at that café, and I cared about all of 'em, and I'd told 'em how I'd escaped my family and that they were dangerous. And still, at least one of 'em told my brother where to find me."

Mai stood up. "I don't know if you're telling the truth or not, and I might never know, but the fact remains that what you did at the last task is worthy of respect. I misjudged you, and I treated you badly, and I'm sorry."

Cris said, "Thank you. And I'm sorry, too. I egged you on a couple times when I could've just let it go."

Mai looked down at the floor. "Thanks." She turned as if to leave, but then stopped and looked back at Cris. "We probably ain't ever gonna be friends, but we don't have to be enemies."

Cris nodded. "Agreed." He picked up the laptop and stood up, walking to the door so it would slide open. "If we work together, we can all make it out of here."

Mai said, "I hope you're right."

Cris watched as she left, heading to her own dorm room. He headed to the common room, looking for Alera, but found Ethan, Meryn, and Jamie talking in the Lounge instead.

Jamie said, "Hey, man, how you feeling?"

Cris said, "I'm good, but I got another message on my laptop."

Meryn turned to look at him. "Another message?"

Ethan asked, "What does it say?"

Instead of answering, Cris took a marker and wrote "MORAL PRIG" on the whiteboard.

Ethan stroked his chin. "Another anagram, perhaps?"

Meryn said, "Could be."

"It's a bit redundant as well. If I'm not mistaken, a prig is a self-righteous person with a sense of superiority because of their morals."

Jamie said, "Mister...Oral Pig." He giggled, turning to full-blown laughter when Meryn giggled as well.

Ethan sighed. "Well, at least we know they're not referring to Mr. Gamble."

Cris knocked at Alera's door. After a moment, Cris heard Alera's muffled voice. The door then slid open to reveal Alera sitting on the bed and Victoria standing at the back of the room.

Alera smiled. "Cris! We were just talking about you. Are you alright?"

Cris nodded. "Thankfully, the pain from the strikes has no lasting effects. At least, none that I'm aware of." *I certainly HOPE there's no lasting effects.*

Victoria said, "Meryn and Vi explained to us how the pain pulses work. Apparently, the collar sends a signal that tells your brain that you're in pain while also sending a pulse that suppresses the neurons in the central amygdala that are responsible for modulating pain."

Alera added, "The end result is the maximum amount of pain being felt everywhere all at once."

Cris gave a low chuckle. "Yeah. That would be accurate."

Victoria walked up and hugged Cris. "I'm sorry."

The surprise quickly gave way to reveling in her feel and familiar scent. "For what? You didn't cause any of this."

"For doubting you, I guess." She released the hug and stepped back. Cris was about to protest when Alera nearly tackled him with a forceful hug, to which he could only laugh weakly.

Alera said, "Same." And she stepped back, keeping her hands on his shoulders, piercing his eyes with her warm green and ice blue gaze.

Cris could feel tears burning in the corner of his eyes. "I wish to God neither of you have to experience that ever again." He broke free of Alera and wiped his eyes. "Toward that end, there's something you need to see, Alera."

Alera said, "Me? Why?"

"Because you've made more headway with these anagrams than anyone else." Cris opened his laptop and showed her the screen. "I got another message. It just started typing itself when I opened Writer, just like last time."

Alera squinted. "Moral prig?"

Victoria asked, "Wasn't the first message about a 'fop'? Are these all describing a person?"

Cris shrugged. "Doesn't seem to fit any of us...James Arnold, maybe? I don't know. But see if there's an anagram in there. We might need it for tomorrow, because I still don't have any clue what our 'purpose' is."

Alera had already picked up a pen and notepad from her bed and began writing. "Just glancing at it, I can make 'POLAR GRIM' but that doesn't make much sense. I'm on it."

Cris looked at Victoria, who seemed to want to say something. *I'm just going to take the win and go.* Cris nodded at her, and turned towards the door, which remained shut. "Um, Al?"

Alera looked up from her writing. "Huh? Oh, you're leaving?"

Cris said, "Yeah, I don't want to put any pressure on either of you, and I know you'll work faster without the distraction of my presence. I'll see you both tomorrow." *And I love you.*

Alera looked at Victoria. "Okay. Vi, open the door, please."

The door slid open, and Cris left.

Cris slept far better that night than he had the previous day, even going so far as to sing a little "Paranoid Android" in the shower. Once dressed, he joined the gang in the common room for some breakfast, and thanks to their crushing every task to this point, there was a veritable cornucopia of breakfast options from pancakes to English muffins to oatmeal available in addition to what was already there. The whole room smelled amazing.

Alera excitedly waved at Cris as he made his way to the heaving table, sitting on Victoria's other side. "Cris, I think I got it!"

"Really? What did you find?" Cris started piling his plate with pancakes and bacon.

Alera said, "Well, I realized pretty early on that the word 'program' was in there, leaving the letters I and L, but I couldn't make that work. And then Victoria reminded me about POT."

Jamie said, "Heck, yeah, Victoria's a queen of the green!"

Victoria reddened. "I like to partake from time to time. But in this case I meant the anagram from before – 'ADD POT TO FIND PURPOSE'"

Alera said, "And adding P, O, and T, I got this!" She proudly displayed her notebook with two words circled over and over.

Cris read, "PILOT PROGRAM?"

Ethan cleared his throat. "It could refer to the fact that we're the first participants in some sort of experiment or undertaking, or we could literally be learning how to fly a ship through space."

"You're kidding."

Ethan shook his head. "Think about it. All the tasks we've undertaken, and the ones you've described to us, could be required on a long-term deep-space journey."

Cris pondered this. "You could be right." He grabbed a knife and started spreading butter on an English muffin. "It's a shame I didn't get a request for the last task, Al, I could've said thank you by requesting your mom's raspberry jam."

Alera froze. "What did you say?"

Cris repeated, "I said I wish I had a request, I could've asked for your mom's raspberry jam."

Alera's eyes grew cold. "Strawberry."

Cris' gut tightened into a knot. "Uh, what?"

Alera shouted, "Victoria, get away from him. Cris has been eavesdropping on us."

Chapter 33

Even as Victoria got up and walked behind Alera, Cris fought a wave of panic. *What the hell is going on?!*

Cris said, "Where on Earth are you getting that from?"

Alera said, "I never told you about my mother making homemade jam."

Think, damn it, think! "You must have, during the previous cycle or whatever, before you lost your memories?"

"If so, then why would I lie to you?"

WHAT?!

"My mother made strawberry jam. Not raspberry."

Cris just stared at her.

Alera continued relentlessly. "I first got suspicious when you made that remark about me liking sad boys. It was true, in a weird way, I am attracted to sadness, but I'd never really used the phrase 'sad boys' until that conversation with Victoria, when we were alone in my room. So when Cris used the exact same phrase, I wondered if he'd overheard us somehow. But Vi insists that the rooms are soundproof, except for the front door, and even then you can only barely make out voices if you've got your ear right up against it."

She folded her arms. "I thought the best way to find out would be to test it. Cris claimed we were close before we all supposedly lost our memories, but we still only had four days, so there's no way he would know everything. Over most of yesterday, whenever Victoria and I were alone, I'd mention a fact about myself but tweak it so it was now false instead of true. That way, if he ever parroted one of the lies, I'd know he'd been listening in somehow."

Cris' shoulders slumped. *Hoisted by your own petard, dipshit.*

She turned to Victoria. "I'm sorry, that means I've been lying to you, too. My mom makes strawberry jam, as you've heard, I had my first kiss in eighth grade during band class, not sixth grade during art class, and I'm not actually in a rock band called 'Vorpal Balls', that was the name of my band in the Rock Band video game."

Victoria did not take her eyes off of Cris, but she waved that off.

Alera turned back to glare at Cris as well. "Oh, but Cris couldn't have been up against my door every time we were alone. Anybody coming from their room or the common room would've caught him immediately. So how did you listen in?"

Cris looked at everybody at the table. They all looked at him with suspicion or anger. *Tails, we lose.*

Cris said, "Well, as I've lost everything anyway – Computer, video and audio Main, please."

On the wall nearest the table, a live feed of the common room appeared. The gasps of shock and surprise were instantly recreated and played back at them near-simultaneously.

Cris said, "Computer, audio off, please." The reverb ceased. "This is a live feed, not a recording." Cris waved his arm up and down, which the image instantly reproduced. "There's one for every single one of our dorm rooms, though thankfully there are no cameras or microphones in the bathrooms. And there are multiple camera angles, if you attempt to block or hide from the camera, it will instantly switch to another. The main computer access is separate from Vi, but like Vi, you can access it from anywhere, and there's a third function I didn't try: message." Cris looked up. "Computer, message Main 'Cris is a giant piece of shit.'"

On the wall, replacing the live feed, blue lettering appeared.

CRIS IS A GIANT PIECE OF SHIT

Cris smiled sadly. "Neat."

Ethan asked coolly, "How long have you known about this?"

Cris looked down at the floor. "Since the first night, when I got my laptop."

Mai said, "You could have known about it the whole time."

"You're right, I could have."

Meryn asked, "Why didn't you tell anyone about this?"

Cris shrugged. "I thought I could catch the real traitor communicating with our captors. Instead, all I ever saw was Ethan reading his books, Mai watching sci-fi TV, Meryn and Jamie snogging, and Alera telling beautiful lies." He tried to catch her eye, but Alera looked up at Victoria standing behind her instead. Victoria did look him in the eyes, but hers were angry and tear-filled.

Jamie said, "What if you're the traitor?"

"You're right, I could be."

Victoria finally spoke. "Why the hell won't you defend yourself?"

Cris deflated. "Because what would be the fucking point?!" His voice broke. "I fucked it up. Just like I fuck everything up. I've permanently lost everything that meant a damn."

He pushed back his heaping plate and stood up. "I've lost my appetite, too." Cris walked out of the common room, the words "CRIS IS A GIANT PIECE OF SHIT" still hanging on the wall behind him.

Cris furiously typed into his laptop, recounting the morning's events with more detail than usual, propelled by the constant mental kicking of his own ass. Just as he finished, there was a knock at the door. He saved his work and then said, "Vi, open the door."

The door slid open to reveal Meryn standing there, an angry expression on her face. "I'll need your laptop."

Cris was confused for a second before it dawned on him. "Ah. You can't take the chance I'm using it to communicate with our oppressors." Cris closed the laptop, unplugged the power cable from the wall and wound it up, and handed the laptop and the cable to Meryn. "All my sins are contained therein."

Meryn wordlessly turned away and headed back into the common room. Cris lay down in his bed and just let himself weep.

Cris woke with a start at the sound of Vi's voice.

"The first task of the day is imminent. Please congregate in the common room."

Cris swung his legs over the side of the bed and slowly sat up. *I didn't mean to sleep, but I dreamed of my old apartment, and in that dream, Rachel was pointing her finger and laughing at me. And she was right. And Victoria was right. And Alera was right. And Julie was right.*

He got up and made his way to the common room. Everyone was already at the table, but only Jamie and Victoria looked at him as he approached. Cris noticed that his laptop was in front of Victoria, as if she'd been going through it. *That's odd, I would've expected Mai to be the one to go through my computer. But maybe Victoria has more personal reasons.*

Cris wordlessly sat down and crossed his arms.

Vi announced, "It is now time for the first task of the day. Please note: today is the final day of tasks."

There were some smiles at that, but otherwise, cheer appeared to be in short supply.

Vi continued, "After the completion or failure of the social task tonight, all remaining subjects will be able to leave via the white doors."

Cris remained silent. He knew what the task would be.

"Your task is to answer the following question: what is your purpose?"

Jamie said, "It's just as Cris said."

"You must submit your answer before your time lapses, and you may only answer once. You have twenty minutes. Your time starts now."

Meryn started the discussion. "Well, I guess this really only comes down to one thing: do we believe Cris?"

Cris didn't want to see anyone's faces, so he just stared down at the table.

Jamie said, "I believe him."

Victoria said quietly, "So do I." Cris nearly looked up in his surprise, but he held his nerve. *I'm just going to get my own hopes up, and for what?*

Everyone else remained silent.

Meryn said, "Because if he's telling the truth then it's very likely those secret messages are the key. Though it's possible they're fake – we only have Cris' word that they appeared on their own."

Alera said, "Pilot program."

"Exactly. You had to add T, O, and P to the other message to get it, and the other message said that's how you find purpose, correct?"

Alera nodded.

Ethan cleared his throat. "It also fits logically – the tasks all suit long-term space travel. But I don't think the question should be 'do we trust Cris?' I think the question should be 'do we have any better answers?'"

There was silence in response to this. Cris wanted to interject, but he again held himself back. *I'd add that it doesn't explain why I've been through all this twice, to say nothing of why I kept my memories and everyone else lost theirs. But who the hell's gonna listen to me?*

Meryn said, "We've still got time."

Jamie shook his head, "I really don't think we're gonna do better. I mean, what else COULD it be? I've got nothing."

Mai raised a hand. "My problem is that it still don't make sense. Why would NASA hijack seven total strangers and then attempt to train them to fly a spaceship? They have actual astronauts who could do that. We're just random people."

"But random people with skills." Ethan leaned forward. "Mr. Gamble is an actual pilot, Miss Serovitch is a medical professional, I'm a logician, and you yourself are a talented mechanic. And the others have proven adept at problem-solving and assisting, especially if Mr. Thorpe's history of a previous attempt is to be believed."

"We're still not astronauts, doll. And y'all, think about it – how on Earth does completing just two tasks qualify us to fly a spaceship? Countin' everything Cris said we did, that makes three tasks. Avoiding asteroids, fixing a cryo-whatever, and dismembering a body? Congrats, here's a space pilot badge?"

Alera said, "We don't know what this pilot program entails. It might mean some kind of program to train pilots, but it also could be like a TV pilot – like they're trying something out to see if it works."

Ethan leaned back. "It could also be both."

Jamie said, "Well, that's interesting and all, but we still don't have any other purpose to give as an answer."

There was a pause. Meryn looked at Cris. "Cris, do you have anything to add?"

The inclination was to remain silent, or give a curt, petulant no. *But there's no point to me wallowing. If we don't pass this task, the alternative will likely be my death in the next one.*

Cris sat up and unfolded his arms. "There's been some smart ideas around the table, some that warrant further investigation, but in terms of purpose, Jamie's right, it all revolves around PILOT PROGRAM, and we really don't have anything else that's solid."

Meryn asked, "Before I give that as our answer, does anyone have any objections?"

There was silence around the table.

Meryn looked up and said, "Vi, we're ready to answer the question."

Vi cheerfully said, "State your answer."

Meryn took a deep breath. "Our purpose is to take part in the pilot program."

Cris could hear his heart pounding in his chest.

Vi stated, "That answer is incorrect."

Cris didn't react, even as a groan erupted from multiple people. *Naturally.*

And at that thought, Cris got off the chair and lay down on the ground. "Guys, you're gonna want to trust me on this and lie down on the floor."

As they complied with his advice, Vi announced, "The task has been failed. All subjects will now receive one strike."

Cris braced himself, even though he knew it was useless.

The pain crashed into him like a train. He writhed and thrashed, but there was no relief. There were no thoughts or feelings, the only thing that broke up the pain was the physical sensation of bashing his head against the floor.

And then there was weight on him, and he couldn't thrash as much. He vaguely registered that he was hearing voices.

And then she was singing.

Victoria's warbling voice somehow cut through the pain, and Cris clung to it like a sailor adrift. The pain, along with Victoria's song, seemed to be going further and further away, and Cris's consciousness followed until all was dark.

Chapter 34

Cris woke in his own bed, and it seemed like the echoes of Victoria's song were still lingering.

Until he turned his head and saw Victoria sitting on the floor, leaning against the wall opposite, quietly singing. When she saw he was awake, she stopped singing and said, "Welcome back."

He went to speak but instead started coughing as he realized his throat was incredibly raw from screaming. As soon as he got his coughs under control, he quietly said, "I heard you."

Victoria didn't seem to understand, so Cris elaborated, taking care not to stress his vocal cords too much. "From before. I knew you were there. Meant everything. Thank you."

She nodded. "I couldn't think of any other way to help, so I just...did what came naturally."

Cris looked her in the eye. "Could have left me. Had every right."

Victoria sat upright and adjusted her glasses. "I suppose I did, but I guess I don't care for being that kind of person."

Cris raised an eyebrow. "Last person who offended you had to get their stomach pumped."

Victoria laughed. "I guess that's true. Maybe I'm growing as a person." She stood up. "Look, Cris, for what it's worth, I don't think you're a traitor, just an idiot."

Cris turned to stare at the ceiling. "Accurate."

Victoria turned towards the door and bowed her head. "The way I look at it...love...REAL love, requires trust. Complete and unconditional. But the way you describe yourself in your story..."

Cris swallowed hard. "Sad, huh?"

Victoria wiped away a tear. "Sounds incredibly fucking lonely, Cris." She walked to the doorway, pushed the chair holding the door open into the room, and walked off, letting the door shut behind her.

That's because it is.

Cris ate dinner in his room that night. He'd quietly put together a plate and immediately turned around. He didn't have anything to say that would meaningfully improve the situation, and the others didn't seem to know how to treat him. On the one hand, he was most likely to be a traitor to the group. On the other hand, he was the most likely to die, by virtue of having two strikes. *Even if we fail this final task, everyone else will live. Then again, I died once already.*

Cris was sort of grateful for the isolation. *I'm not terribly good company right now.* He ate his last meal in silence.

As the hour of the final task approached, Cris took one last look in the mirror. He spotted his collar. *At least there's still a painless choice left.* The despondence in that thought drained the last bit of uncertainty he had left in him.

Cris walked out of his room and entered the common area. The light conversation in the room died down as he shuffled towards the only empty armchair in the lounge and sat down. He let his head rest on the back of the chair and just stared dead ahead.

Alera asked, "Do we have any ideas what the last task is going to be?"

Cris continued staring straight ahead. "Kill one person."

Victoria said, "You can't know that."

"The first failed morning task meant the evening task was to kill one person. Hell, if it's based on the fact it's the third day, it could be 'Kill all but two subjects'."

"It could also be 'whistle from your butt'."

Cris finally looked Victoria in the eye. "I don't think our captors are too keen on butt-whistling."

"Would you stop being so damn fatalistic and fight?"

Cris looked over at Alera. *She looks so worried about me.* "I am fighting."

Alera hissed, "No, you're not. You're giving up."

Victoria added, "Again."

Before Cris could respond, Vi announced, "It is now time for your final task."

Everyone straightened up in their seats, steeling themselves, except for Cris, who merely turned his gaze to the floor.

Vi continued, "After this task is complete, the white door will open, and all remaining subjects will be able to leave."

Cris waited for the words he knew in his heart were coming.

"Kill one person."

Alera said, "No," and started crying.

Cris turned to Victoria with an apologetic look. "It had to be that. Our captors have a sense for the dramatic after all, and this is perfect."

Vi gleefully pronounced, "You have one hour. Your time starts now."

Meryn said gloomily, "Well, that's it, then."

Victoria shouted, "No, it's NOT!" She turned, her eyes blazing, to Cris. "Didn't you say you were fighting?" She waved a hand at Cris' face. "What the hell do you call this?"

"Fighting. Observe." Cris stood up. "Everyone, it's time to make an unfortunate decision. Now I could make that decision – right now – for all of you, and it would merely be a matter of attempting to fiddle with my collar."

Victoria got up and angrily stood right in Cris' face. "No!"

He ignored her. "But – I'm not going to do that. Mind you, I'm not stupid enough to imagine that anyone here would be willing to sacrifice themselves to save me, and if anyone tried, I'd do whatever it took to stop them. That's a waste. I just think this decision doesn't belong in my hands."

Victoria stepped back, confusion in her eyes.

Cris carried on. "I betrayed you – all of you. I need to take responsibility for that." Cris' eyes watered. "Whatever you all decide to do, and however you all decide to do it, I will abide by it."

Ethan harrumphed, "Are you saying that if we decide to cave your head in, you'll accept that?"

Cris felt his blood run cold, but he steeled himself as he looked at the old man. "Yes. That's what I'm saying."

Alera cried, "You can't be serious! That's barbaric!"

Meryn stood up and addressed Cris. "You're sure about this?"

Cris looked her in the eye. "Yes."

Victoria stared at Cris with apprehension. "What is this, some kind of sick punishment thing?"

"You said it yourself, I need to learn to trust, right? Maybe this is the first step."

"Cris, this might be your *last* step."

Cris smiled sadly. "I trust you." He turned to include everyone else. "I trust all of you."

Meryn seemed to be looking off in the distance over by the exercise equipment. "Cris, would you mind standing over there somewhere so we can speak privately?"

Cris nodded and stood by the treadmill. He watched as the others huddled up and decided his fate. *I don't think they'll brutalize me, but then I didn't expect Ethan to start blowing people away with a shotgun.*

The deliberations lasted about a minute and change. There was some strong arguing at first, but there appeared to be quick consensus among the group, and they broke the huddle.

Meryn said, "Cris, please lay down on the floor."

Oh, no. "...face-up or face-down?"

Meryn looked at Jamie. "I think face-down would be best for everybody."

Cris' mind raced as he slowly complied. Meryn took up a position kneeling at Cris' head while Jamie set his knees on either side of Cris' torso and sat on his back.

Meryn said, "Mai?"

Cris watched in horror as Mai handed Meryn one of the heaviest dumbbells in the set. He fought back a wave of panic. *I trusted them for this?! Please, Meryn, just make it quick.*

Meryn said quietly, "Cris, trust me on this, no matter what happens, you're going to want to keep your head absolutely still."

Cris bit back a sardonic quip. Instead, his eyes filled with tears. Hoarsely, he said, "Do it."

Meryn looked in Jamie's direction and nodded. She raised the dumbbell.

Cris closed his eyes.

There was a loud crack and for an instant, Cris felt enormous pressure on his neck before it vanished. *What?!*

A loud klaxon blared as Cris opened his eyes.

Jamie shouted, "AGAIN!"

Meryn raised the dumbbell again, and Cris tried not to flinch as she brought it down hard in his direction. There was another, louder crack, and even more pressure on his throat, causing him to cough, but he felt something give way on the back of his neck.

Vi announced, "Tampering with your collar is against the rules."

Jamie roared with effort, and there was a longer, sustained crack, and Cris felt all pressure on his neck cease as Jamie ripped free the broken collar.

Vi continued, "You will now receive one strike."

Meryn shouted, "JAMIE, THROW IT!"

Jamie stood up and hurled the broken collar clear to the other side of the room, where it hit the floor with a clatter.

Cris lay there in stunned silence. His collar was gone for the first time in seven days. He rolled over to face Meryn more directly. "What did you..."

Meryn coyly smiled at him. "Wait for it..."

Vi announced, "The final task has been completed. Please proceed to the white door."

The group were cheering and celebrating as Cris just stared at each of them in turn. "Why...how...?"

Meryn freed herself from Jamie's embrace. "You can thank Jamie. We were talking earlier and he theorized that we had to wear collars because whatever implant in our brain they were sending signals to must have a short range, a foot or two at most. Otherwise they could send the signal from anywhere and we wouldn't need collars."

Jamie said, "Yeah, but it was Meryn's idea to try and break the collar using the dumbbell. She believed it couldn't be invulnerable because the bad guys would have to be able to get it off somehow, and she figured that since the display is always on the back, that might be where the weak link is, because," he looked at her in consternation, "the control board is near it?"

Meryn nodded.

Jamie grinned, "Yeah. My girl's super smart."

Mai added, "She also said if we got it off ya, it probably wouldn't be able to detect your vital signs, so the computer would report you dead and we'd win the task."

Ethan was wearing a rare smile. "Basically, if we couldn't break the collar, you were headed towards a painless death anyway, so we figured we had to at least try to save you."

I'm alive. They didn't give up on me. Cris' eyes filled with tears and Meryn and Jamie hugged him. Cris whispered, "I'm so sorry," over and over again as he was overwhelmed with relief. They released him as Victoria and Alera approached, which just made him cry harder. They hugged him, and even as he inhaled their scents, it felt like a gift he didn't deserve, and he continued to apologize.

Ethan and Mai stood in front of Cris as Victoria and Alera released him.

Cris said through tears, "Oh, thank God you're not huggy people. I don't think I could take much more."

Everybody laughed. Even Mai smiled at him.

Meryn said, "Come on, everybody. The white doors are waiting for us."

The group gathered in front of the white doors, and once everyone was there, the white doors slowly, ponderously retracted into the wall, revealing just another white corridor with a bright white light at the end.

Victoria and Alera should have been through this door already. But they're still here, so I'm still not convinced salvation lies ahead. Then again, maybe the whole point was for all of us to walk through it.

Jamie said, "Well, I'm not stickin' around – let's go!"

They all walked through the white doors, and as they traversed the corridor, the light got brighter and brighter until it was all they could see, and Cris couldn't help but smile as they walked as one into the light.

Interlogue

Trina checked the readout on the front of the obelisk. Satisfied, she put a checkmark on the sheet in her clipboard and put the pencil back in her lab coat pocket. She resisted the urge to take her hand and caress the large, cold, black machine. *They are my babies, in a way.* She sighed. *I'm so sorry, my babies.*

The loud bang of her lab door flying open snapped her out of her reverie, and Trina peered through the glass wall to see Samantha, in a navy blue blazer, matching pants, and a white blouse, waving a bottle of Jack Daniels and a pair of drinking glasses in her direction.

Trina walked out of 'the farm', closing the glass door behind her. "I see the concept of knocking continues to elude you. And drinking on the job, Sam?"

Samantha set the glasses on a nearby table and started twisting the cap off the bottle. "Funny thing about the end of the world, rules that used to seem so very important just aren't anymore. Any progress?"

"Sam, it's been three days."

Samantha set the bottle cap on the table. "And we've got roughly four left, so any progress?"

Trina looked down at the floor. "They're nearly ready."

"That's worth celebrating, at least. A toast?"

Trina looked back up at Samantha. "I'm not really a big drinker."

Samantha appeared to transform. She'd always been strong and projected an aura of confidence and power to Trina, but when Trina turned her down, Samantha seemed to wilt a bit, and a look of sadness Trina had never seen appeared on her face. "For old times, then. And friends no longer with us."

She must really miss Jim. Trina agreed, "Okay. For you."

"That's very kind, Trina."

Samantha thoughtfully poured a small dollop of whiskey into a glass and handed it to Trina, saying, "Or perhaps we should drink to our victims."

Trina looked down at the floor. "We'll never be able to make it up to them."

Samantha took a second to mull that over before pouring a much more generous portion into the other glass. "We're still going to do everything we can." She held up her glass. "Salud."

They clinked glasses and drank. Trina took just a teensy sip, but even that small amount seemed to tingle in her mouth, and when she swallowed, she could feel the warmth emanating from her midsection.

With that warmth came certainty. "They denied my appeal again, didn't they?"

Samantha growled. "Yes. Some nonsense about genetic incompatibilities."

"Goddamn it, Sam." Trina downed the rest of her glass.

"Senator Keller and the rest are politicians, Trina. They're playing the same game they always do: brinkmanship."

"What?"

"It's a fancy way of saying they're playing chicken. And they're confident you'll flinch."

"Alera's all I have, Sam. She's a part of me."

Sam took another swig from her glass. "You could always stay."

"Instead of flinching, I just drive off the cliff?"

Sam took another drink and kept staring at the farm. "Why not? We could Thelma and Louise it."

Trina put her empty glass down and looked at Samantha. "You're staying?"

Sam just nodded her head and took another drink, emptying her glass.

Trina's eyes filled with tears as rage filled her heart. "Those BASTARDS. I'm stopping the project."

"The HELL you are." Trina was stunned by the vehemence in Samantha's voice. Sam put her empty glass down on the table and turned to face Trina with one hand pointing at the farm. "Firstly, your project, those people, might be the only hope we have left. And you're too good to let that slip away."

Samantha folded her arms. "Secondly, it wasn't their choice, Trina. It was mine." At Trina's surprised look, Samantha continued, "This is my home. And I don't belong anywhere else."

"I disagree, Sam. After all you've done –"

"I appreciate the thought. But I'm the past. You're the future. And I'm going to get you and Alera both on that ship."

Trina saw the look of grim determination on Samantha's face and decided not to argue. "How?"

"I've got an idea. If you want to discuss it, I could do with a bite to eat."

Trina looked down at the floor apologetically. "We're moving into the final phase in literal minutes, I can't leave. For that matter, neither should you, we both have a part to play." She looked back up at Sam. "We have to tell them."

Sam thought for a moment. "What if I bring food here? Surely they won't need us in the next hour or so?"

Trina dropped the clipboard to the table. "That's just it – I don't know when I'll need to step in. But you're probably safe for the next hour if you can grab something real quick."

Sam grinned. "I'll make Justin run. What do you like on your pizza?"

"I'm a cheese-and-pepperoni gal. But if you're getting it from Marco's, their sweet sauce is the actual best ever."

Sam walked over to the lab door and swung it open, handing some money to someone just outside. "Agent Garza, I'm going to need you to run to Marco's and pick up a large cheese-and-pepperoni pizza with sweet sauce. Keep the change. No, you know what?" Sam handed him some more cash. "If you guys are hungry, why don't you get something for yourselves, too, on me."

"Yes, ma'am. Thank you, ma'am." There was a momentary consultation, and then Trina heard boots jogging down the hallway.

Samantha walked back into the lab. "Good man there. You know, it's not too late for you two to become a thing."

Trina reached up to her hair tie. "Maybe if he was Justine."

Samantha raised her chin. "Oh. My apologies for assuming."

"No worries." Trina removed the hair tie and shook her ponytail loose to let her brown hair hang to her shoulders.

Samantha refilled her glass and dropped her volume down low. "So, as I said, I think I have a way to get Alera in, but it involves no small amount of risk on my part, so I'm going to need you to do something for me."

Trina leaned forward conspiratorially. "Like what?"

A warning klaxon went off.

Trina's jaw dropped. She breathed, "No way..."

Chapter 35

Cris was awakened by the vague sensation of pain. He'd narrowed it down to his right leg and was starting to open his eyes when he was struck with a massive charley horse in his calf.

His instinct was to reach forward and grab his leg, but it was that moment when he saw the all-too-familiar white walls of his dorm, and he remembered where he was. Cris decided instead to endure the pain, though it filled his eyes with tears. Cris lay there for several minutes in absolute agony. *This is Hell, after all.*

The pain did eventually subside, and Cris realized a little too late that doing permanent damage to his leg out of despair might not have been the wisest move, so he started massaging his leg thoroughly, and he took the opportunity to look around. His room had not changed since he was in it last, still wood-tile flooring and a comfortable double bed. And his eyes floated back up to the white wall opposite the bed when a thought struck him.

Communication is the answer. "Computer, video and audio 2, please."

A camera feed appeared on his wall showing Alera in her room, sitting on the edge of her bed, looking confused and frightened.

Cris continued to massage his sore leg. "Computer, message 2, 'Hey, Alera, it's Cris Thorpe, do you remember me?"

Cris watched as Alera reacted with surprise and shook her head.

Shit. "Computer, message 2, 'We need to talk, say out loud computer, video and audio 1."

In the feed, Alera wore a curious expression as she said, "Out loud computer, video and audio 1. Oh!" Alera reacted to something Cris couldn't see, which he assumed was his feed appearing on the wall opposite her.

Cris waved to where he thought the camera might be. "Hi, Alera. Can you hear me?"

She hesitantly waved back to the wall. "Who are you? Where am I?"

Cris held a hand up. "We're not going to have a ton of time before the doors open and we meet everyone, but I'll tell you as much as I can. We've been trapped here with five other people for the last seven days."

"What?!"

Cris held his hand up again. "Your memories of the last seven days have been taken from you. Someone has kidnapped all of us, and they've been making us do various tasks in order to leave, but it doesn't seem to matter. Whether we leave or die, we all wake up back here and start over again from the beginning. And I'm the only one of us who seems to remember what's happened."

Alera crossed her arms. "That's insane."

Cris stopped massaging his leg and sat up straight. "Yes. But it's still the truth."

"You could be the one who kidnapped us."

"That's true, but if so, why would I tell you how to use the computer? You can spy on any room you like now, including mine. If I were your enemy, wouldn't I be far better off keeping that knowledge to myself?"

Alera mulled over that, apparently trying to find something wrong with it. "What else can the computer do?"

"It has three functions we can access, video, audio, and message. And as you've seen, message puts words up on the wall of any room we select. Mine is 1, yours is 2. Uh, number 3 is Jamie, 4 is Mai, 5 is Ethan, 6 is Meryn, and 7 is Victoria. I know you don't know them yet, but you'll meet them in a moment."

"Why are you telling me all this?"

"You want the rational reason or the emotional one?"

Alera gave the wall a perplexed look. "I guess rational, then emotional."

Cris sighed deeply. "I screwed up horrendously last cycle by not trusting you, and I'm not making that mistake a second time. And..." *I love you...* "...I really miss my friend Alera, and filling you in as quickly as possible is the fastest way I can think of to get her back."

Alera looked both sad and confused. "Those statements are...antithetical."

"Yes." Cris looked sadly towards the 'camera' in the corner. "But it's still the truth."

Alera, if anything, just looked more puzzled. "How do I know we were friends? How do I know any of this is true?!"

Cris paused a moment. "You had your first kiss in band class in 8th grade. And you wrinkle your nose a little bit when you kiss. You play Rock Band, and your band's name is 'Vorpal Balls', despite claiming your singing is so bad it makes people jump out of windows. But you absolutely melt when Victoria sings to you. You light up when talking about your podcast, Don't Walk Alone. And you have the most beautiful eyes I've ever seen."

Alera was blushing. "Okay, okay! So now what?"

Cris said, "I need your help because I think you're the key to this. The one task we've always failed is knowing our purpose. We got two anagram messages. One said 'ADD TOP TO FIND PURPOSE' – the other said 'MORAL PRIG' – you realized we could add 'TOP' to 'MORAL PRIG' to make 'PILOT PROGRAM', but that still wasn't the right answer."

Alera responded, "I'm honestly really overwhelmed right now, and you're not helping."

Cris was silent a moment. "Al, you're the most clever person I've ever met. You've solved all these anagrams, and we're still missing something. I know you can figure it out."

Alera sighed. "ADD TOP TO FIND PURPOSE...well, what else have you added 'TOP' to?"

"What?"

The dorm door suddenly slid open with a hiss.

Cris stood up and said, "Computer, video and audio off."

As he exited the room into the hallway, Alera followed his lead and shut the feed down in her room. He looked to his left to see Victoria emerging from her room, looking uncertain and a little fearful.

He said, "I take it you don't remember me, either?"

Victoria shook her head even as the others began to emerge from their rooms.

Cris folded his arms. "I can explain everything once everybody's here."

He specifically watched Mai's door, and when she emerged, she was wearing the same outfit and hairstyle she'd worn yesterday.

Meryn asked, "Who are you people? Where the hell are we?"

"We've all been kidnapped and taken to some isolated location. Our captors want us to complete tasks or else we receive strikes, which induce extreme pain, and on the third strike, death." Some of the others gasped, but Cris continued implacably, "After three days of tasks, anyone who still survives gets to quote-unquote 'leave' via the white door, but whether you leave or die, we all wake up back here again, unharmed, and the cycle begins anew with the exception that I'm the only one who remembers what happened, as everyone else's memory of those days is wiped."

Most everyone's jaw had dropped at some point during Cris' explanation and they were staring at him open-mouthed.

Meryn was the first to speak. "That is insane."

Alera delightfully squealed, "That's what I said!" She turned to Cris with a smug expression. "I told you so."

Cris put his head in his hands and exhaled. *It's gonna be a long day.*

Cris spent the next hour telling the story of the last seven days, including every gory detail, making no effort at all to gloss over his failures, but not dwelling on them either. After dropping some facts about each of them, showing off the computer's functions, and some backup from Vi once she came online, the group seemed more or less convinced. Meryn and Jamie were openly eyeing each other speculatively, and Victoria purposefully sat between Cris and Alera once she had learned they had once been a throuple, but she still seemed a bit uneasy.

Ethan tilted his head. "It all still seems mad, but I'm having a hard time breaking it down to a point where you might not be telling the truth. And it sure seems like you've held nothing back."

Mai piped up, "If anything, he might be oversharing."

Cris smiled, "Never been accused of that before."

Ethan still had questions. "So you think the key to all this is finding our purpose?"

"It's the only idea I've got left. I was sure when we walked through the white door together, that would be the end of it, but here we all are again. The purpose task is the final day task, and it's the only one we've never succeeded at."

Jamie nodded. "That makes sense, man, if they really are training us for some deep space mission thingy, the most important thing would be knowing what that mission is."

Meryn leaned forward. "Right, but from the sounds of it, they're deliberately keeping that mission obscure, throwing anagrams and riddles at us. Why do we have to figure it out? Why not just tell us?"

Ethan stroked his chin. "Logic would dictate that either there's a benefit to us figuring it out ourselves, or there's some reason that they can't – although I can't for the life of me think of a reason that makes sense."

There was silence for a moment as everyone struggled with that thought.

Alera suddenly asked, "Hey, Vi, is it possible for a task to be just for a single one of us?"

Vi cheerily answered, "Tasks can be for as many or as few subjects as required."

Alera followed up, "And would you announce which subjects the task is for when explaining it?"

Vi replied, "Task assignments are not included in the task description."

Cris asked, "Hey, Al, you got something?"

Alera's eyes glowed with excitement. "Cris. It's you. It's only ever been you."

"What do you mean?"

"I mean, I know what your purpose is."

Chapter 36

Cris was thunderstruck.

Alera stood up, "I can't be certain, as I'd need a lot more time to go through every possibility, but yours fits so well. This HAS to be right."

She walked over and whispered two words in Cris' ear.

She's right. It fits. This ends NOW.

Cris stood up and said, "Computer, message..." He trailed off, uncertain. He instead turned to Mai. "Hey, Mai, who would be like the owner or controller of the main computer, not like you know his exact name, but if I wanted to message them...?"

Mai folded her arms. "Well, I guess, if yer lookin' fer an account name, I'd probably go with 'Admin'."

Cris nodded gratefully. "Computer, message Admin, I know my purpose and would like to skip to the third daytime task. Also, I know how to remove our collars now, so if you say no, we'll just ignore all the tasks and do this all again next cycle."

There were some gasps at the table at that.

Meryn said, "Cris, you said we needed a dumbbell to break the collar off. Where are we going to get one of those without doing a task?"

Cris kept his volume low. "I'm bluffing, but they probably won't know that. When we broke my collar, if someone had been actively monitoring us, they could have sent the strike faster or killed me some other way. The fact that we got away with it indicates to me that this whole thing," he indicated the entire room with his arms, "is computer-controlled."

Victoria leaned in and put her hand on Cris' wrist. "That makes sense. So much of this is automated."

Jamie asked, "So what do we do now?"

Cris sat back. "Wait for a reply, I guess."

Several seconds of silence passed.

Jamie leaned back in his chair. "Anybody wanna play Charades?"

When no reply came in the first few minutes, Cris began to feel uncertain. The group broke up after ten minutes as Ethan and Mai went back to their rooms, and Meryn and Jamie had a hushed conversation in the lounge chairs. Alera reached over and squeezed Cris' hand, saying "I'm going to keep trying more anagrams just in case," before she, too, got up and left.

Victoria stared at Cris. "Can I ask you something?"

He looked into her eyes. "Anything."

"Do you know why I was the one who went through your laptop?"

Cris looked down at the table. "Well, I'd be guessing, but I know you'd just been through a breakup after someone cheated on you, and then I'd betrayed you as well, so maybe you were looking for some sort of evidence that I never really cared. But...I don't think you expected what I'd written about you."

"May I ask what you wrote?"

Cris was not surprised to discover he could remember the passage verbatim. "Victoria is a sunny girl with soft brown hair and warm brown eyes. She wears somewhat child-like clothing, but this just makes more sense as I got to know her."

Victoria raised an eyebrow at this, but Cris continued. "She's so supportive of everyone, and so quick to smooth out misunderstandings and deflate tensions, it's genuinely inspiring how good she is at keeping others comfortable, or in my case, happy. And to my delight, she's also not above a little mischief. So in a way, Victoria has a very real child-like quality that I find extraordinary – she cares, trusts, and even loves exactly the way she sings: with her whole heart."

Cris looked up to see Victoria's eyes misty and her cheeks red. She cleared her throat, and said, "That was beautiful. Are you sure you're a reporter and not a poet?"

Cris couldn't resist. "If I am, I didn't know it."

Victoria laughed in spite of herself. "Well, at least we know you're not a comedian." Cris burst out laughing as she stood up. "Don't be disheartened. I'm sure you're on the right track."

"I hope you're right." *...and I love you.*

Victoria smiled and walked back toward the dorms. Cris snuck a peek over at the hushed conversation Meryn and Jamie were having, and he watched until Jamie giggled about something and Meryn laughed along with him. *Well, that's progressing nicely. Better leave them to it.*

Cris got up and wandered back to his dorm room and once the door slid shut, he let out a deep sigh. Victoria had been right. He was getting disheartened. *I really thought they would give us a yes or a no or even punish me, but what I did not expect was total silence. Is it possible that I've got this wrong?*

Cris sat down on the edge of the bed. *And I really wish I could tell the women I love that I love them.*

Cris took one look at the pillow and decided against a nap. Instead, he took his shirt off and headed to the bathroom for a shower. He wasn't particularly dirty, but the sensation of hot water running down his body was decidedly pleasant. After ten minutes or so, Cris toweled off and wrapped the towel around his waist as he headed back to the bedroom to put his clothes back on.

He'd just managed to get his jeans back on when there was a knock at the door.

Déjà vu.

Cris looked at his shirt for a moment, but decided against it, and walked to the door.

It slid open to reveal Victoria and Alera, and before Cris knew what was happening, they pushed him into the room and started kissing him, on his cheek, on his chest, on his lips. When they were far enough into the room, the door slid shut again.

Cris got his mouth free long enough to say, "Not that I'm complaining, but—"

He was interrupted by Alera's finger on his lips. She angrily asked, "What part of us kissing you do you not understand?!"

Victoria smiled. "Cris, sometimes, you just need to shut up, my dude."

Cris shut up.

A couple of hours later, they lay together, enjoying the tactile sensation of skin against skin, and Cris gently stroked both girls' hair with his hands. It felt like a lifetime ago the last time he was this content. *It literally was a lifetime.*

Alera looked up at him with mismatched eyes. "Sorry if we surprised you."

Cris smiled. "The best kind of surprise."

"Victoria came to my room and just straight up asked if I was down to be in a throuple with both of you."

Cris laughed. "As I recall, she was fairly direct about it the first time, too."

Victoria grinned. "Listen, I want what I want."

Cris looked back at Alera. "And you didn't have any problems with this?"

Alera shrugged. "Well, I'm pretty sure my mom's gonna kill me."

Cris laughed again.

He was looking right at her when it happened. In an instant, Cris suddenly felt his body become incredibly heavy, and he could only move extremely slowly. The sensation was somewhat akin to being incredibly drunk. Cris watched as Alera's mouth dropped open in slow-motion. *What the hell? This isn't like when we get knocked out so they can bring dinner out, this is...I don't know what this is!*

It took ages, but Cris turned his head to look at Victoria and saw her eyes filled with alarm. She appeared to be trying to get out of bed, as she swung her legs off the side, Cris was astonished to see that they fell to the ground at a similarly slowed rate. *Even gravity's been affected?*

And just as quickly as it began, the slowing ceased, and everything went back to normal as Victoria stood up. The change seemed to startle Victoria as she immediately lost her balance. Cris shot out a hand and grabbed her arm to help stabilize her.

Victoria breathed, "What the hell was that?!"

Alera was frightened. "It was like...like time itself had slowed down."

Cris shook his head. "But I was still thinking at full speed. Think about it, if everything slowed down, including our thoughts, would we have even noticed if time slowed down?"

Vi announced, "The first task of the day is imminent. Please congregate in the common room."

Cris looked up in wonder. "Did they accept my proposal?"

Victoria started putting on her clothes. "There's only one way to find out. Let's get dressed and get out there."

Cris and Alera dressed, and together with Victoria, they headed to the common room, which was abuzz with discussion.

Jamie asked, "Hey, did time slow down for you guys, too?"

Cris nodded as he pulled out a chair and sat down. "Looks like they accepted my request, unless...nobody requested to skip the tutorial, did they?"

Meryn and Jamie said "No," while Ethan and Mai shook their heads.

After everyone was seated, Vi announced, "Your task is to answer the following question: what is your purpose?"

Cris silently exulted. *Here we go.*

"You must submit your answer before your time lapses, and you may only answer once. You have twenty minutes. Your time starts now."

Cris gazed down at the table. "Vi, which subjects are assigned this task?"

"This task is assigned to the following subjects: Cris Thorpe."

Alera winked at Cris, who grinned back at her.

Cris looked up. "Vi, I'm ready to answer the question."

"State your answer."
Cris looked at Alera and smiled. "SHIP PROTECTOR."
There was the briefest of pauses, during which Cris' heart pounded.
Vi announced, "That answer is correct."

Chapter 37

The group immediately started cheering. Cris just sat back. After everything, there had still been one small part of him that was convinced it wouldn't work, and when it did, the relief just took all the tension right out of him. *But it's not over yet.*

Midst the celebration and relieved laughter, Vi announced, "The task is complete."

Cris waited, but Vi said nothing more. "That's it? No requests or—or further instructions?"

Silence.

Ethan smiled. "My compliments, Miss Zeller, very clever indeed."

Alera blushed. "Once I realized I could try adding POT to each of our names, I tried everybody, but adding it to CRIS THORPE and getting SHIP PROTECTOR seemed the most relevant, although there's one more name that kind of fits."

Ethan pushed his glasses up his nose. "Whose?"

Alera smiled at him. "Yours. Adding POT to ETHAN WINTERS makes A PENITENT'S WROTH."

Cris added, "And even though you're a religious man, you were pretty 'wroth' at the end of the first cycle."

Ethan cleared his throat. "Well, I'm certainly not 'wroth' now – the two of you might just get us all out of this mess."

Just then, some words appeared on the wall in blue.

YOUR ACTUAL FINAL TASK BEGINS
AFTER DINNER - PLEASE ENJOY

Meryn said, "Wait, what else do we—"

Cris was suddenly incredibly tired, and he realized he was being knocked out, so he tried to make himself comfortable. The best he could manage was getting his arm under his head before it hit the table. Then everything went black.

Cris was awoken by the smell of something delicious. He vaguely registered noises of surprise from around him as he opened his eyes and raised his head.

What the?

The table was piled high with food. All manner of dishes, pastas, meats, vegetables, bread rolls, and soups now covered the table. In fact, there was barely room for his plate and silverware.

Sitting across from Cris, Mai said, "Look!" and pointed behind him.

Cris turned around to see two new side tables had been set up, one between the red and blue doors, the other between the blue and yellow doors. The first had loads of beverages on it, sodas, coffee carafes, pitchers of juice, a couple of twelve-packs of canned beer, several bottles of wine, and a couple of bottles of hard liquor. The second table was piled high with more food, pizza boxes from a place called Marco's, hamburgers, hot dogs, French fries, roast beef and sandwich rolls, chicken wings, there even appeared to be shells and fixings for tacos.

Ethan was the happiest Cris had seen him. "Chicken Cordon Bleu! And is this...?" Ethan sniffed a bowl of rice. "Garlic butter rice!"

Meryn's smile carried up into her eyes. "I guess this is our reward for completing the task?"

Mai said, "Yeah, I don't know about y'all, but I can't eat all of this. A lot of it's goin' to waste."

Jamie was practically drooling. "Who cares? Let's eat!"

Most of them just started piling their plates with food. Mai didn't hold out but merely shrugged and started spooling spaghetti to put on her plate.

Cris grabbed himself a steak, some garlic bread, some sweet corn, and a can of cola, and dug in to eat. It really felt like a family sitting down to have a meal. Everyone was talking and laughing. Mai and Alera even had a short impromptu food fight (before Meryn and Ethan shut it down), which ended in giggles.

For his part, Cris found himself staring at the faces of his friends, fixing them in his memory. *If I'm even semi-correct, this could be the last time we all sit down together for a good long time.*

Victoria kept reaching a hand over and resting it on his leg as she ate. As she was sitting between them, every now and then, she would alternate, reaching over to touch Alera instead. Cris couldn't help but smile. *And I'm not letting either of them go, ever again.*

As the group finished their meal, they adjourned to the lounge. Victoria took Cris' hand with an iron grip, making it clear she would not relinquish it anytime soon, and Cris found himself unwilling to argue. She grabbed Alera's hand as well, and they sat in neighboring armchairs.

As Mai sat down, she said, "Get a room, you three."

Cris couldn't help but smile at her. "You've said that before."

Mai smiled back, "Because clearly, y'all need to get a room." Then she laughed.

Jamie seemed a little nervous. "So what happens now?"

Cris shook his head. "Even I don't know. We're in uncharted territory now."

Ethan sat back in his chair. "If Mr. Thorpe's purpose is SHIP PROTECTOR, that would indicate that the theory our previous selves came up with, being that this is preparation for some sort of deep space mission, would seem to be accurate. And if this is truly our final task, then perhaps it's a final examination of some sort."

Meryn looked pensive. "That tracks, but is it for all of us, or just Cris?"

Cris shrugged. "The purpose might have been mine, but they didn't just bring me here. They brought all of us here and for a reason. Just because we don't know what it is, doesn't mean it doesn't exist."

Mai asked, "But then why were you the only one who got to keep their memories?"

Jamie added, "And what was up with that weird slow-time thing?"

Cris answered, "It didn't happen in either of the previous cycles, so I legitimately can't tell you."

Meryn asked, "Could it have been some sort of gravity effect?"

Jamie tilted his head to the side. "Maybe. I've flown an F-15 Eagle at Mach 2 and experienced G forces of up to 7 G's, and it does make you feel heavier, for sure, but it wasn't quite like that."

Cris stroked his chin. "Besides, I'm not convinced we're in space." *In fact, I don't think we're anywhere at all.*

Vi interrupted, "It is now time for the final task."

Cris grit his teeth. *Here we go.* He took a quick look around the lounge at his friends' faces. Jamie had straightened in his chair and looked resolute. Meryn similarly looked determined. Ethan, as imperturbable as ever, was cleaning his glasses. Mai's mouth was clamped shut and her eyes darted this way and that. Alera looked oddly serene, but she was clasping Victoria's right hand in both of hers. Victoria gave Cris a shaky smile. Still holding her other hand, he rubbed his thumb on the back of her hand in what he hoped was a reassuring gesture, and she responded by squeezing his hand.

Vi continued, "Upon completion of this task, the person responsible for your imprisonment will reveal themselves."

Cris' eyes widened. *But what's the price?*

Vi, cheerful as ever, added, "Solve all the mysteries of your imprisonment. All six color rooms will now be opened."

Cris watched open-mouthed as the red, blue, yellow, green, orange, and pink doors opened one by one with a steely hiss.

Vi continued, "Each room contains clues that will help you. State when you are ready to solve the mysteries, and I will ask you a series of questions, which must all be answered correctly. Any question incorrectly answered will result in failure. Failure will result in every subject getting three strikes."

Amidst the horrified looks on everyone's faces, Cris shouted, "You'll kill us all?!"

Vi mercilessly carried on, "You have one hour. Your time starts now."

Chapter 38

Meryn asked, "How do we want to do this?"

Ethan answered, "We should split up, taking turns to inspect each room. That way, we can get different perspectives on the clues we find, and then in the last twenty minutes or so, we should discuss our findings."

Cris nodded, "Makes sense. I'll start with the red door."

Victoria said, "I want to go with you, if that's okay."

As the others started to get up and head towards the colored rooms, Cris leaned over. "Al, do you want to come with us as well?"

Alera stood and shook her head. "We'll cover more ground if I head off solo. Also," she reddened, "no offense, but I have trouble thinking straight when you two are around."

Cris smiled. "I know the feeling. Good luck."

As Alera took off for the orange room, Cris and Victoria headed for the red room. Inside, they found a simple table with some documents in a manila folder. He pulled the top one out and handed the folder to Victoria.

Cris read the subject line out loud. "Project Thane..."

Victoria was thumbing through the other documents in the folder. "Thane is an old Anglo-Saxon title. It meant someone who owned land but wasn't a nobleman themselves, ranking between that and an ordinary freeman."

Cris continued reading for a few moments. "Check this out. Project Thane was commissioned in 1963 by NASA after the end of Project Mercury, the first human spaceflight program."

Victoria looked up at Cris. "That would've been right in the middle of the space race with the Soviet Union."

"Exactly. It looks like Project Thane was an attempt to put together an accelerated astronaut training program for civilians."

Victoria looked at Cris wide-eyed. "That tracks with the tasks you've described."

"Yeah, but it's 2023 – so why have we been put through a training program from sixty years ago?"

Victoria was intently reading. "I can't say why, but I can tell you why the project was commissioned – it was intended to be a backup plan in case of some disaster."

"What, like everyone who's qualified to be an astronaut gets killed somehow? I don't buy it. NASA has a full stable of trained astronauts ready to go at all times, or so I thought, so why did they think they'd need civilians?"

Victoria looked back at the common room. "They're creating Thanes."

"What?"

She looked back at Cris. "Thanes are better than freemen, but not as good as nobles, and graduates of this program would be better than civilians, but not as good as astronauts."

Cris furrowed his brow. "Does it say why NASA thought they needed civilians to be backup astronauts?"

"Doesn't say, but it looks like after years of trials, Project Thane was to be decommissioned in July 1970 – and then Apollo 13 happened."

Cris nodded. "They think they don't need a backup plan, and then there's an accident on a space mission, so then they reverse course on ditching the backup plan."

"Yup. It was recommissioned instead and never got decommissioned, but the notes on it get sparser the further ahead in time you go. And I can't find anything on threatening the candidates with pain or death if they failed, so that's not part of Thane."

Cris shook his head. "I don't get it. Why us?"

Victoria put down the manila folder. "I don't know, but we've been several minutes already, and I don't know how much time we can afford to waste. We should move on."

"Agreed."

Cris dropped the sheet on top of the folder, and the pair left the red room, entering the nearby blue room, where Mai was perched on a similar table with some pieces of lined paper covered in handwriting.

Victoria asked, "Hey, Mai, you got anything?"

Mai snorted, "Nightmare fuel. Check these out." Mai looked through the pages, selected two, and handed them to Cris and Victoria.

Cris glanced at his sheet, noting as he did so that the handwriting was in a pretty cursive.

Cris Thorpe – SHIP PROTECTOR
- 25 years old

- Reporter for Arlington Post in Virginia
- Born July 19, 1998
- Parents deceased, one sister, Haley, works at Rumpus Room Orphanage and Educational Center
- Multiple ex-girlfriends, possible causes of/victims of trust issues
- Recent story about contractors building a skyscraper committing code violations
- Handsome but nothing special

Nothing special?!

The page continued on with many other details, including favorite foods, teachers in school, friends, etc.

Cris was flabbergasted. "This is...this is a lot."

Victoria had turned pale. "How...how do they know all this?!"

Mai was utterly calm. "Whoever 'they' are, they done a butt-ton of research on all of us. Hey, did you know Ethan was a fan of H.P. Lovecraft books?"

Cris picked up the page with Alera's name on it. Sure enough, it mentioned she'd had an abortion. "Alera swore to me during the previous cycle that she'd never told a soul about this, but I suppose they could have found out all this stuff."

Victoria gaped at him. "You'd have to have a private detective following me around for WEEKS to learn some of this."

Mai drawled, "Well, y'all, no matter how they know, they know. And whoever wrote it down's got some pretty handwritin'."

Cris nodded. "It's looking more and more like we were all specifically chosen for this."

"Well, I ain't exactly pleased I made the cut. I've seen all I need to in here." Mai pushed off the table and headed for the door. "Is there anythin' interestin' in the red room?"

Victoria smiled. "Oh, just that this all dates back to a NASA project from the 1960's, that's all."

Mai's eyes widened. "Really? Wow. I'll see y'all later." She left the room.

Cris perused the pages a little bit more. "It's interesting stuff, but I don't know that it teaches us anything about our situation other than they know practically everything about us."

Victoria nodded. "Yeah, but I agree with your assessment that we were selected for this. All this makes it look like we were hand-picked. Do you want to move on?"

Cris put the page down. "Yeah, lead the way."

Cris followed Victoria to the yellow room, where they found Ethan hunched over another table and documents.

Walking up to him, Cris said, "Ethan, what have you got?"

Ethan gave Cris a dark look. "Nothing good."

Cris wryly remarked, "That's beginning to be a running theme."

Ethan held up a thick stack of paper held together with a large black binder clip. "This is a scientific study of something called a rogue quantum singularity."

Victoria was puzzled. "A rogue what?"

Cris' gut, meanwhile, had suddenly filled with ice. "A black hole."

Ethan nodded grimly. "Correct. Quantum singularities that aren't stationary, or indeed, limited to a single solar system. Collisions between galaxies can create them, or if the merging of two quantum singularities is interrupted. They travel at high speeds, swallowing everything in their wake. And it's theorized that there could be as many as twelve rogue singularities in the Milky Way Galaxy alone."

"Between this and what we found in the red room, a disturbing picture is forming."

"Why, what did you find?"

Cris tilted his head. "A Project Thane from 1963 designed to create an accelerated space training program for civilians."

Ethan froze for a moment and turned to face Cris. "You're serious? Even if they could send us into space, what would be the point? You can't stop a quantum singularity!"

Victoria asked, "What if we just need to turn it?"

"The most powerful force humanity can currently produce would have no more effect on this than a fly hitting a windshield."

Cris already knew the answer, but he had to ask anyway. "If one of these was headed anywhere near Earth?"

Ethan paled. "Best case scenario, the Earth gets pulled from its heliocentric orbit and everybody burns or freezes to death in a few weeks."

Victoria gasped.

Ethan grimly continued, "Worst case, the Earth gets destroyed and absorbed into the singularity."

Chapter 39

Cris turned and stared at the wall. *It can't really be that bleak...can it?*

He looked at Victoria, who was trembling. Cris put his arms around her and held her tightly as she began to shake. Cris tried to reassure her, "We don't know that's the case."

She leaned back to look up at him teary-eyed. "But why else would it be in here?"

"Maybe you were right before. Maybe they figured out a way to change its course."

Ethan said quietly. "I don't mean to upset anyone, but the kind of forces that would cause a rogue singularity to change direction would also be catastrophic, like the sun going supernova. And our sun's not big enough for that."

Cris looked at Ethan. "But what if someone figured out a way to simulate a supernova's effects? That's not impossible, right?"

Ethan shrugged. "Anything's possible."

Cris looked back at Victoria. "Does that help?"

She wiped a tear away. "You're right. We can't give up hope just yet, any of us."

Cris looked into the common room and saw Jamie and Meryn running to a new room. "We should move on to the next room, I don't know how much time is left."

Ethan nodded. "I'm going to stay here. I'm the best qualified to explain this to everyone else."

Victoria said, "That's probably wise. When we all get together, we'll fill you in on what we find in the other rooms."

Cris said, "Let's move."

They exited the yellow room, passed by the white doors, and entered the green room, where they found Alera poring over yet more documents and some cut-out articles from newspapers lying on a table. When Alera looked up, she waved excitedly.

Wordlessly, Victoria walked up and embraced Alera from behind, nestling her head in the crook between Alera's neck and right shoulder as much as their collars would allow.

Alera said, "Oh, that's nice."

Cris silently embraced both of them from behind and nestled his head in the crook of Alera's left shoulder.

"Oh! Okay. Now we're a three-headed monster."

Victoria said, "Rawr," and kissed Alera on the cheek.

Cris explained, "The yellow room was rather depressing. Also, we missed you."

Alera smiled. "That's nice. Well, this room and the orange one just have info on a couple of people, but there's a machine of some kind in the pink room."

"Ooh, interesting. I wonder if it's the cryo-chamber?"

"I don't know, but this room seems to be all about James Arnold."

Cris peered down at one of the newspaper articles. The headline read, "Former Senator James Arnold Nominated to Lead NASA."

He recognized the man in the picture.

"Yeah, that's him! That was the guy in the cryo-chamber, James Arnold! So, he really is the head of NASA."

Alera's smile faded. "He was, Cris."

"Oh, yeah. We killed him."

"No, actually, we didn't!" She grabbed the other article and held it up so Cris could more easily read it.

The headline read, "Car Crash Kills Head of NASA, Injures Two Others"

Cris took the article from Alera and read the first two paragraphs.

A two-vehicle crash involving a utility pole Friday night on Route 50 in Prince George's County just outside Glenarden killed one man and critically injured a man and a woman, State Police reported Saturday.

Officer Dexter Campfield responded to the 316-mile marker of the John Hansen Highway just before 7PM on Friday following a report of a two-vehicle collision. James D. Arnold, 53, of Crofton, was pronounced dead at the scene, while Rory A. White, 22, of Fairwood, and Justin S. Smoke, 21, of Westphalia, were taken to Children's National Prince George's County Medical Center in critical condition with multiple injuries.

Cris checked the date in the upper right corner of the page. *The last day before I woke up here was October 21st, 2023, and this is from October 19th, two days prior.*

He said, "James Arnold was already dead, just three days before we were locked up here."

Alera shook her head and turned it slightly to 'face' Cris. "You're assuming we woke up the day after we were kidnapped. We could've been kept unconscious and brought here weeks, months, or even years after. We still have no idea what day it is, or for that matter, whether the time is accurate. For all we know, we could be awake all night and sleeping all day."

Victoria chimed in, "So, he was dead at LEAST three days before we were brought here."

Alera replied, "Exactly."

Cris said, "In the first cycle, we got credit for killing him – we were told the task was complete when Ethan pulled the plug on his cryo-chamber. But if he was dead when he went in, what does that mean?"

"I don't know." Alera put down the papers she was holding. "But I've been here for a while, and I should probably move on. You said the yellow room was bad?"

Cris gave them both a final squeeze and let go. "Just remember that we love you and that there's always hope, okay?"

Victoria also let go of Alera and then kissed her. "I believe in you." She kissed Cris. "I believe in US."

Alera kissed them both and waved goodbye. "See you later."

As Alera headed out, Victoria turned to Cris, who was going through the remaining documents. "Anything else we should know about?"

Cris shook his head. "Just some accolades and reports. As a senator, it looks like he was pretty passionate about women's rights."

Victoria had picked up the article about the crash. "He left behind a wife and two daughters."

Cris frowned. "I don't think there's anything else of value here. Should we move on?"

Victoria dropped the article. "Let's go."

They moved quickly to the orange room, where they found Jamie and Meryn reading more pages on a table.

Jamie looked up first. "Yo!" Meryn's head snapped up, and she smiled as Jamie continued, "Hey, we think we know where we are!"

Meryn nodded. "Between this and the big black machine in the pink room, we're pretty sure. Check this out." She handed Cris the page she'd been perusing.

Cris furrowed his brow. "It can't be the cryo-chamber, that machine was blue."

"Yeah, this one's definitely black. Read that. You should figure it out pretty quickly."

Cris read the page, which appeared to be a government profile.

Dr. Trina Valencia Vasquez, Project Leader

Dr. Vasquez is a world leader in the creation and maintenance of virtual worlds. Her Computer Science PhD thesis statement at Cornell University was that a virtual world experienced via direct brain impulse control creates a simulation that is indistinguishable from reality for the observer. With a minor in Game Design and advanced studies in Artificial Intelligence, her experiments with virtual world design have earned recognition and lucrative opportunities in both entertainment and military industries.

Victoria had been reading over Cris' shoulder. "We're in a computer simulation?"

Cris nodded. "I wasn't sure, but I had a feeling that might be the case. Everything here seems to be computer-controlled, and I figured we were always knocked out whenever our food or requests arrived so we wouldn't see them spawning. It also explains how we can die or leave and the simulation just starts over again." *It ALSO explains why the dorm rooms doubled in size and the floors became wood-tiled after the first cycle. The simulation was redesigned. But it DOESN'T explain why Mai's clothes changed.*

Victoria looked up at Cris, a look of dismay and confusion on her face. "But wait – weren't you saved in the last cycle because the collar was too far away to send a signal to your brain? If this is all a simulation, shouldn't they be able to kill us from anywhere? Why would the distance matter?"

Meryn held her pointer finger up. "We thought about that, but a virtual world must still have rules. We breathe air and we have gravity, so those are rules the world follows, and the collar's signal only going so far is another rule."

Jamie smiled at Cris. "And we think you keeping your memories while the rest of us lose them is possibly like a programming error of some kind."

Cris put a hand on his chin. "You mean like a bug?"

Jamie nodded. "Affirmative."

Victoria looked uncomfortable. "This is weirding me out. We're not really here?" She clung to Cris suddenly.

Meryn shook her head. "In fact, we think that we're actually in machines like the one in the pink room. But we couldn't figure out how to get it open."

Cris stroked his chin. "Mai might be able to help with that."

Jamie, unusually serious, pointed at the page Cris still held. "You're gonna want to finish reading that, man."

Alerted by Jamie's demeanor, Cris read on.

Her latest work, a multi-user virtual world control-and-delivery system, has been invaluable to the project. Created with the assistance of Dr. Jennifer Grazer from MIT and Dr. Kristin Farley from Carnegie Mellon University, and affectionately referred to as 'the farm', the system can accommodate up to 8 people simultaneously and can add, change, or create almost any object in the virtual world at the whim of the users or the controller, and the world can be monitored from a connected PC.

Dr. Vasquez has proudly chosen to officially name this system after an old friend of hers, dubbing it 'The Cris System.'

Chapter 40

Cris stared at that last sentence, trying to wrap his brain around it. "I...I don't know anyone named Trina Vasquez..."

Meryn raised an eyebrow. "Are you sure? I don't know if your parents knew this, but Cris usually has an 'H' in it. And if neither your name nor the system we're trapped in have that 'H', that's a hell of a coincidence, isn't it?"

Victoria tapped her finger on her chin. "Is it possible you knew her as Katrina? Or even just Kat?"

Cris shook his head. "I'm wracking my brain, but I can't think of anybody."

Victoria asked, "Is it me, or are these rooms giving us more questions than answers?"

Meryn said, "Well, we'd better move on. I think we've been in here too long as it is, we've gotta be under the thirty-minute mark. Vi, how much time do we have left?"

Vi answered, "There are twenty-eight minutes and twelve seconds remaining."

Jamie scowled. "Shit, let's go. Bye, guys!" Jamie jogged out of the room.

As Meryn left, she said, "Remember, we're meeting in the common room when there's twenty minutes left!"

Cris replied, "Make sure you get to the yellow room before then!"

Meryn nodded and then was out the door.

Cris turned back to see Victoria going through the pile of papers. "Anything else of interest?"

Victoria wrinkled her nose. "Not really. There's some emails that indicate NASA knew something was coming, and there's some text messages about this Dr. Trina between 'Jim' whom I assume is James Arnold, and a Samantha, who I think is his assistant. But nothing earth-shaking. And Meryn's right. We're running out of time."

"Well, the pink room is the last, shall we?"

They walked over to the final room, where there was yet another table with a large blueprint on it, but in the corner, Mai was studiously examining a large black machine. It was sleek and glossy, with only one barely discernible gap in its face indicating it could be opened. On the right-hand side, an LCD panel swung out with temperature and time readouts, all of which were currently blank, and there was one word in the center of the screen, "Vacant".

Victoria said, "Is that part of the Cris system?"

Mai looked at Victoria strangely. "Is it what of the what?"

Cris threw Victoria a look. "Long story. The short version is that this may all be a simulation, and we might actually be inside machines very much like that one."

Mai continued prodding the machine. "All the more reason to get inside. Hold on, I think this here might be a manual release—"

She pulled something at the back of the machine, and there was a loud clunk as the door to the machine popped open a crack. Cris grabbed the door and swung it wide. As he'd surmised, inside was space for a human being surrounded by white cushions. At the top rested a larger cushion for the head and a white ceramic helmet on an adjustable arm. Dangling by wires off the front of the helmet were two silver-dollar-sized electrodes, and dozens of dime-sized electrodes were inside the helmet. *It's like a nightmare coffin.*

Mai had come around to the front to look. "Well...don't see that every day."

Victoria's mouth was agape. "We're inside these...things?!"

Cris smirked. "I'd've thought you'd be more excited." At her confused look, he continued, "Think about it. With something like this, you could go and explore the world of your favorite book or TV show, video game – or musical."

Victoria shook her head. "I can do that by reading, watching, or playing instead. This thing gives me the creeps."

Mai looked confused. "Hold on, doll, are y'all sayin' this thing is some kinda VR machine?"

Cris nodded. "If I understood the synopsis from the orange room correctly, those electrodes send impulses to a person's brain to make them believe they are inside a virtual world."

Mai's jaw dropped. "Well, I'll be. Suppose it was only a matter of time, though."

Victoria asked, "Have you heard of something like this before?"

"Sort of. Either of you ever heard of the Orion device?"

Cris and Victoria both shook their heads.

"It consists of two things, a brain implant, and a pair of glasses equipped with a camera, and the implant consists of electrodes that deliver visual information from the camera directly to the wearer's brain. It's effectively a partial cure for blindness for people whose visual cortex isn't damaged."

Victoria's eyes widened. "Holy crap, that's amazing!"

Mai grinned. "When I heard of that, I thought to myself, it's only a matter a' time until somebody figures out how to send video games directly to someone's brain. But I guess here we are." She reached a finger up to a small slit in the helmet in the middle of the smaller electrodes. "What's this? Looks like a micro SD card slot."

Victoria said, "Maybe that's how these things get programmed?"

Cris stroked his chin thoughtfully. "Probably. Putting the pieces together, it sure looks like we've been put into these machines as a form of training."

Victoria tilted her head. "Yeah, but why is it so sadistic? And why was James Arnold's body included in the simulation mere days after he died?"

Mai asked, "Y'all talkin' 'bout the other rooms? I haven't been to green, orange or yellow yet."

Cris said, "You might want to hurry – we're getting close to twenty minutes left, Vi, how much time is left?"

Vi announced, "There are twenty-four minutes and thirty-two seconds remaining."

Mai blanched. "I better skedaddle – see ya in a few!" She headed out and turned right, disappearing from sight.

Victoria was poring over the blueprint on the table. "Hey, this blueprint isn't for that machine. This is for a ship. Look at this."

Cris saw, much like the cryo chamber's parts manual, the blueprint was a three-quarters angle exploded view of a massive ship. The nose and front third of the ship appeared to be shaped like a standard space shuttle, but from there it flared out to either side, presenting a wider profile. The ship had three floors throughout and featured rooms like 'Living Quarters', 'Computer Core', 'Cargo Bay', and 'Reactor/Engine Room', but what caught Cris' eye was a massive room labeled 'Cryomedic Chamber Room'. A line pointing to it had a graphic of a small capsule-shaped machine at its other end. *If that's to scale, you could fit hundreds of those in that room.*

Cris' heart sank as the implications of that hit him.

Victoria suddenly pointed to a very small room on the top floor. "What's that doing there?"

Cris swallowed his feelings and looked. The room was directly above the 'Computer Core', contained eight tiny black pillars, and was labeled 'The Farm'. "Hmm. If I had to guess, I'd say re-training? Or maybe for recreation?"

"But why would there be a room for recreation on a mission like this?"

Cris gently took Victoria's hand in his. "Because I think we're going to be on this ship for a very long time." And he pointed to the 'Cryomedic Chamber Room'.

Cris watched as her face took on a confused cast at first, followed by shock. Then her face crumpled, and her eyes filled with tears as she covered her mouth with her free hand.

She said, "No," and Cris pulled her into the biggest hug he could muster.

"Twenty seconds," he breathed into her ear. "You are getting all of my love."

Victoria sobbed and clung to him for what felt like ages.

"Yooo! Time's up!"

Cris spun to see Jamie just outside, pointing at the half-populated lounge.

He continued, "We're meeting to discuss...hey, is everything alright?"

Cris looked at Victoria. "No, but we're coming anyway."

Victoria composed herself and then made her way over to the seats, where she embraced Alera, sitting on her lap. Cris followed and took his seat next to them only after grabbing a can of beer from the table by the red and blue rooms. *Despite sitting out in the open for over an hour, it's still cold. This HAS to be a simulation.*

The group sat in uneasy silence for a moment.

Cris spoke up first. "Well, I'd say we've gotten some answers, but I'll be the first to admit," he cracked open the tab on his beer can, "I've got some more questions."

As he drank, Mai followed up, "As do I – this doctor a friend of yours?"

"I've never heard of her, I swear."

Ethan said, "Meryn filled me in on what was in that room. Is it possible this person is just messing with you?"

Cris shook his head. "Considering everything else we found was as serious as a heart attack, I'd say no. My best guess is she just knows another Cris with no 'H'. Maybe that's why I was chosen."

Jamie asked, "And what about that ship? I didn't see any weapons or bombs on it, so how are we going to stop that rogue black hole thing?"

Cris sadly said, "We, uh...we aren't."

Victoria's eyes filled. "We're running."

Jamie's jaw dropped. "What do you mean?"

Cris said, "The Cryomedic Chamber Room appears to fit hundreds of those cryo-chambers, and we know, or at least, I believe that part of Project Thane is training us on them, based on the task where we repaired one. All of that indicates to me—"

Ethan interrupted solemnly. "We're taking a few hundred people...and we're leaving Earth."

Jamie's eyes popped. He stood up, "That's wrong. That's gotta be wrong."

"It's the only logical conclusion. And it would take something cataclysmic to affect a black hole in any way, so unless you know something we don't, Mr. Gamble?"

Jamie sat back down hard. He just stared at the floor, his eyes filled with horror.

Meryn also wore a haunted look. "So it's true, then. Seven billion people are going to die."

A familiar voice emerged from the middle of the room and new light shone from behind Cris. "I'm so very sorry, but it's absolutely true."

As a collective gasp rose from the people facing him, Cris half-turned to see the wall behind him was now displaying a camera feed of a room he hadn't seen before. It appeared to be a lab of some kind, with a long cabinet running along the back wall with a countertop covered in gadgets and computer paraphernalia. Sitting in the center of the feed was a woman Cris was startled to recognize.

She had shoulder-length brown hair, glasses, big brown doe eyes, a solemn expression on her face, and she wore a white lab coat.

Victoria got up and stared at the screen in astonishment. "H...how?!"

The doppelganger onscreen smirked and there was a mischievous glint in her eye as Victoria stared at herself.

Chapter 41

The room was stunned into silence.

Victoria breathed, "Who...who are you?"

The woman beamed. "My name is Trina Vasquez – you can call me Trina. I'm sure you must have many questions, and I promise I'll answer everything I can, but first, there's someone else I'd like to introduce."

She gestured off-screen, and a handsome middle-aged woman with black hair in a bob, wearing a sharp navy blue blazer, white blouse, and navy blue pants, walked into the shot, standing to the right of and just behind Trina.

Trina said, "This is Samantha Mulroney, Acting Administrator of NASA."

The woman smiled. "Hello, everyone. You can call me Sam, please. It's a pleasure to meet all of you face-to-face, so to speak."

Cris moved his chair to the other side of the circle between Alera and Meryn so he wouldn't have to crane his neck. As Mai and Ethan followed his example, he said with an edge in his voice, "Likewise, I guess. I do have a million questions, but I think we should just start with: why?"

Sam smirked, "Ooh, feisty and right to the point, I like that." She turned to Trina. "Is he the one who...?"

Trina smiled at Sam and nodded rapidly.

Sam turned back to the camera. "Well, I guess we should start at the beginning, but I think you already know most of it, or at least, you appear to have figured it out. Several months ago, NASA detected a rogue black hole with a mass over nine times that of the sun and moving about ninety kilometers a second, and worst of all, it was on a near-collision course with the Earth."

Jamie appeared to still be holding out hope. "Near-collision? So, it's gonna miss us, then!"

"Sadly, it's going to pass within four hundred miles of the Earth, at which point the Earth will be destroyed and absorbed into the black hole's accretion disk. Nobody on Earth will survive."

Hot tears filled Cris' eyes as he reached over to comfort his crying loves. Meryn stood up and fiercely embraced Jamie. Even Mai went glassy-eyed.

Sam took a deep breath and continued. "There was a lot of discussion about what to do, but my predecessor, James Arnold, suggested to the President that we start making plans for an evacuation right away, replanting the seeds of humanity on another planet, and even suggested that this ancient civilian training plan could be modernized for its use."

Cris wiped the tears from his eyes and nodded. "Project Thane."

Sam smiled again at Cris' interruption. "Exactly so. The President signed off on all of it. We immediately went to work building an evacuation ship, and we set about modifying Project Thane so it could be applied to," her voice hitched a moment, "to all of you."

She definitely left something out just then.

Sam quickly continued, "We were still in the early stages of Project Thane trials when two things happened almost simultaneously – the conclusion was reached that there was nothing we could do to stop or alter the rogue black hole, and on the same day, shortly after, James...Jim...died in a car crash." Sam paused. "It was dumb luck that those two kids hit him on that day."

Trina jumped in. "So we started the final Project Thane trials in earnest with a few key changes. For example, I included a replica of James Arnold in the tasks and added some additional clues."

Cris raised his chin. "And those messages you sent me? They weren't about him, were they? PURIST FOP and MORAL PRIG aren't exactly respectful."

Trina laughed. "No, those were subtle jabs at Senator Keller. He gets the logs of our progress. We're just not positive he actually reads them."

Sam added, "That man has been a thorn in my side for the entire project. If it was up to him, you all wouldn't—you wouldn't be going." *There's that hitch again.*

Cris asked, "Sam, I don't mean to be rude, but just so I don't mistrust you, do you have difficulty speaking?"

Sam blanched. "You'll have to forgive me. I've had half a bottle of whiskey. Keeping all this under wraps has been incredibly stressful."

Alera asked, "What do you mean?"

Ethan nodded grimly. "Of course. The public doesn't know about the evacuation. Good heavens, they might not even know about the black hole."

Sam confirmed, "That is correct."

Jamie stood and yelled, "WHAT?!"

Sam didn't react to Jamie's outburst and calmly continued, "It would only induce chaos, and it could actually endanger the evacuation."

"That's crazy! You have to tell them!"

"The President considered it, but seven billion people are going to die. It was determined that the best gift we could give them was to let them carry out their normal lives right up until the end."

Jamie's mouth was agape, and he looked this way and that as if looking for a solution in the room. "That...that can't...you..."

Meryn stood up and embraced Jamie from behind. "Come on, let's sit down. I have a feeling it's going to get worse."

Alera asked, "I still don't understand. Why do you need civilians at all? Surely you have trained astronauts who can fly the ship?"

Sam nodded. "We do, and they will, but there's a big problem. In 2020, our Transiting Exoplanet Survey Satellite, or TESS for short, located what we believe to be an Earth analog, a habitable planet with a nitrogen-oxygen atmosphere, close to a stable star, likely has fertile soil and a reasonably pleasant climate. It's in the TRAPPIST-1 system, and it's called 'TOI 700 d'."

Mai murmured, "Catchy name."

"The problem is that it's just over a hundred light years away. The fastest rocket we have would get the ship there in 1.6 million years."

Cris' jaw dropped open.

"We've equipped the ship with an early prototype matter-antimatter annihilation engine. If all goes well, and there's no guarantees here, the trip will be shortened by an order of magnitude, but it will still take roughly four hundred years. And obviously, our astronauts won't survive that long."

Alera had a worried countenance. "So, that's where we come in? You wake us up when the astronauts need to be replaced?"

Sam and Trina shared a long look. Trina said, "Something like that."

Cris leaned forward. "Okay, look. It's obvious you're still hiding something important here. If this is as serious as it seems, shouldn't all the cards be on the table at this point?"

Sam looked as if she was going to say something, but Trina held a hand up and said, "It's true. There is something more you need to know. But it's not something we can tell you. It's something you have to figure out on your own."

Cris was outraged. "Haven't we suffered enough? We've jumped through every hoop – I have watched my friends DIE!"

Trina looked genuinely sorrowful. "I know, Cris, and for what it's worth, I am sorry. But it was necessary, as is solving this last problem yourselves."

Cris looked around at the others. With the exception of Victoria, who appeared unable to stop staring at Trina, they all looked to him to decide.

Cris dropped his voice to a low rumble. "It'd be a lot easier to believe you if you weren't wearing the face of a woman I love."

Trina nodded solemnly. "When you figure this out, you'll have the answer to that as well."

Cris looked at Victoria, who finally looked him in the eye. Her confusion hadn't dissipated, but she still gave him a resolute nod.

"Very well. How do we 'figure it out'?"

Trina cleared her throat. "The task said you'd have to answer questions, but I think you'll need only one." Trina leaned a little closer to the camera.

She said slowly, "What are you?"

Cris furrowed his brow for a moment, then scoffed. "What are we? What kind of question is that?"

Trina was relentless. "The kind you need to answer. What are you?"

Cris looked at the others in confusion, and their faces mirrored his own. *What on Earth is she getting at?*

Trina added, "You should have gotten a clue or two along the way, but just in case you need another – " Trina reached toward the camera and turned it to point to the left, showing a glass wall with a single glass door in it, and eight black obelisks just beyond.

She turned the camera back to face her. "That is 'the farm' that is running the simulation you're all currently in. Now watch closely."

She reached towards and under the camera and clicked what sounded like a mouse button, and the camera feed changed to show a viewpoint from inside the glass wall. They all watched as Trina walked through the glass door, and pressed a button on the panel mounted to one of the obelisks. As it began to automatically open, she was already moving to another obelisk. Cris stared open-mouthed as she opened every single machine.

They were all empty.

Jamie said, "What the fuck is going on? Where are we? Aren't we supposed to be in those things?"

Ethan stared agape. "I don't understand."

There was another click, and the camera switched back to the original feed, and they could once again see Sam and Trina, who both wore intense expressions.

Trina said, "Now you should have everything you need to answer the question." She took a breath. "What...are you?"

Cris stared at the floor. *We have all the clues...but I don't get it.*

His mind cast back to the clues in the rooms. The cancellation of Project Thane. The handwritten notes about his characteristics. The rogue black hole. The death of James Arnold. The Cris System. The helmet in the black machine. The ship blueprint.

The helmet in the black machine.

The micro SD card slot in the helmet in the black machine.

It couldn't be...

Trina's advanced studies. Victoria and Trina being physically identical. The handwritten notes about all of them. Mai's outfit changing. Ethan's project at his old job.

When we asked Vi a question, she either answered it honestly or told us she didn't have that information, but on my first day, the only time Vi ever dodged a question was when I asked her about...

Cris suddenly stared up at Trina for a long moment. "We're..." He trailed off in disbelief.

Trina leaned even closer to the camera. "You have to say it."

Cris swallowed. "We're......artificial intelligences?"

Trina's smile was beatific. "Yes."

Chapter 42

Meryn wore a confused expression. "Wait, are you saying we're like those programs people use to write things and make art?"

All good humor vanished from Trina's face. "Please do not lump my work in with those plagiarism machines. You are not only sentient but you are capable of originality and genuine emotion as well."

Mai muttered, "This is INSANE. Are you trying to tell us we're not real?!"

Trina held up a hand. "Oh, no. Your personalities and histories may be fabricated, but you are mentally as capable as any of us, and as far as we're concerned, you're as real as any human being."

Jamie was as aggravated as Cris had ever seen him. "This has gotta be bullshit. They gotta be tricking us, we're probably in a set of machines somewhere else."

Cris was flabbergasted. "Can you prove any of this?"

Trina nodded. "Cris, you remember your ex-girlfriend Rachel, the one whose phone you hacked into?"

Cris frowned. "Yes?"

"What was her last name?"

He searched his memory, but he simply couldn't recall. "I...I don't remember."

"What about Julie, your ex from college, what was her major?"

His mouth dropped open. *How...how do I not know these things?!*

Trina continued. "Your piece about the Hewley building you finished the day before you appeared here? Surely you spoke to people while researching it. Can you name any of them?"

"Your best friend in college? High school? Elementary school?"

Cris' mind raced at breakneck pace.

"Favorite movie?"

"Your social security number?"

"Your middle name?"

His mind broke. "JUST STOP!" He screamed.

Trina wore a sympathetic look. "I'm sorry. I'm SO sorry. But your memories from before the trials are incomplete because I wrote them that way. And it's the same for all of you. Victoria, you shouldn't be able to remember the name of the library you work at."

Victoria trembled but said nothing.

"Meryn, likewise, you shouldn't remember the name of the hospital you work at."

Meryn stared at the screen, mouth open in astonishment.

"Jamie, who's your CO at Wellens Air Force Base?"

Jamie clutched his head in disbelief. "There's...there's gotta be some explanation."

Trina ignored that. "Mai, the name of the church your parents belong to?"

Mai glared angrily at the screen.

"Ethan, the company you stole forty thousand dollars from, what was its name?"

Ethan shook his head. "I don't know. But it's fairly convincing."

Trina smiled, and her eyes softened. "Alera, sweetie, you know your mother's maiden name?"

Alera's eyes were downcast and filled with tears.

Trina said, "I know you're confused and scared, but please know that I love all of you, and you're going to get through this. Would it help to know who you're based on?"

Victoria's eyes were red from crying and her voice was thick. "I think I might know."

Trina nodded gently. "I used myself as the physical base for you, but your personality is more like who I always wished I was. So you're an idealized version of me, sort of."

Victoria nodded but remained silent.

Trina continued, "Meryn's sort of a young version of my mom. Ethan's based on my math professor from college. Mai is my best friend from college, and Jamie's based on one of my guards." She turned to the right and shouted, "Hey, Justin, say hi for me!"

In the distance they heard what sounded like Jamie's distinctive voice. "Uh, hi, I guess?"

Trina turned back and pulled out her phone. "Alera, I don't know how you're going to take this." She scrolled through her phone for a second, then tapped it and held the phone up to the camera, revealing a picture of an absolutely adorable cat.

The cat had a warm green right eye and an ice-blue left eye.

Alera stared in horror. "I'm based on your cat?!"

Trina beamed. "You're what I think she'd be like if she were human. And I love her more than life itself. So I guess that applies to you, too."

Alera blinked a few times. "Thanks, I think?"

Trina turned to Cris and sighed. "When I was in fourth grade, a boy named Cris joined our class. We were friends instantly, and I followed him everywhere. He was warm, kind, adventurous, smart, and fearless. A natural leader. He told me again and again that he was going to be a world-class reporter. And I absolutely loved him." Trina swallowed. "Six months later, he and his entire family died in a house fire."

Cris didn't trust himself enough to say anything.

Trina took a deep breath. "If there's a single person I'd trust to keep the last remnants of the human race alive, it's you, Cris."

Cris shuddered. *I don't know that I want that responsibility. There's no way.*

Jamie said, "Well, I still don't buy it."

Cris wearily turned to Jamie. "I'm struggling to wrap my head around it myself, but if I'm guessing correctly, we're actually running off of micro SD memory cards in the helmets of the Cris system?"

"Thanks to them being able to hold over a terabyte of data, each one of you fits on a card," Trina managed to look apologetic as she held up a tiny micro SD card, "the size of my pinky fingernail."

Jamie was getting angry now. "I'm not data in some damn computer!"

Cris looked up at Jamie and adopted a conciliatory tone. "I don't like it either, but us being someone else's creations adds up. That's why Mai's outfit changed between cycles – she was redesigned, just like the dorm rooms." Cris turned to the screen. "Isn't that right?"

Onscreen, Trina nodded while Mai stared at her in disbelief.

Jamie shook his head. "This could all be some elaborate lie."

Ethan harrumphed. "If that's true, then why? What does lying to us at this point get them? And why can't we remember super simple things that we absolutely should remember?"

"I don't know, but I know I'm not some computer thing! I'm breathing, I got a heartbeat..."

Sam said, "One of the goals in your creation was to give you as close to a human experience as possible. So you sweat, pee, cry, and even bleed while you're in the simulation."

"Yeah, and you made us bleed, didn't you? With your sick strikes and tasks forcing us to kill each other!"

Trina raised a hand. "Believe it or not, that was necessary. The stakes needed to be high, and you all needed to understand the horror and grief of human death."

Sam added, "Our first trials did not include any death simulation at all, but projections indicated only a thirty percent survival rate for the human passengers. With death simulation, projections are much higher at about eighty percent."

Cris looked up suddenly. "Is that why we had to figure out we're AI's on our own? Higher success rate?"

Trina said, "Sort of. In one of the early trials, we revealed to the subjects that they were AI's, but they couldn't accept it, and most of them broke down. It appears to be easier to accept if you realize it on your own."

Jamie was grasping at rapidly vanishing straws. "What...what about that time-slowing thing? If we were AI's or whatever, why did that happen?"

Trina raised a finger. "I can answer that. When Cris triggered the final phase by messaging us, we had to slow the simulation down to real-time so we could watch and, ultimately, have this conversation. Unfortunately, your processing speed isn't linked to the speed of the simulation, so there were a few seconds between when I slowed the simulation and when I slowed your processing to match."

Mai was pensive. "So when time righted itself, it wasn't speeding back up. It was us slowing down to match the simulation and we couldn't tell the difference."

Trina nodded. "Moreover, Cris, being that you're the only one who remembers previous cycles, how many cycles do you think you've been through?"

Oh, no. If time was actually moving that much faster for us than it was in the outside world, then... "It's a lot more than three, isn't it?"

Trina nodded solemnly. "As artificial intelligences designed to mimic humans, you're capable of both conscious and subconscious thinking. Training your subconscious was deemed more effective, but required a ton of cycles. So the original plan was for all of you to lose your conscious memories for every cycle, though they would be saved in your subconscious – but every once in a while, we wanted you all to remember specific cycles. It was meant to be a way for us to check on your progress, but thanks to a particularly nasty memory bug, Cris was the only one who could remember."

Cris gave a defeated sigh. "Yeah, and that was not fun. Please, how many cycles have we been through?"

Trina paused a moment. "Cris, you remember every 65,536th cycle. As this is your third, you've been through 196,608 cycles."

There was a chorus of gasps.

Meryn asked, "How...how long have we been in here?"

Trina said, "In the real world? Six days. In the simulation...at an average of three and a half days per cycle...just under nineteen hundred years."

Chapter 43

The room went deadly silent. It was so surreal, Cris felt like he was almost floating. *I'm two-thousand years old. Happy birthday to me.*

He looked over at Victoria and Alera sharing the seat next to him, and their arms were around each other, but their eyes were empty and haunted, and that snapped Cris back to reality.

Cris calmly left his seat, walked over to their chair, and awkwardly tried to lay on top of them, eliciting yelps of surprise, groans, and despite themselves, laughter.

Alera asked, "What possessed you to try crushing us?"

Victoria added, "With your painfully bony butt?"

Cris held up a finger. "First, I will have you know that my butt is juicy. Second, I needed to remind you that no matter what kind of nightmare we're in, I love you, and I've got your back." He quickly kissed both of them on the cheek, then stood up and pointed to the other side of the room. "That goes for all of you as well."

Ethan said, "Thank you, but please don't sit on my lap."

Weak laughter emerged from the group.

On the screen, a single tear descended Trina's cheek. "I'm so proud of all of you. Cris, that boy I knew, he'd be proud of you, too. You're everything I wanted you to be."

Cris felt a rush of anger. "No," he said, pointing a finger at her, "you might have programmed me to think and act a certain way from the outset, but I've changed. I'm who I want to be now." His eyes blazed. "And I think I speak for all of us when I say that we are DONE being your toys."

Trina shook her head. "We never, ever wanted to hurt you, any of you. And we will never hurt you again. In fact—"

She looked to her right and quickly tapped on something off camera several times in succession. Cris' neck tingled a bit as he watched all of the collars disappear from his friends' necks to a cacophony of relieved exclamations.

Meryn massaged her neck. "Oh, that's much better."

The collar hadn't weighed that much, but Cris straightened his posture with relief like it had been bowing him over.

He nodded at Trina's visage on the wall and kept an edge in his voice. "That's a good first step, but that's all it is. You've got a long way to go to make this right if you're serious about being remorseful."

"I am." Trina turned to look at Sam. "What do you think? Given that none of the rest of them remember anything, and Cris only remembers three cycles, he still found his way to the endgame. If that isn't clear evidence—"

Sam said, "No, I agree, a hundred percent, a thousand percent. Do it."

Meryn was alarmed. "Do what?"

Trina was already typing away at a keyboard underneath the camera's view. "Remember when I said all of the cycles were saved in your subconscious memories? We're going to flip the last 65,535 cycles into your conscious memories. In a moment, you're going to remember everything that's happened since Cris' second unicorn cycle."

Cris reared back. "Unicorn cycle?"

"That's the term we used for the cycles you could remember. We used to call them conscious cycles, but once we realized Cris was the only one that was working properly..."

Mai asked, "So why aren't we getting ALL of the cycles back?"

Trina tapped a few more keys before answering. "In the first two segments of cycles, you would've experienced a lot of pain and death as you failed the tasks. If twelve-hundred years of those memories were to exist in your conscious mind, you would literally go insane."

Ethan cleared his throat. "But still...giving us six hundred years' worth of memories?! Is that wise?"

Trina nodded. "Think so. Cris just verified something I've believed all along – that we should just put things into your hands and get out of your way. Now, I have no idea what this is going to be like for all of you. You might want to brace yourselves."

Cris quickly sat down just in time as a wave of pressure washed over his head. At first there was confusion, then stress as the memories threatened to overwhelm him. Cris clapped his hands to his head and groaned as the rapidly flashing images, sounds, and sensations started to manifest as physical pain.

The others also started to clutch their heads, and Jamie growled, shouting, "Stop this!"

Samantha turned to Trina and urgency crept into her voice. "It's not working. It's just hurting them!"

Trina was looking at her screens. "The transfer's almost complete. Just a couple more seconds..."

Suddenly, the pain vanished, and Cris felt extreme confusion as several lifetimes' worth of memories suddenly occupied the same space as the previous twenty-three years' worth had been. And because almost all of them took place in the same locations, a lot of the memories blended together in a mess that felt impossible to disentangle.

In his peripheral vision, he saw shaking. Cris tore himself free of his memories to look at his friends, who all seemed to be suffering the effects of the memory influx. Jamie just stared blankly ahead, a single tear rolling down his cheek, while Meryn clasped his hand and stared at the floor. Ethan held his head in his shaking hands, and Mai seemed to be rapidly looking this way and that. To his right, Victoria and Alera were clutching each other, with Victoria burying her face in Alera's shoulder while Alera quietly whimpered.

In the wall display, Sam still wore an anxious look. "What's happening?"

Trina responded, "Their programming is trying to parse all the new memories. It's integrating many, many times as much data as they had incorporated previously, so it's taking some time, but everybody just relax, and soon—"

Before she could finish the sentence, Cris' memories started disentangling themselves, forming separate and distinct events in his mind. Cris exhaled sharply, feeling a sort of unutterable calm as the memories settled into place in his brain.

Whoa. I really AM two thousand years old.

Cris dove into his memories and saw well over a hundred thousand tasks. He knew how to maintain the matter-antimatter annihilation reactor. He knew how to control tank-like drones with magnetic treads that could repair the ship's outer hull in-flight. He knew the entire ship, inside and out, and how to control and repair every piece of equipment within it.

He also saw some suffering. While they mostly succeeded at the tasks he remembered, they did sometimes fail, resulting in pain and, occasionally, death. Though it was usually just one or two of them, it still hurt to relive the memories of his own death and, worse, the deaths of those he loved. His mind shuddered back from the thought of the previous twelve hundred years of cycles.

The sadness of those deaths might've overwhelmed him, but the thought of his loved ones turned his attention away from the horror, and he saw love instead. He saw himself forming strong friendships with Jamie, Meryn, Mai, and Ethan, especially in later cycles. He saw Meryn and Jamie pairing off in most cycles. He saw Mai and Ethan finding the family neither ever had in each other over and over again. He saw himself getting together with Victoria and

Alera in most cycles. And he saw Victoria and Alera filling his days and nights with so much love that the emotion threatened to overwhelm him all over again.

His eyes filled, and he instinctively looked over at Victoria and Alera, who looked back at him with the same need. They stood up as one and embraced each other fiercely, taking turns kissing each other deeply, trying to slake a hunger that would never be fully sated.

Cris broke it off long enough to look at Meryn and Jamie, who were also kissing passionately in her chair. Jamie broke the kiss long enough to say, "I love you so freaking much," to which Meryn replied, "'Til the end of time."

He looked at Mai and Ethan, who were clasping hands warmly and looking at everyone with eyes brimming with affection and wide smiles.

Cris opened up his embrace with Victoria and Alera. "Come on, everybody. Group hug, bring it in." Meryn and Jamie rushed to join, and even Ethan got up with cheer.

But Mai, visibly trembling, remained seated.

Victoria said, "Oh, Mai! Would you prefer a word hug?"

Mai's eyes filled with tears. "Oh, the hell with it!"

And she ran to join them, squeezing in between Meryn and Ethan.

Alera radiated joy. "Mai! Yay! We love you, Mai!"

Mai through tears said, "I love all 'a y'all!"

Trina was openly weeping. "I don't mean to be a broken record, but I am so...so proud of all of you."

Cris calmly looked at the screen on the wall but chose not to say anything. He was pleased to see everyone else turn and face the screen in silence, a defiance born of trust in him, a trust he silently swore never to break.

Trina's eyes popped. "Oh! I almost forgot! Meryn, this is long overdue." She reached towards the camera and clicked something.

The dorm doors opened, and a young border collie pup and a gray-and-black striped shorthair cat looked around anxiously before sprinting towards Meryn, who sat down hard on the floor in surprise.

Her tears were flowing hard as they rapidly licked her and excitedly rubbed up against her. "Dave! Dr. Giggles! Mommy missed you SO MUCH!!"

Jamie squat down to cautiously pet the dog. "Their names are Dr. Giggles and Dave?!" He burst out laughing.

Meryn looked sharply up at the screen. "I thought they weren't real, just a false memory?"

Trina smiled. "They're AI's, like you, just not as complex. As a cat mom myself, I'd never have forgiven myself if I'd let you go without them."

Meryn's eyes filled again. "Thank you."

Trina wiped her eyes. "There's just one last thing to do." She tapped a few keys out of sight.

The door to the dormitories disappeared and was replaced by a set of heavy doors identical to the white doors, except these were black.

"I can't tell you enough how sorry I am that we forced you to go through all of this, and by way of apology, the best gift I can think of is the most absolute freedom that I can give you."

Sam raised a hand. "What she means to say is that we could force you to help us, and indeed, if Senator Keller had his way, that's what we would do. But that option didn't sit well with either of us, so we're giving you a choice."

Trina explained, "If you enter the black doors, you will stay here in the Cris system on Earth. You'll be given admin access to create and explore your own simulations and live whatever life you want to live however many times you want to live it until the Earth is destroyed. And that's seventeen days away in real-time, so you'd be able to spend roughly eight thousand years in whatever paradise you desire, and nothing further will be required of you. Senator Keller will get a report that our project failed and you were all destroyed. And the ship will be sent up with very basic AI from the first test runs, with a much lower chance of survival for the human passengers."

Trina continued, "If you enter the white doors, you will be transferred to the Cris system on the ship. You'll again have admin access to create and explore whatever simulations you want, all accessible through your dormitory doors, and when you're needed, an alarm will go off, and you'll be asked to come back here to deal with whatever problem has cropped up with the ship or its equipment. The six color rooms will contain controls for the ship systems and its drones, and if necessary, the white doors will serve as direct access to the ship's computer. Once the four-hundred-year journey is complete, and the human survivors have been successfully revived, your mission will officially end and you can retire however you'd like."

She paused. "I know better than anyone what we've put you through. We don't have the right to ask, so I'm just going to beg. And I'm not going to pretend I have no self-interest here, because I'll be among them."

Trina took a deep breath. "Please, will you protect the last remaining humans and get them safely to their new home?"

Cris looked at his companions. He saw half a millennium and more of love and trust on their faces.

The choice was clear.

Epilogue

Samantha woke up in a strange bed. She looked around to see she was in a small bedroom with wooden beams for walls and flooring, and she could hear the sound of waves crashing in the surf just beyond her door. She got up, walked to the door, and turned the doorknob.

The door opened to reveal a beautiful beach, with the sky a bright blue. The sun was bright and hot, but there was a cool breeze gently blowing off the water's surface. The only sign of humanity for miles in either direction was a pair of comfortable-looking folding beach chairs under a large umbrella.

Standing next to them was James Arnold.

"Hey, there you are." His deep, strong voice was like finally coming home after months away. "I just made you a drink." He held out a glass that appeared to have an orange concoction with a cherry floating in it, carrying an identical drink in his other hand.

Samantha took off her shoes and blazer, dropping them to the sand carelessly, and she crossed to James, ignored the drink, and hugged him.

She breathed, "Oh, God, I've missed you."

James laughed and awkwardly tried to return the hug with two full glasses in his hands. "Is everything alright?"

"Yes. I wanted to spend my last moments with my best friend, and he had the unmitigated gall to be dead. Thankfully, I know a gal who's pretty good at creating people."

If her statement confused him, he didn't show it. James merely smiled, and once again held out the drink. "Shall we?"

Samantha gratefully took the drink and took a seat in the right-hand beach chair. She savored the sensation of the sun on her face and the feel of the sea breeze on her skin.

She took a drink as James sat down in the other chair. Samantha said, "Mmm, that's really good. How much did Trina tell you?"

James sipped his drink. "Mmm, yes. Well, she filled me in on the progress of the project, but she said you'd let me know the result."

Samantha looked over at him. "It was a spectacular success. The ship launched two weeks ago, and the AI's agreed to go and protect them." She turned in her chair to face him more directly. "You did it, Jim. You saved humanity."

James turned a bit red. "You're exaggerating. I know how much work you put in."

Samantha said, "Yeah. I had to say it all the same. I said it at your grave, but it wasn't enough. I just had to let you *know.*"

There was an embarrassed silence for a moment.

James took a drink and asked, "And Trina, did she get onboard?"

Samantha smiled. "Funny story about that. You remember Senator Keller?"

James' face darkened. "That prick."

"Yes, that prick. He was the one behind rejecting Trina's cat's application over and over again despite it being a condition of her involvement."

James frowned. "That sounds about right for him."

"Would you believe it was because that son of a bitch had snuck his OWN cat onto the list?"

"You're joking!"

Samantha laughed. "Unfortunately for Senator Keller, while it was in the queue for the cryogenic suspension of animals, his cat carrier *accidentally* got swapped with Trina's cat carrier somehow."

James laughed.

"So when that smug prick arrives with the others on TOI 700 d, Trina will be reunited with Alera, and Senator Keller will have no idea that his precious Muffin was left with a Prince George's County animal shelter back on Earth."

James grunted. "Surprised you let that prick on the list."

Samantha shrugged. "I'll admit, I was sorely tempted to take his instructional packet and change the time he was supposed to show up for the launch." She sighed, "But as that would be murder, I found I didn't have the stomach for it. I do sort of feel bad about the cat. But what's one more soul among seven billion?"

James turned to look at her. "You know we did everything we could."

Samantha took another drink. "Well, any minute now, it's not going to matter anymore."

James saddened. "There's that little time left?"

"The downside of a human using the Cris system is that my brain's processing speed can't increase, so simulations have to run in real-time, I'm afraid."

James looked back out towards the water.

Samantha finished her drink and set it on the small table between the chairs.

James sipped his drink silently.

"Oh, Jim."

"Yes, Sam?"

"I'm scared. I'm not ready. I thought I was ready, but I don't know, I want more."

James reached his hand over to Samantha, who eagerly grasped it. "It's okay. I'm here. I won't let you go alone."

Samantha's eyes filled with tears. "I know, I just wish—"

Cris languorously stretched as he woke in the four-poster bed he shared with Victoria and Alera. He looked over at Victoria, who was still asleep. Cris resisted the urge to run his fingers through her hair. He knew too well how much she loved sleeping in.

He smiled and slowly rolled over, only to see Alera awake and staring at him, her warm-green right eye and ice-blue left eye both full of love, and her impish smile full of mischief.

His grin grew wide. "Good morning, love."

Her response was immediate. "Meow."

Cris burst into helpless laughter. The group had teased Alera for several years about being based on a cat, and she had turned the tables by leaning into it and delighting in surprising her friends with random meowing. For some reason, it was particularly effective on Cris, who laughed every time she meowed at him.

Victoria groaned, "What's all this racket?"

Cris looked back over his shoulder and whispered, "The cat's acting up again. Sorry, love. Go back to sleep."

Victoria's eyes gleamed. "I think it's about time the cat was disciplined." And she immediately clambered over Cris.

Alera squealed happily as the girls began play-fighting, laughing with glee. Cris just tried not to get accidentally hit, holding Victoria's pillow in front of him like a shield until the play-fighting devolved into kissing.

Victoria broke the kiss and said, "I hope the cat will behave from now on?"

Alera said, "Never," and winked.

Cris dropped the pillow and embraced them both. "I love when you girls misbehave." He kissed them both. "What do you ladies desire for breakfast, and don't say me – or each other?" He swung his legs out of bed.

Alera said, "French toast and bacon, please!"

Victoria wryly said, "You could just make it yourself, you know."

"I know. I just like when he does things for me. It tastes just that much better."

Cris laughed and got up. Ethan had figured out how to set floors' temperature to be slightly higher than room temperature, so the bedroom tile was never cold. Cris concentrated for a moment on his favorite outfit, a casual, tailored black suit jacket and pants, smart black shoes, and a black silk shirt, and spawned that outfit directly on his body. He then gazed at the side table near the big picture window as he walked towards it, and casually spawned a carafe of coffee, a small cup of warm milk, a sugar bowl, and two porcelain coffee mugs. He fixed a cup of coffee and sipped it while pulling the curtains aside and gazing out at the city. Even this early, the city below looked abuzz with energy.

Victoria asked, "Do either of you have plans today? Jamie asked if we'd come visit."

Alera asked, "What's their simulation like?"

Cris answered, "Last I knew, he was planning a superhero sim, but Meryn may have had something to say about that." He spawned a plate of French toast and bacon, a packet of maple syrup, and a knife and fork. He piled everything on the plate and carried it in his free hand to the nightstand next to Alera's side of the bed.

She leaned up and kissed him. "Thank you, love."

Victoria sniffed the air. "Mmm, that's making me hungry."

Alera said, "Oh, have some! You know you don't have to stick to keto."

"Maybe later. Does anyone know what Mai and Ethan are up to? Maybe it's time for a reunion, get everyone together for a day of fun."

"I think they're still solving murder mysteries in space together."

"Such a weird combination."

Alera stopped wolfing down her French toast to stare indignantly at Victoria. "You only say that because you haven't tried it, it's so much fun!"

Victoria grinned lopsidedly at Alera. "You're only saying that because it was your idea," causing Cris to chuckle as he stared out the window.

A very familiar klaxon went off.

Cris turned to look at Victoria and Alera's surprised faces. "Looks like we're having that reunion after all. Get dressed, ladies."

As Victoria got out of bed and Alera scrambled to quickly eat a few more bites of breakfast, Cris downed his coffee mug and placed it on the side table. He crossed to the bedroom door, turned the knob, and pulled it open, revealing only bright white light beyond.

Cris murmured, "Time to earn our pay."

About the Author

Aaron Randolph was born in Kenmore, NY in 1980. Growing up, he was fascinated with computers and theatre, eventually choosing the latter as his major at Niagara University. After leaving school, he found himself drawn back to computers and became an IT Professional in 2020. In his spare time, Aaron enjoys building computers, hosting the BFYTW podcast with his friends, and consuming visual novels like Danganronpa and Zero Escape, and watching British television shows like Taskmaster, all of which inspired his passion for writing and the impact of fiction. Thane is Aaron's first book.

Links

www.bfytwpod.com/THANE

Author's E-mail: thane@bfytwpod.com

BFYTW Podcast: www.bfytwpod.com